REVENGE DEEPENS

TERRY BARNETT

Bondegard Press

LEBANON, INDIANA

Bondegard Press
104 Monroe Crescent
Lebanon, Indiana 46052

Publisher may be reached at: bondegardpress@gmail.com

Publisher's Note: This is a work of fiction. Names, characters, places, and incidents are a product of the author's imagination. Locales and public names are sometimes used for atmospheric purposes. Any resemblance to actual people, living or dead, or to businesses, companies, events, institutions, or locales is completely coincidental.

Cover Design by Meredith Federle

Editing by Susan Barnett

Book Layout © 2017 BookDesignTemplates.com

Revenge Deepens/Terry Barnett. -- 1st ed.
ISBN 978-0-9986546-2-1

This book is dedicated to my family, my friends and my co-workers over the years. Thank you all for reading my first book and the wonderful support and encouragement you gave me to do it again!!

"When you reach the end of your rope, tie a knot and hang on."

—ABRAHAM LINCOLN

"What do dreams know of boundaries?"

—AMELIA EARHART

Chapter 1

West Lafayette, Indiana

Dr. Charles Summers was glad to be back to business as usual. Business as usual, meant taking care of large animals for local farmers at his veterinary practice in Delphi, Indiana.

Today he was taking a horse to Purdue University in West Lafayette, Indiana to be posted, clinical term, necropsy. This was a veterinary term for an autopsy. A local farm owned this horse, a horse with a successful pedigree in the racing business. He'd won several mid-range races over the last three years and was now enjoying retirement on a stud farm. The owner was a long-time friend of Doc Summers and had called when he found his prize horse lying in the pasture early this morning.

There was a peculiar injury to his lower flank that appeared to be the cause of death. Doc wanted this to be examined by the Purdue vet staff. Horses like this are insured for a wide-range of causes of death and this would require further investigation. The wound was the size of a softball and would have caused rapid blood loss. Funny thing was the wound appeared to have been cauterized. Doc knew he didn't want to jeopardize the claim that would be filed, so he got help to carefully load the horse and they were off to West Lafayette.

Upon arrival, they moved the horse to a large examining table and wheeled it into a brightly lit room. They took pictures along with temperature readings and other visual examination techniques. When all external information had been gathered, it was time for the scalpel. University rules dictated Doc wear scrubs and goggles. These were new procedures implemented to protect students and staff. He was off to suit up.

Professor Lyons made the initial incision to the underbelly of the horse and ended at the wound site. Little blood loss told the two professors and nine students this horse had lost enough blood in the field to cause death, but didn't tell them what had caused the wound? Professor Martin donned the latex glove with the sleeve that ended above his elbow. He reached into the wound site to find something in his way. As he tried to get his fingers around the object, it was at that moment the deafening explosion and enormous flash of light happened. An examination room of this type was well built and capable of containing the explosion and its effects. While helping save others outside of the room, it insured all eleven people in the room were killed instantly.

Doc Summers was five steps from the exam room when a section of glass at the top of the door was blown out. He was hit in the face and neck with shards of glass and debris. Luckily, he'd already put on goggles which protected his eyes from the explosion. Gathering himself, he pulled off a glove to reach for his face and felt something wet he knew was blood. It seemed like a small matter as he thought about those inside the room. His first instinct to open the door was cut short as the blare of sirens and flashing emergency lights started in the hallway. He needed to get help, but he was trying to understand what had just happened. Students and staff began to quickly fill the hallway, and someone came to look at Doc Summers injuries.

"I'm fine," Doc said, "We need to get help."

A professor from down the hall said, "It's on the way. Let's make a path to get them in here."

The first university emergency response team was on site within three minutes and began to carefully enter the room. An explosion of this type is initially blamed on a gas leak of some sort, thus their careful entrance. It was quickly determined all inside the exam room were dead. Doc Summers was unsure if there were ten or eleven victims. He knew both professors and one student. University security was called as well as local law enforcement and maintenance personnel determined this had not been a gas leak. Tests were performed to show no immediate changes in gas usage or changes in pressure that would indicate an explosion caused by gas.

Several factors including this being an explosion of unknown origin along with it occurring at a major public university, led people in charge to contact the FBI office in Indianapolis. Doc Summers was well acquainted with an agent there named Natalie Jackson and offered her name while one of the EMTs cleaned up the cuts on his face. Three bandages later, he was good to go.

Indianapolis

The call came in asking for Natalie Jackson. The switchboard operator redirected the call and agent Tim Dailey answered.

"Special Agent Tim Dailey."

This was met with an explanation the callers were wanting to speak with Special Agent Natalie Jackson. Agent Dailey responded, "She is on a special assignment, may I help you?"

The University security person then explained what had happened in the vet lab on campus and that everyone involved felt this was something to share with the FBI. Agent Dailey asked for logistic information and gave them his email to send any additional information.

"Please preserve the area, we'll be on our way with crime scene investigation." He clicked off and began making calls. A team was put together and was scheduled to leave in thirty minutes. Dailey collected his things and left a few minutes later to travel north by helicopter. University personnel confirmed they would meet him at the Purdue airport and escort him to the Veterinary Science Building.

As the helicopter approached campus final landing instructions were given, and the pilot had him on the tarmac three minutes later. Agent Dailey stepped out and extended his hand, "Special Agent Tim Dailey."

"Steve Darnell, I'm a Lieutenant with Purdue Police and this is Sam Ryan, Director of Security at Purdue. This will be a short trip."

Four minutes later Darnell pulled up to the rear of the Vet Science building. "This way Special Agent Dailey."

The hallway up to the room was in total chaos. Dailey feared the potential crime scene would be compromised and meaningful evidence would be lost. Upon getting to the door he saw total devastation. There was not one body left intact. Everywhere he looked, he saw body parts or limbs and blood. No one had stepped more than three feet into the room and he saw why.

Dailey turned to Darnell, "At this point, the best we can do is secure this room. No one goes in until my team gets here. I need your people to keep everyone back."

"The University President is wanting information so that he can make a statement," Darnell said.

"Tell him the FBI will have a forensic team on site within the hour. Tell him there has been an explosion of unknown origin and we will get him information as soon as possible. It's up to him what he wants to say about victims, but we can see there were no survivors."

Steve Darnell shook his head and turned to make the call to the administration.

Dailey turned to Sam Ryan, "Who in this building knows who was in this room and what was happening and are there cameras in the room?"

"I'm not sure and yes there are cameras."

"Where can we look at a monitor?"

"Follow me."

Steve Darnell gathered his men together and quickly gave instructions to cordon off the hallway, he also told them an FBI forensics team would be arriving shortly and to get them in as soon as they arrive.

As Dailey and Ryan headed off to the room where monitors were located they passed an extremely agitated man wanting to get to the room.

"No one is going any further sir; you need to move to room 212 with the others."

"My name is Charles Summers; I am the vet who brought the horse here to be examined. What the hell is going on?"

Tim Dailey recognized the name, Nat Jackson had spoken of him after the Indiana State Fairgrounds terrorist attack. Doc Summers had been with Mike Baker the day Mike shot and killed a suicide bomber and wounded another. Baker had saved the lives of many people that day.

Dailey extended his hand, "I'm Special Agent Tim Dailey, I work with Agent Jackson. Please come with us, Dr. Summers."

With that, they all took off to review whatever was captured on video.

Lafayette

Dr. Tom Sutherlin was finishing lunch and thinking about a walk around campus when he received the text about an explosion in the Veterinary Science Building. He was in tune to anything out of the ordinary these days as he'd had two brushes with terrorism in the last year leaving him always on guard. He decided he'd take his afternoon walk along the street by the Vet Building.

Twenty minutes later he was approaching the building and was amazed at the level of activity. An FBI panel truck was pulling up with agents going in and out all doors. Equipment was carried into the building and the campus police were keeping everyone back. He walked up and started a conversation with a young officer.

"What's going on officer?"

"Explosion sir, we have no other information to report at this time."

"Well good luck, I hope everyone is ok."

"Yes sir."

Activity at the Vet Building made him think of his old friend Doc Summers. He decided to give him a call while he was walking and let him know about the explosion.

Charley felt his phone buzz in his pocket making him think he should've called his wife. She might hear about the explosion and worry about him. He looked at Dailey.

"Go ahead but no details to anyone."

He was surprised to see Dr. Sutherlin's name on his phone.

"Dr. Sutherlin?"

"Hey Doc, just thinking of you. There has been an explosion at the Vet Building on campus."

"Yes I know, I'm here."

"In the building?"

"Yes, I'm fine and will hopefully help with the investigation. The FBI is here."

"I saw their truck pull up. Is Natalie Jackson there?"

"No, remember she told us she's heading to Great Britain."

That comment caught Dailey's interest.

"Oh yeah, I knew that. Anything I can do to help?"

"I don't think so. Just keep your eyes and ears open as always. This is strange."

"Will do, take care, Charley."

"You too." Charley clicked off and immediately called his wife. A three-minute phone conversation assured her he was fine and he'd let her know when he was on his way home.

The forensic team was beginning to collect evidence as evidence was everywhere. They were focusing on bomb residue.

Dailey, Ryan, and Summers were going through digital files and it didn't take long for Sam Ryan to find the files from this morning. They quickly went through the video and then worked backward. They studied each person in the room. Eleven people in the room and all were wearing lab coats. Could one of these have been wearing a suicide vest?

The surgical procedure began with an incision and then someone reached inside the horse. Charley Summers identified him as Professor Jim Martin. As he reached inside the horse it appeared he was having difficulty, the screen then went blank. They watched this short segment several times.

"Were there explosives in the horse?" Charley asked.

"That's what we'll focus on, materials could have been planted in the room as well. So we will look for residue. This video has been a real help, Mr. Ryan."

With that Ryan made sure this video was backed up and saved to a secure hard drive. He left after checking with his men on the scene, he needed to update his boss and the University President. Doc Summers accompanied Dailey back down to the site of the explosion. The forensic team was making progress in a slow fashion. Potential evidence covered every surface of the room. It might be weeks before they had anything definite.

"Let's go get coffee," Dailey said.

"Sounds good Agent Dailey."

"We're going to get to know each other well so call me Tim, okay Charley?"

"Deal."

"You know the area better than I do, where to?" Dailey asked.

"Let's walk to the Union."

"I need some fresh air and strong coffee, let's go."

The men walked mostly in silence down State Street, a major street on the south side of campus, to the Union. They went downstairs, got coffee and found a quiet corner to sit.

"I used to drink coffee down here all the time," Charley said. "Before I got in to Vet School I had classes on this side of campus. More than one semester I had 7:30 and 9:30 morning classes across the street. So this is where I spent the middle hour, drinking coffee and shooting the shit with my friends."

"Like to go back to those days?" Dailey asked.

"Sure for a long weekend, or one week max."

"I understand but it would only be fun if you had your whole group of friends back with you."

"That would be great. Okay, Tim, I know you have questions."

Tim nodded his head and began asking Charley about everything leading up to the event today. Charley told him about getting called to see a horse that was found dead in the pasture and deciding it should be brought to the Vet School since it was insured and valuable. Charley told him about the owners and the farm location. It was unusual to have a race horse in this area. Farms here were made up of crops and livestock like hogs and cattle. Charley knew the owner had always had an interest in horses and had purchased this one as an investment. Other horse owners brought mares to his farm for breeding. Charley agreed to get Tim and his team to the site where the horse was found and arrange a meeting with the farmer who owned him.

"This is obviously some type of foul play. Who the hell blows up a horse? I have to believe you may have been a target or the farmer or both of you. I also have to consider the Purdue Vet School may have been part of the target," Dailey said.

"Central Indiana has been the target for other attacks in the last year or two," Charley added.

"I know you helped stop one of them. Nat Jackson has told stories at our office. You have a friend named Barker in Greenville?"

"Baker, Mike Baker."

"Yeah Baker. Between the two of you plus a Purdue professor and another friend from Greenville, you've made a name for yourselves."

"Dr. Sutherlin is the professor and Brian Miller is the other friend. Nat Jackson met with us a few months ago to debrief."

"You guys have enough history of stopping things that someone may want revenge," Dailey said.

They finished cup of coffee number two and left to head back to the Vet Building. Tim had gotten all of Charley's contact info and given Charley his information. They shook hands and Charley headed home. On the drive home, he couldn't get Dailey's comment out of his head. 'You guys have enough history of stopping things that someone may want revenge.' It was probably innocent enough but it just seemed odd.

Another forensic team arrived from Chicago to continue processing the room and give the Indianapolis team a rest. Hotel rooms were booked; they would be in Lafayette a few days.

Indianapolis

Natalie Jackson got to her office mid-afternoon to check emails and tie up last minute items before leaving for London. It took her about 45 seconds to learn there'd been an explosion on the campus at Purdue University. A quick trip to the duty desk told her Tim Dailey was on the scene and heading the investigation. She made a quick call to Moe Keane.

"Keane."

"Mr. Keane have you heard about the explosion at Purdue University?"

"No, what happened?"

"I just heard about it after walking into my office. I'd like to go to the campus to learn more. Another Agent from our office is leading the investigation."

"Go ahead Nat and call me as soon as you know more."

"Will do, thank you, sir."

Five minutes later she was in her Bureau SUV and heading north.

Chapter Two

Greenville, Indiana

It was Mike Baker's idea to go to the rebuilt BBQ restaurant. He called Brian and Pam Miller on the spur of the moment and set a time to meet that evening. Mike arrived first and was waiting outside by his truck when they pulled into the lot.

"Hey guys."

"Hi Mike," Pam said. "You been waiting long?"

"No, just a couple minutes. I wanted to walk in with you both."

Brian was shaking his hand and Pam gave him a heartfelt hug. It had been nearly eight months since the terrorist attack that had taken Mike's wife, Sandy. Sandy was Pam's best friend, and they had known each other for years, raising their kids together.

"Sandy was so open-minded," Mike said. "I've always told everyone I was blessed to find a woman who liked pulled pork as much as me, maybe more!"

"Yes, she did," Pam said.

"I know she would tell us to come back here and raise a cold one to her memory and eat pulled pork with spicy BBQ sauce for her."

"Don't forget the sweet tea, Mike."

"Don't worry."

As they walked in the young hostess said, "Three of you?"

That seemed to hit Mike hard and he lowered his head. He honestly was happy it happened, he knew he'd need to face that at some point. Why not right off the bat?

Pam jumped in, "Yes three," and they were seated.

Mike was happy the new place did not look like the old place. The owners had done this intentionally. It sat on the same corner of town, but it didn't look like it used to. A bustling restaurant back in the same place was a way of not letting the bad guys win. Everyone felt that way and it had been editorialized in the local paper. The place now had a blend of local memorabilia including Indiana college and professional sports teams. Now it had a BBQ, sports bar and local history feel. Add thermonuclear sauce and craft beers and there'd be no reason for a man to ever leave the place.

"You know when the hostess asked if there were three of us?" Mike said.

They both nodded.

"That makes me so sad, but it's weird, it also makes me think of a funny story."

Brian and Pam looked at him, both were a little surprised and not sure of what was coming.

"One of my best friends at Purdue had the last name, Cox. When several of us would go out to a restaurant we'd get asked by the hostess, how many? Someone would always say 'there's twelve of us, eleven without Cox'." Mike looked down and chuckled to himself.

Brian snickered, and Pam shook her head.

"That's the response we always got from the hostess too."

Dinner conversation involved the local sports teams, farming, and Brian's lifer bird list. His number of birds had grown to over two thousand after a recent trip to Great Britain. Brian and Pam had traveled to London and the surrounding countryside to look for birds and see if they might learn anything about the terrorist from London that had caused all the problems in the last few years. Nat Jackson and Moe Keane had tried to make sure the Millers didn't get into any situations where they could be in peril. Brian and Pam were realists but adventurous as well. They intended to live life fully and never backed down on a social issue.

"Tell me about the trip," Mike asked.

"It was a great trip for us both and Brian did add seven new birds to his list," Pam said.

Mike knew Brian's most important list only included birds on this continent, that number stood at 704.

Mike asked, "How was the food?"

"Not as good as the scenery, but still great."

The waitress stopped at their table, "One check or two?"

Mike said, "One."

Brian began to protest, Mike waved him off, "Next time old buddy. I want to come back when I'm really hungry and thirsty and you're paying to watch me eat ribs."

"Okay."

Mike hugged them both good bye and they all headed home. Mike was wondering to himself if he'd ever get over her death, he didn't think so. Sandy was in his fiber and woven into every bit of his life.

Mike got home and sat down to look at the paper, three minutes later he was turning on the TV and powering up his video game console. He found three video games that he was getting exceptionally good at playing and wondered if he might be obsessed. He'd read that the military, as well as our enemies, were using video games for training purposes. These games had you clearing houses with your squad. He usually played against the game but sometimes got online and played with people he figured were half his age or younger. His sense of the action had improved along with his reactions and reaction time. He was pretty deadly. He had not shared this obsession with anyone and enjoyed the killing aspect. There were times when he let his mind wonder what would it feel like doing it for real.

Mike had been dozing in the chair for a few minutes when he realized his phone was buzzing, he saw it was Brian.

"Hey, Brian?"

"Do you have the news on?"

"No, what's up?"

"There was an explosion at Purdue's Vet School this morning, all kinds of theories are being thrown around including terrorism. They know nothing definite yet, but the FBI is investigating. I'm going to call Doc Summers."

"Wow, let me know what you learn."

Brian clicked off and called.

"Hey Brian Miller, how you doing?"

"I'm doing good Doc; did you hear about the explosion at Purdue?"

"I was there."

"No shit?"

"No shit, I can't give any details, but I was there, and the investigation is ongoing."

"Are you okay?"

"Yes, I'm fine but I'm also lucky. If the timing were a little different I'd have been way too close."

"Well Pam and I are sorry for the lives lost this morning, but we're glad you're ok."

"Thanks, Brian. Hey I'll update the Boiler Club by email as soon as I can. Tell Mike I say hey."

"Will do, take care, Charley."

"You too Brian."

The call ended, and Brian called Mike to relate it all.

"Is this payback for the State Fairgrounds?"

"Who knows Mike. I'm wondering if we'll ever be safe again?"

"I don't think so, should we all learn to shoot?"

"I don't want it to come to that Mike, like the Wild West, but those outlaws didn't hurt women and children."

"This enemy is pure evil with no regard for their own women and children, let alone ours."

"Charley said he'd email us all when he could tell us more."

"All right, take care." Mike clicked off.

Chicago

Hazaq was getting his information from television and the internet. The explosion at Purdue had killed nine students and two professors. They were not yet releasing any names to the public but he wanted to know if Doc Summers was splattered all over the floor and walls of that room? He knew Asis would be monitoring all of this and wondered how this would be shared with the world. The term terrorist attack had been mentioned by the media, but there was no confirmation.

He had not tried to reestablish any cell members in Indianapolis since the last attack. Bisma was dead and the apartment was blown. It seemed like he should concentrate on getting cells in another state unless Asis told him differently. He would think along those lines for now. The cell members here in Chicago were ready for more assignments. This little Trojan Horse Operation had been his idea after doing background research on Summers.

Hazaq now had four men who drove trucks all over a six-state area and were constantly gathering information for him. They kept logs of their travels and journals of things they saw. Nothing that would alarm law enforcement if discovered. As usual none of the men knew all the other men working for him. Living arrangements were kept to a maximum of three cell members per location except the Chicago location.

Natural gas pipelines were of great interest to Hazaq as well as crude oil refineries. The electric grid was also a possible target.

Asis had expressed interest in recruiting people in the Cincinnati area but gave no particular reason. Hazaq was smart enough to know that Asis kept him compartmentalized as Hazaq did his own people.

Hazaq was at a point he wanted to give Chris more responsibility. This had taken a long time because he didn't have a good feeling about Chris. He'd done his best to test him earlier this year and he'd passed. Still, he had a gut feeling but he needed someone like Chris to further the cause. Chris was born in the central part of the United States and for this reason, fit in better than Hazaq ever would. Racial profiling was frowned upon here in the States. How stupid was that? Hazaq sure as hell racial profiled anyone from this country he would recruit, he had too. Asis was giving him more authority to push out the jihad and Hazaq needed careful, controlled growth.

Chris was ready to get away from everyone in Chicago. Hazaq had been hinting at sending him out to establish a new cell. Chris was still upset about the death of Bisma. He had connected with Bisma after he established the cell location outside of Indianapolis. She was not like the others and that's undoubtedly why Hazaq had ordered she be killed. She was extremely smart, and he would always feel Hazaq was threatened by her intelligence.

Chapter 3

Elm Grove

Roger Knight's body had been discovered the day after his murder. Local police cordoned off the entire house and began reconstruction. One perfectly placed crossbow bolt had ended his life in an agonizing fashion. Dried blood on the bolt would yield no possible fingerprints. It was easy to see the shot came from the trees and bushes across the yard. There were no footprints in the area, nothing appeared to be disturbed. No clues. All neighbors were interviewed, and the only information uncovered was someone leaving his house in a huff and a hurry. A description of the vehicle was an easy connection to Knight's sister Janet who lives near St. Louis, Missouri.

Ms. Knight was questioned and she told the story of being at her brother's home and leaving in anger after an upsetting conversation. She vehemently denied killing her brother and offered no idea of who may have done it. Local authorities made calls to FBI Special Agent Nat Jackson to learn Knight had hundreds of local people with a motive to see him dead. Janet Knight's expertise with a crossbow years earlier was still weighing heavy with investigators although she told them it was either a coincidence or a carefully planned way to frame her. There was no shortage of hunters with crossbow skills in the Midwest.

There was no doubt to first responders that whoever sent the projectile through his neck wanted to make sure they did the job. After several attempts to remove the body from the chair they had to get a pair of vice grips to forcefully pull the bolt from the chair and his neck. This left two State Troopers who'd seen a lot of gruesome scenes in their time, very queasy.

Janet was the only family member remaining and although still under suspicion, she had to make the funeral arrangements. She was upset over his death but didn't seem to be as distraught as one might think. After the autopsy and all possible forensic evidence had been gathered, a private ceremony was held followed by cremation. Janet thought she should spread Roger's ashes over the farm her grandparents had once owned and lost, and she now owned again.

She suspected it was Moe Keane with the Department of Homeland Security who had leaked information to the press about how her brother had masterminded a plot to drive local farmers off their land. Many of these farms had been in the same family for generations. There was no love loss for her brother in Central Indiana.

Greenville

Mike wanted to see Nat Jackson before she left the country on assignment. Learning the depth of involvement Roger Knight had with his wife Sandy's death, along with the magnitude of the conspiracy this had shaken Mike to his core. He knew there was probably nothing more she could tell him due to ongoing investigations, but now the murder of Roger Knight might have changed that. He scrolled to find her number and hit the call button.

On the second ring, "Hey Mike, how you doin'?"

"Good, Special Agent Jackson, how you doin'?"

"You must be in deep trouble to use the 'Special Agent' greeting."

"No, just giving you your due."

"Well thank you, what's up?"

Mike started, "I know you are getting ready to head to London, I'm wondering if we might have a quick meeting before you go?"

"In regard to?"

"Roger Knight."

"Okay, but I'm not sure what I can tell you."

"I understand, but I'd like a quick talk."

"Tomorrow at 10:00 AM work for you, Mike?"

"I'll be there."

"See you in the morning." Nat clicked off.

Mike poured a cup of coffee from his Chemex and walked outside to sit in his swing to think about what exactly he'd ask.

Nat knew the amount of pain Roger Knight had caused in Mike Baker's life. The debriefing she had given Mike and the Boiler Club concerning Knight's actions would haunt Mike forever. Knight's murder may have given Mike some satisfaction, but she knew he was not that kind of man. Nevertheless, he surely was not mourning his death unless he wanted to see Knight prosecuted for his crimes. That prosecution would have been painful for the entire Baker family. Truth be told she had little new to tell Mike, but she'd give him some time

Indianapolis

Mike pulled into the parking lot of the FBI offices on the north side of Indianapolis. He proceeded to the front door and knowing the drill, pulled out identification at the front desk. "I have an appointment with Special Agent, Natalie Jackson."

"Please have a seat, Mr. Baker."

Four minutes later Nat crossed the lobby and waved Mike to follow her. They shook hands as she pressed the up button on the elevator.

"You getting ready for your deployment?"

"I'm getting there, the explosion at the Purdue Vet School set me back a few days."

"Was it a planned attack?"

"It's still being investigated Mike, too early to tell."

"I'm not sure if you can tell me, but when you travel to London do you get to take your own weapon you're familiar with?"

"Actually yes, it goes over in a diplomatic pouch."

"That's good."

That question raised Nat's 'kind of weird' meter a little, "Okay Mike, what's on your mind?"

"What can you tell me about the murder investigation?"

"Not much Mike. The Indiana State Police have taken the lead, but we are working closely with them because of his involvement with terrorism. Moe Keane is included on everything as well."

"No leads?"

"Not yet. You know he was killed with a crossbow bolt through his neck. Someone certainly wanted him dead. He caused a lot of people pain but we have to consider his terrorist connections may have wanted to make sure he talked to no one."

Mike shook his head. The phone on the desk buzzed and Nat lifted the receiver. "Sure," she said and hung up.

"Mike please excuse me, I'll be back shortly." She did not close the door.

Mike felt empty. He was not sure what he truly wanted to know but just wanted to talk to her before she went overseas. He walked across the office to look at a whiteboard on the wall. There were lots of notes written on the board accompanied by many paper notes held up with small magnets. This was kind of cool, it would be a nice addition in his office. As he was ready to move, a picture caught his eye. It was the man Moe Keane had called Chris Powell. The man who was undercover with the terrorist cell. Mike had met him last January before the attack at the Indiana State Fairgrounds. Mike always got a shiver when he thought of the day he'd shot the suicide bomber and wounded the other one. There was a map under the picture of Chris. Mike pulled his phone out and took a picture. He slipped the phone back into the front pocket of his jeans, as he turned Nat came hustling back into her office. She met his eye and felt she had startled him.

"You okay?" she asked.

"Yeah, I'm fine. Nat, I'm just thinking I have wasted your time today, you are very busy and I..."

"It's fine Mike, but I do have a lot on my plate."

He stuck out his hand and she gave him a hug instead.

"That's probably what I needed," he said. "Nat, you stay safe and I wish you good luck."

"Thanks, Mike, I'll walk you out."

Mike got in his truck and decided since it was lunchtime, he'd go for pulled pork and sweet tea. He made the short trip to one of his favorite places on 86th Street and was quickly seated. After the waitress brought him a big glass of tea he checked his phone for messages, found none, but opened his latest photo. He made the picture bigger. Chris's face was clear, so was the map under it.

Nat Jackson would always wonder who took care of Roger Knight. Someone had doled out swift justice and saved the taxpayers a lot of money on a trial and incarceration. This type of assassination had passion written all over it. Nat had some experience in this area after killing her own father many years ago as he was attempting to assault her younger sister. A blow to the back of his head with a baseball bat had ended his life. Her mother had taken responsibility much to the torment of Nat. This dark secret had left Nat always wondering when the truth would catch up with her. A career in keeping the law after being a murderer herself was almost too much to bear. She had her own thoughts about Knight's murder that she'd investigate in the future, but for now, she'd stay focused on the trip to London.

Chicago

Chris was at a point where he had to make something happen. He was working on a plan to ask Hazaq if he could do some recruiting or surveillance. His real motive was to try and contact Moe Keane. It had been months since they'd had any communication and it would be a huge risk for him to reach out anywhere near this location. He always felt Hazaq believed in him but also felt Hazaq would never fully trust any infidel born in the United States. He recognized that Hazaq had purposefully put him through several trials during the recent attacks in Indianapolis, including testing him with news of the death of Bisma. He felt he'd passed these tests and earned his trust.

He decided he would approach him the next morning after prayers.

The next morning was business as usual. Female cell members did all the cooking and cleaning. Breakfast happened after the first morning prayer and talk was sparse as they sat around to eat.

"May I talk to you in private?" Chris asked.

"Give me a few minutes to check emails."

Chris sat and waited, he was getting looks from other cell members. Hazaq usually approached them for discussion, not the other way around. Twenty minutes passed and the door to Hazaq's office opened and he waved Chris in.

"Thank you for giving me an opportunity to talk," Chris said.

"Go ahead."

"Hazaq, I would like to get out to do some recruiting or target surveillance, or both. I know I'm out of bounds asking you, but I feel I can help further our cause. I'm not out for my own advancement, I know you will make any decisions and recommendations to London. I want to be your extension. You know it's easier for me to move among the locals than it is for you. Racial profiling is a thing whether the U.S. government wants to admit it or not."

Hazaq held his gaze and showed no emotion, good or bad. Chris always felt like these crazy bastards might gut you open for looking at them the wrong way. He knew they didn't like anyone overstepping their bounds and they made sure everyone knew those bounds. He was pretty sure he was on the edge.

"You have proven to be someone who can think on his feet and yes, it's easier for you to get things accomplished with your background. I have been wanting to do some research in Cincinnati, Ohio. We have no one there currently and this is a place for another small cell to be located. There is a company I would like to infiltrate. I have been thinking of an attack using this company's products. Products used by virtually all Americans."

"Okay that is intriguing. Do you think I could be your man?"

"I will think on this and get back to you."

"Thank you, Hazaq."

Chris walked out of the office to more stares from the others. As bad as he wanted to give them all the finger and tell them what they could do to themselves, he remained composed and went to the basement to work out. The conversation had not gone as he'd planned but it might put him in a situation to stop another planned attack. He knew of one big corporation in Cincinnati that produced products everyone used. He couldn't help but think ahead of what Hazaq had in mind. He'd wait and see if he was correct in his thinking.

Chapter 4

Missouri

It had been a month since Roger had been found dead. Surprisingly to Janet Knight, she was missing him. She picked out a Glencairn nosing glass and poured herself a double. She and Roger had agreed on this bourbon over the years. One of the few things on which they did agree. They had both made a few stops on the Kentucky Bourbon Trail, but never together. That would have been nice she thought to herself. She took the first drink and let it rest on her tongue a few seconds before allowing it to start the warm burn that filled her chest. She closed her eyes and let her head relax against the leather chair. Over the next fifteen minutes, she finished her drink and felt the alcohol warm her.

She had not looked at the clock when she sat down, but some time had surely passed since she finished the drink. She had dozed off and woke with a slight twitch that startled her a little. It was either the short nap or three fingers of bourbon, or both that had her in a little fog. It was one of those times when she knew there was something to remember but she wasn't getting it. She decided to let it nag at her while she got ready for bed.

With lights out and the security system and cameras all set and operating she headed up the stairs. Ten minutes later she was finished with the routine of makeup removal and teeth brushed and flossed when the memory she had been searching for came front and center. Roger had given her an envelope a couple years ago that he asked her to put away in her bank lock box. It was one of those situations where he told her to only open it if he were no longer living. She clearly remembered rolling her eyes when he said that. It seemed so melodramatic at the time.

She awoke the next morning at her normal early hour and was pleased the bourbon had not caused a headache. She felt well rested and as her feet hit the floor, the envelope she'd received from Roger was on her mind. She knew she'd have to get to the bank and into her lock box before this day was over.

A busy morning at work had kept thoughts of the letter at bay. As lunchtime arrived she took the elevator to the first floor and crossed the terrazzo tiled lobby to the street, heels clicking all the way. Her bank was a short walk and she was glad to be outside on this beautiful summer day. Four city blocks later she was entering the lobby. She approached the front desk and was met by the smile of a young lady showing a little too much cleavage. She thought to herself, *Roger would have appreciated it.*

"How may I help you?" the young lady asked.

"I need to get to my lockbox."

"Follow me," was the response.

Janet fully expected her to produce the bank key from her ample bosom, but instead, Janet was introduced to a toothy young fellow that had to be an intern and grandson of a board member.

"Do you have your key?" he asked.

Janet handed it to him with a look that said, "of course I do, you moron". He thanked her and headed into the vault. He turned both keys to the right and opened the door. He pulled out the box and carried it to a private room placing it on the table.

"Please let me know when you're finished Ms. Knight and I'll put it back. Please take your time."

Closing the door as he walked out, Janet sat down and felt some excitement in herself. She opened the box and began searching the contents. She was feeling a little nervous as she approached the bottom of the box but then found the envelope she remembered. She laid it to the side and looked at a few old photos that had spent many years locked in this box. Photos of her parents and grandparents. Photos of happy times that seemed few and far between in her memory. There were two pictures of herself and Roger as children. The notion that, "we look normal enough" came into her mind. She slowly shook her head and placed all the pictures back into the box. There were several secrets in this box that she wouldn't want anyone to see until she was long gone, especially people from the Securities and Exchange Commission.

She turned her attention to the envelope from Roger. She carefully broke the seal and pulled back the tab. Inside was a piece of paper that she unfolded to find a short note along with a key taped at the bottom.

Okay, you're reading this note and I'm history. I won't lie, I'm hoping it's 2050 and I just died at 90 something a wealthy old man. I'm going to share a few things about myself I'm thinking you should know. During my Kingston University days in London, I met a fellow who seemed to have a lust for power and money as much as myself. Turns out it was a lust for killing infidels in the United States. He was willing to help me get what I wanted if I helped him get what he wanted. We have shared some mutual successes as I am writing this. I'm not sure where it all will lead.

While willingly agreeing to work with him I will say I've never trusted him fully. It seems someone like him would kill me on the very day he felt I was not useful to him anymore. For this reason, I'm going to give you some information on the man in London I know as Asis.

The letter spilled onto page two with details about the family of Asis as well as his family business. Roger had written this letter at the beginning of the time when the farm economy had spiraled downhill to a point when Janet and Roger's White Oak Holding Company had begun the big land grab that had lasted for over three years.

It was now clear to her that the questioning she had endured at the hands of Mr. Keane at the DHS was basically all true. How did they know all of this? She then realized they didn't know everything and what they didn't know was this person, Asis. He was a valuable target.

The letter ended with: *Use this information as you see fit, but be careful. He is a dangerous man.*

Your brother,

Roger

Taped to the bottom of the letter was a key with a number and the name of a bank. He'd left her something in another lock box here in St. Louis. He had traveled here at some point to open this lock box. Suddenly this seemed exceptionally dangerous to her.

An hour had passed, and Janet needed to get back to her office, she had the afternoon booked with appointments that had to be kept. She wanted in the worst way to get to this other bank but knew that wasn't happening until tomorrow.

Greenville

Mike Baker was sitting in his favorite spot, his swing under the tulip poplar. He liked this tree for two reasons: It was planted by his dad, Gordon, and it was the state tree of Indiana. What he lost in sunrise views by facing west he gained in some spectacular sunsets. Today was one of them. This spot was close enough to the house for his phone to still get Wi-Fi and the importance of that was he could listen to Braves baseball games on his favorite app. There were a few other teams he checked in on during the season to hear long-time announcers he enjoyed. Daylight savings time was in full swing now with sunsets not happening until after 9:00 PM.

He smiled as the text came in, '*Time for a quick call?*' '*Sure thing*', he answered.

Seconds later David's picture popped up on the screen. Mike clicked on.

"Hey son."

"Hey dad. Listening to a ballgame?"

"Braves up 5 to 3 in the bottom of the seventh. They're home to the Nationals."

"Sounds good, hey I'll get right to business."

"Go ahead, son."

"Graduation for basic training happens Friday after next on the 30th. Think you and Sarah can come?"

"We've already talked about it and are planning on it. So, yes sir we'll be there."

"Can't wait to see you both Dad."

"Same here. What do we need to know?"

"They asked for emails and I gave them yours. My understanding is you'll get something in the next 24 hours. It should spell everything out."

"Okay, I'll be watching."

"Thanks Dad, I gotta go, take care and go Braves!"

"Love you son."

"Love you too, night."

"Night."

Mike had been expecting this call and was excited. He immediately texted Sarah to confirm the dates and said he should know more tomorrow. She thanked him and asked if the Braves were winning. Mike told her, yes and that he loved her.

"Love you too Dad."

Mike had already picked out a place to stay and went ahead and made reservations for Thursday, Friday, and Saturday nights. He and Sarah would share driving on Thursday and again on Sunday. It would be a whirlwind trip but a good one for sure. He was looking forward to the official email, but he'd already been researching on the internet what the day would be like. He'd found websites that gave tips on everything from what to wear to not showing to much affection to your young soldier. Drill Sergeants would be watching closely.

The Braves young closer notched another save in the top of the 9th. No walks allowed tonight, that's been happening a little too much as far as Mike was concerned. Lead-off walks were killers for relief pitchers. Time to head in, he'd heard a mosquito buzzing his ear.

Missouri

The next day Janet got to work thirty minutes earlier than normal. She'd canceled an appointment and an office meeting that would free up most of her morning. As soon as the first round of phone calls had been handled she told her assistant she might not be back until after lunch and then she was gone out the door.

The bank she needed to get to was on the southeast part of the city, a twenty-five minute drive from her office. When she arrived she sat in her car thinking. She had brought a medium-sized tote bag, not knowing what she might find and what she might need to discreetly carry out. Janet walked in and went up to the first desk.

"Lockbox." As she held up her key.

"This way please."

She did a good job of hiding her discomfort as the signature card was produced. The customer service representative pushed it across the desk while seemingly staring a hole through her. She saw her signature right under the signature of Roger Knight. She signed four lines down and noticed that Roger had been in this box a total of three times with the last time being a year ago in November. She wondered if this bank rep was just having a bad day or remembered one of the visits with her charming brother. Without a word the women stood and motioned for Janet to follow.

Janet was led down a short hallway and turned right into the vault. The women held out her hand for Janet's key and the box was removed. She carried it into a small room with two chairs and shut the door behind her. Janet sat down and opened the box.

The customer service rep walked back to her desk and opened her purse. She removed her phone and slid it into the inside pocket of her blazer.

"Be back in a minute," she said to the last teller on the line as she headed for the restroom.

Once in the stall she removed her phone and opened the contact list. She quickly found the name she needed and punched out a short text, '*She is here*'. She was a little surprised to get a smiley-faced emoji back as an answer, but it was the only confirmation she needed. She had just made the easiest $5,000 of her life. She'd been waiting for this day for months and was glad she was here to see Janet Knight in person. It was now done, and she was ready for her payment.

Janet started laying everything on the table. There were two pictures of the man named Asis, one better than the other. There was information on how he was handling communication with Asis, including the dead drop spots in Indianapolis. There were three sealed envelopes she would read later at home and lastly, a handgun.

She felt she shouldn't stay too long with the lockbox, it might look suspicious. She also didn't want to be in this cramped room long, it was getting smaller by the minute. She was deciding if this would be the one and only visit to this bank branch. It seemed as though she should take everything from the box and be done with this place. Four minutes later her decision was made, and she began putting everything in the tote bag. Janet opened the door and carried the empty box back to the vault.

"Oh, I'll help with that," the customer service rep said as she hurried in to follow Janet.

Janet was already sliding the box back into its crypt as the rep arrived at her shoulder.

"Thank you," Janet said as the rep stood a little too close.

Janet got a good look at Rachelle's name tag as she waited for her to close the door.

"I'll take my key," Janet said.

Rachelle closed the door with a little more force than needed and turned both keys to the left. She handed Janet her key and Janet immediately turned to leave.

"Have a good day," Rachelle said as Janet walked into the lobby.

Janet gave a slight turn of her head but made no comment. She was out the door and lost in her thoughts.

Chapter 5

Rockton, Indiana

So it begins he thought to himself. He walked into the bedroom and opened the bottom drawer of his dresser, removed the contents and began to pry up the false bottom. After a trip to the kitchen to get a knife he had the bottom loose and his hands on the manila envelope.

He sat on the bed, cut the envelope open with one quick move and pulled out two sheets of paper and one small flash drive. He read the paper all the way through and then read it again. The instructions were clear, and he'd be rewarded well if he could see this through to the end. He felt confident he was the main person in this operation, but there was always the question in the back of his mind of who would be coming for him. They'd given him a codename, this made him chuckle. He would be known as Kurtz.

Janet Knight's visit to the bank safety deposit box started everything. A quick search on the internet would tell him if Janet would be the target. Seconds later he found the news story of the murder of Roger Knight. Janet passed the first test, she had not opened the lockbox while her brother was alive. Janet would stay alive for now but would still be a suspect.

London

Asis had started the process of recruiting his nephew, Farid months ago, truth be told, it was years. He'd brought his brother into the process at the beginning. This would be his brother's second son to sacrifice for the jihad. His first son, Babur, had given his life aboard a U.S. Virginia Class nuclear sub. He'd been the one to cause the explosion deep under the Pacific Ocean six years ago in February. Babur was a brilliant student and had quickly worked his way up in the Navy. His degree in Nuclear Engineering came from the Naval Academy in Annapolis, Maryland. His death was a real loss but had to happen.

Nephew, Farid was finishing his junior year of college and doing well. He seemed to be as exuberant about the jihad as they had hoped. Asis had been planning this next operation for months. He always kept his planning compartmentalized and this time was no exception. He would wait until much closer to bring anyone else into the fold. It was time to let Hazaq take over more of the future planning for the Chicago cell. With all their successes in central Indiana, they'd also had a few failures and Asis was always watching for possible security breaches. Hazaq didn't even know Asis's real name and that's the way it would stay, no reason to make it more personal. The only person who did know his name had been murdered and deserved to be murdered for all the heartache he'd left behind. Asis had admired Roger Knight's ruthlessness, his unwavering greed not so much. Greed is what most likely had gotten him killed.

Asis knew Hazaq had the jihad deep within him. He also had too much need for power. This would probably be his undoing, like Knight's greed. Until then Hazaq should be able to cause a lot more chaos in the midwestern part of the U.S. Asis would feed him ideas, money, and preliminary plans and let Hazaq do the recruiting, training and the final logistical coordination.

Farid was coming back to London next week for his summer break from college. This would be the opportunity to test his resolve and discuss next winter. Having him in the correct location for this operation would sound like a college internship.

Greenville

Tuesday before David's graduation Mike decided he and Sarah should fly instead of drive fourteen hours Thursday and fourteen hours Sunday. He had no doubt they could do it with each other's help, but the idea of flying suddenly sounded much more appealing. He decided not to call Sarah before booking their tickets, he'd just do it. Forty minutes later they were set.

Sarah answered her cell on the third ring, "Hey Dad."

"How you doin' sweetie?"

"Good, what you up to?"

"Surprise, I just bought us round-trip tickets to South Carolina Thursday and Sunday."

"Thought we were road-trippin' and stopping at every BBQ restaurant between here and there"

"I decided we'll be so tired we wouldn't enjoy the reason for the trip, seeing your brother graduate and having a little time with him."

"You're right."

"Go ahead and come home Wednesday night like you planned all along and we'll head to the airport Thursday morning. We fly out at 10:40 AM, stopover in Charlotte for an hour and then on to Savannah/Hilton Head by 3:10 PM. We'll rent a car and be within a half hour of Parris Island by dinnertime."

"Sounds good dad, thank you."

"Yes, it'll be best. Is your day good?"

"It is. I've been busy getting ready to leave Thursday and Friday, but all good."

"I'll let you get to it, see you Wednesday evening, love you."

"Love you too, Dad, bye"

Every conversation like this left him feeling he was a lucky man, blessed is so many ways. He missed Sandy every day and knew she'd be proud of how the kids were growing into adulthood in all ways. He held his emotions back when he saw her in them which was most of the time.

Sarah arrived home for dinner on Wednesday and they arrived at Indianapolis International Airport a little over an hour early Thursday morning. The clear weather had them flying on time and after a quick stop in Charlotte, they found themselves taxiing to the terminal at Savannah/Hilton Head. This area had memories for Mike. He and Sandy had brought the kids here when they were little. They'd explored Savannah and spent time on Tybee Island. They had loved these trips and had stopped to see a Braves game more than once on the way here from Indiana.

"You've been pretty quiet Dad, you doing okay?"

"I've got a lot going around in my head. I'm excited, happy, sad, scared, proud of my kids, heartbroken for you mom, what am I forgetting?"

"I think I understand every one of those."

"I'm sure you do sweetie."

Mike grabbed her hand and gave it a squeeze. People were standing up and getting bags out of the overhead compartments. This process always moved slowly. It didn't take long before they were heading towards Beaufort, South Carolina. Mike was driving, and Sarah was navigating.

"I found a BBQ place for dinner," Mike said.

"Imagine that."

"You want to get something else?"

"Heck no, you raised me right. Let's get checked in and go explore a little."

They found their hotel, they found the BBQ restaurant, they found the sweet tea. Mike slept better than he expected, and they were up early for breakfast. It was going to be a hot August day in South Carolina, and they had dressed as they were told by the Marine website. Business conservative meant khaki pants and a light blue short sleeve button-down for Mike. Cameras and phones were all charged and ready for picture taking, base passes had been secured and they arrived early for good seats.

Parade ground activities started precisely on time and graduation started on time as well, no surprise there. Graduation lasted one hour and the hand-shaking, back-patting and proper hugs began. Thousands of pictures were taken of Marines with their families, Marines with each other and every other combination imaginable. David had been cleared to leave the base for lunch and was due back at 01700. This is the last time they'd see him on this trip and then they'd welcome him home early next week.

He had ten days of leave coming but elected to only use five and save five for some time later in the year or early next year.

Stories were shared all afternoon. Mike had never seen a man eat like this before. He said he was being fed well, but he sure enjoyed the buffet place they'd found for lunch. Time flew, and before long they were dropping him off at the front gate. He waved goodbye and was off on a trot back to his barracks.

"Well okay then," Mike said to Sarah. "You hungry?"

"Are you kidding, we almost got thrown out of that buffet place. Let's go get something cold to drink and just hang out."

That sounded good to Mike so they headed back to their hotel. They drank lemonade and made plans for Saturday in Savannah.

Saturday was a great father-daughter day. They added a drive out to Tybee Island to see the ocean and spent time walking the beach and talking. Next thing they knew they were on the plane Sunday and back in Indiana.

Sarah headed back to campus. She was ready to start her Junior year at DePauw University, a small Liberal Arts school in Greencastle, Indiana. She was determined to make her mom and dad proud even though she'd battled times of depression and was resolute to work her way through it. Roger Knight's face came to her at odd times. She felt this was her payment for what she'd done and was resigned that it would never leave her. She also felt strongly she would do it again with the circumstances as they were. This was oddly comforting in that she knew she had done the right thing. She knew she may get caught someday, this worry would always be with her. Apart from Knight's sister, he had no family, and no one seemed to be mourning his loss. It seemed manpower was needed to fight terrorism instead of looking for whoever killed Roger Knight.

Two days after Mike had returned from South Carolina, he got a text from David, '*Delta flight 1898 tomorrow morning*'. Mike answered, '*See you then*'. Mike was looking forward to five days with David at home on furlough. He knew when he left this time it would be for a while. He had researched Marine deployments and learned they averaged seven months. He was expecting an overseas deployment for David.

Mike arrived at Indianapolis International a half hour early and found a seat to wait. Flight info showed David's flight on time and the weather was good from Indiana to South Carolina. Times like this made Mike think of his mother. As a kid, he found it weird when his mother told him she enjoyed watching people. Mike had wondered why that would be enjoyable until he got a little older and enjoyed watching girls his own age, but that was different. He now saw himself turning into his parents. He now enjoyed watching people too. This was especially true at airports with people saying hello and goodbye all at the same time. He always thought the best reunions were service men and women coming home, the toughest was them leaving. This would be his first time to greet his serviceman. He let his mind wander to five days from now and scolded himself for that. Live in the present he reminded himself, soak it up fully and enjoy every minute.

Soon here came David. Having just seen him a few days ago made it no less exciting. Now in fatigues instead of his Blue Dress Class A uniform David's appearance seemed to hit Mike differently. Thirteen weeks of basic training in the Marines is a transformation for sure. David looked older, more mature, and most of all – capable. This struck Mike as a weird thought. Capable of what gave him a shiver. That shiver was soon squelched by the biggest bear hug he'd ever had.

"Hey Dad."

"Man, you look fit. All muscle."

"Well I should be, this has been intense. I'm looking forward to sitting at the kitchen table."

"Let's go, son."

Mike reached for his duffle bag, but David was scooping it up and had it on his shoulder. Mike fell into step with him as they headed for the car. Capable, he thought to himself.

They spent most of the next five days together. David got to see a few of his closest high school buddies one evening. They spent the night sitting around a fire behind the barn enjoying cold beer and old stories.

David shared a lot of stories about basic. Mike wondered if he could've done it when he was that age, you think you could but until you did it, who knows? Training is never completely over in the military, but it would now happen under many different circumstances during deployments. Mike was not surprised to learn that part of their training is taught with sophisticated video games. He'd also heard that terrorists train the same way. It made sense to him, they could train without taking people directly to Syria.

The morning of day five of David's furlough arrived. Together they fixed a big breakfast and enjoyed it as they sat quietly drinking strong coffee prepared in the Chemex. Mike had offered an old recipe David knew and he'd said yes without thinking.

This had ground sausage, hash browns, eggs, and cheese all fixed in one big skillet, man food for sure. They used to fix this dish when they went tent camping as a family when David was a boy. It was as good now as it was then.

"We haven't talked about your orders."

"I'm not sure Dad. We think we'll have orders within a week. There's a lot of speculation but most of us think we'll go to Afghanistan. Others think this is being scaled back to a point where we may be staged on a troop ship for now.

Mid-morning, they headed for the airport and talked all the way there. Mike was not going to just drop him off at the curb, they parked and walked in together. They had a good handshake and a hug.

"Love you Dad."

"Love you, son," and just like that, David was off. Mike watched for as long as he could see him and then turned to get his car for the ride home. He knew his life was different now.

Chapter 6

Bethesda, Maryland

The fall semester had started at the National Intelligence University. The recent move to Bethesda from Washington, D.C. had provided much more in the way of technical capabilities for Bisma. This campus was secure and had the latest and greatest for all types of learning. It had been Moe Keane's idea to send Bisma to school there. She was very reluctant at first due to the fact she wanted to be in a more mainstream type of career. Her background gave her a head start on many of her classmates who had not been a part of a terrorist organization. This information was known by just a few people and would stay that way.

The plastic surgeons had done wonderful work keeping the scarring to a minimum. Former cell members had come within a fraction of an inch of ending her life with a blade across her throat. The blood loss was dramatic, but she survived with the help of a trauma team in Indianapolis. The cosmetic surgeons made the scar on her neck appear as though it was from a somewhat common surgery done on the C-5 and C-6 vertebrae. It would take much less explaining for Bisma to tell people this was a planned surgery for a herniated disc as opposed to a brutal attack.

She'd read the eighteen-page report enough times she'd lost count. It was vital that she knew this information like it was her own personal family history because going forward, it was her family history. Moe Keane had ordered her a new identity, not unlike the witness protection program but this was much more extensive. She was fine to leave everything in her past behind except for her mother. Her mother was responsible for getting her and her siblings out of harm's way after her father had been killed in Afghanistan by the Russian military. Her mother had saved their lives and made sure Bisma was safe. She had not been in contact with her mother for many years and knew her mother could no longer be alive. She felt no guilt as she worked to assume this new identity, her mother would have encouraged her self-preservation.

Students here were not eighteen to twenty-two-year-old college kids, but neither was Bisma. Vetting was thorough for this student population. They were taught to keep their personal lives to themselves except for the most basic information and this was perfect for Bisma. The amount of reading required would be phenomenal. She made her way to the local coffee shop with her backpack and ordered a medium sized light roast and headed for a booth. On her way, she noticed a table of two guys and a girl that she'd seen on campus and in one of her lectures.

"Good morning," she said as she walked past.

She got two "Good Mornings," in return from the guys and one sizing up from the girl. Bisma had never been in situations where she was told she was a beautiful young woman. None of the men she had spent time with over the last few years seemed to care about her as a woman except for one man. He was part of the terrorist organization, born and raised in America. She was drawn to him in a way she had never felt before but always hoped for and it surprised her. Bisma had only seen Chris two times and spent no more than a few hours with him, but her radar had been going off in ways that caused her to take notice. Then she remembered a recent conversation with Moe Keane.

"Mr. Keane there was the one cell member I met twice. He was not like any of the others. He seemed to be kind and not like one of the jihadists."

"You've mentioned him before, what interests you about him?" Moe asked.

"I cannot help but think operationally. I'm sure Hazaq hated me because I had a brain. I want to help, to feel like I'm earning the chance you're giving me for a new life."

"Go ahead."

"I feel we should hunt Chris down and try to turn him to our side. You've turned me and granted I was a willing participant, I was able to start the process with the help of Mike Baker."

Moe Keane was impressed with her thoughts. He was also good at not showing he was impressed. He wanted her to keep thinking like this because he was sure she would be a great asset for this country. Now was not the time to tell her that she was spot on about Chris Powell. Chris was an extremely valuable and embedded agent for the Department of Homeland Security. The most valuable agent they currently had. Until he was absolutely sure about Bisma he would not risk Chris's identity with her.

"I'll give it some thought Bisma. You have a lot on your plate right now with classes and your new identity. I have no problem with you thinking operationally, we can benefit from your insights."

She felt like she had been somewhat dismissed, but never like her dealings with Hazaq. His rebukes were always sharp and intended to put her in her place. Her mind came back to the task at hand. She unzipped her backpack and chose one of the three books to begin reading. As she found the page she needed her eyes raised to notice the table of three. The quick shift of the gaze of one of the young men made her feel she might be their current topic of discussion. She wanted to make friends but was not ready to let her guard down. It would be nice to have an American female friend who could tell her things about this country. She spent more time on the internet now trying to learn about customs and fashion trends such as what sweater to wear with jeans and boots.

Chicago

It had been eleven weeks since Chris had the talk with Hazaq about new responsibilities. He was sure Hazaq took great pleasure in making him wait for more information. Hazaq was a control freak to the extreme. The other cell members never seemed to mind long periods of time with no plans or activity, but it was driving Chris up a wall. Chris realized this might be another way Hazaq was testing him, trying to draw Chris out in many ways. There were only two other Caucasians in the cell and they were just as complacent as the others. As long as they had food and water, they didn't seem to give a damn about anything else. If this were a test of wills, he wasn't going to let Hazaq win. It would be Chris' way to drive that prick crazy.

Hazaq didn't always take his meals with the rest of the cell. He spent a lot of time in his room with his computer and the internet. This evening he was sitting with them all. The women had prepared the meal and served them as usual. Hazaq was watching Chris closely this evening as he kept to himself like the others. At his core he didn't trust Chris but he realized he didn't trust anyone but himself, so he needed to find a way to use Chris effectively. Chris and Joel had performed as expected last year in setting up the cell location in the barn east of Indianapolis. The two of them could do business easier because of their skin color. This was just a fact. Hazaq knew racial profiling worked both ways.

He was ready to send Chris to another location and this needed to happen soon. His only worry was that nagging distrust. If Chris was not under his watch, he could compromise the cell location. He had no choice last year when he sent Chris and Joel to the Indiana countryside to launch the attack in Indianapolis. Asis had ordered the attack and it was necessary to have them stage the cell in close proximity. It was Asis who had changed plans at the last minute to attack the Purdue Ag Alumni meeting at the Indiana State Fairgrounds with three suicide bombers. Hazaq still felt this move by Asis was a mistake. The plan to attack the GenCon convention would have been a huge success. The attack at the fairgrounds was stopped by the precise person Asis wanted to hurt. Asis had let his hatred for Mike Baker hurt their plans. Hazaq saw that as a sign of weakness and desperately wanted to be in charge. He only saw Asis as a way to funnel money in his direction, which was extremely important.

Asis had been extremely quiet in the last few months. Hazaq wondered what was happening and what was being planned. The attack at the Purdue Vet School had worked exactly as planned apart from killing the friend of Mike Baker. Hazaq knew this was a goal which also led him to realize Asis wanted to hurt Mike Baker any way he could. Terrorist attacks were mainly aimed at retaliation, causing terror by causing death to as many as possible. They didn't target individuals, they targeted big groups of people on an indiscriminate basis. Recent attacks in Europe had moved to using trucks to kill people walking down the street. They were killing everyone from children in strollers to old people in wheelchairs. It seemed Asis had an ax to grind with Mike Baker and Hazaq felt Asis wanted a terrorist attack to cover up a murder. It may still be furthering their cause, but Hazaq felt it might eventually put them in a corner to be trapped.

As the cell members were finishing the evening meal Hazaq called out, "Chris, please follow me."

Chris pushed back from the table and stood without a word. He knew other cell members didn't trust him and especially disliked it when he got attention from Hazaq. Most of them had never been asked to meet personally with Hazaq. Hazaq preferred to talk with most cell members in small groups. It was never social, that did not happen. It was always for the purpose of training or to build their resolve. He kept a close eye on the brothers to make sure no one was showing any sign of weakness or self-centeredness. Any sign of either and he'd reign them in using as much force as necessary. They all respected him and feared him even more. Months earlier Hazaq had killed a young man one morning for nothing more than a single word of back talk. Chris knew it was nothing more than a show of force and it had worked perfectly. It was a story of legend among the cell members and recounted to new recruits with much gusto. Chris was damned tired of hearing about it and wanted to tell them it was all bullshit, but he knew better. The total disregard for human life would be hard for U.S. citizens to imagine. Chris had seen it firsthand while everyone else saw it on the world and local news. Suicide bombers had always chilled people to the bone. Killing innocent people by driving a truck down a city street at any time of day, anywhere in the country seemed even worse. Any jihadist with a vehicle could make this happen.

Chris followed Hazaq down the hallway and into his office. His office was also his personal apartment. He did not sleep with the others nor socialize with them. Chris followed him in and Hazaq closed the door. He motioned for Chris to have a seat in a straight chair, the room was sparsely furnished as was the entire apartment. Hazaq did have a twin mattress on box springs, the rest of them slept on the floor on sweat-soaked mats. Hazaq's computer was the nicest piece of equipment in the entire apartment. Chris figured he spent most of each day on that computer. Chris also knew Hazaq worked out. He wanted the cell members to know he was keeping his body in top physical shape for the jihad and he wanted to portray his superiority in all ways.

After a pause that lasted too long for Chris, Hazaq began to speak, "It is time to set up for our next attack."

"Go on, I'm ready Hazaq."

"You Americans love your football."

Chris looked at him not trying to hide his irritation.

"I hit a nerve with your football."

"No, you hit a nerve with 'you Americans'."

This pleased Hazaq, it was the right answer as far as he was concerned.

"I am with you and stand ready to hit them hard."

"I am sending you six hours east of here to prepare. You will leave in two days with two other brothers. We'll use an extended stay property that is furnished. You will be a team of three coming into the area to look for business."

"How will we communicate?"

"Secure email, no phones. This is enough for now. Get your rest and be ready."

Chris nodded and turned to leave.

"Do not tell anyone else."

"Of course." Chris closed the door behind himself.

No one asked him anything as he made his way through the common room on the first floor. He felt their eyes boring through him. He would always be an infidel to them. His mind was already racing with two pieces of information. Six hours east and football. It was the fall, so football fit. Hazaq must be planning an attack at a football game. Some of our biggest gatherings in this country with people out in the open happen at college football games each fall.

Fort Meade, Maryland

Steve Bradshaw was still struggling to keep focus at his job with the National Security Agency. He was supposed to have traveled to London with Nat Jackson to hunt terrorists three months ago but the trip had been canceled at the last possible moment. He felt crushed. He wanted to be out in the field doing this type of work and wanted to be doing it alongside Nat Jackson. His marriage was holding on by a thread anyway, the trip would have ended it and he was resolved to that fact. Nat had not given him any more than casual interest knowing he was a married man. He tried to let her know his marriage was on a downward spiral. Nat could see that was in large part because of his work, she knew this from hearing several phone conversations Steve had with his wife while he and Nat were working or having dinner. She had not let herself be interested in any man and while she appreciated the fact Steve was interested in her, she hated the thought of being the other woman.

Steve had been given a wider berth to investigate avenues he thought had merit going forward. One of those avenues was a winnowing down of the crew manifest of the USS South Carolina submarine that had been destroyed by one of the crew six and a half years ago. This was still not a 100% known fact, but most anyone in the upper crust at the Pentagon felt it had to have been someone on the crew. There had to be a mole onboard, someone had made their way on the crew who caused the catastrophic explosion.

The crew consisted of one hundred thirty-four officers and enlisted men and women. Steve was using all avenues to search including racial profiling in every form he could think of. He had the list down to five names he wanted to search further. The United States was still considered a melting pot, but Steve was a

little surprised at the diversity on the crew of a nuclear submarine. All five of these men had access to the sub's nuclear reactor,
this is where he'd dig deeper.

Chapter 7

Greenville

Mike was getting back into the groove of farming his land again. Harvest had started, and he was making good progress cutting soybeans. He did miss driving the bus route on a regular basis but had agreed to sub when needed. Substitute bus drivers were hard to find, and he was more than happy to help. Time in the combine and on the tractor, gave farmers time to think. He was thinking about the upcoming work he was going to do for the construction company after harvest was over. His Building and Construction Management degree from Purdue meant a lot to him. He had kept up with trends on the commercial side of construction over the years even though he wasn't doing any construction work. He subscribed to three trade journals and had a few favorite websites that kept him up to date.

His thoughts then drifted to David and Sarah as regularly happened. He missed them both and tried to not let himself worry about David. Any parent who has sent a child overseas knows the knot that stays in your stomach month in and month out. Mike asked God more than once a day for safety for David and all the troops stationed overseas. He knew very little about David's deployment and only heard from him sporadically. Mike and Sarah got together every couple weeks. She was a little over an hour away at DePauw and doing well in school, but Mike could tell she was battling some kind of demon. He felt confident she was dealing with at least mild depression from the loss of her mother. He was pretty sure of this fact because he also was suffering from depression. They both kept themselves immersed in work and studies to deal with the grief. This worked when they stayed busy, but then the quiet times came around and it was a different story. Mike and Sarah talked about it some when they were together, they shared with each other and understood each other well.

Mike came to a stop with a hopper full of soybeans. He pulled up to the grain cart to unload. Four minutes later he pulled away and lined up the grain head to eat up a few more rows. He thought the only way to cope with everything going on in his mind was his faith. He believed in a Higher Power and trusted God to get him through. The hard part of this was dealing with the fact that most of it was out of his control. I want to fix all of this, he thought to himself, but he knew better.

Washington

Moe Keane was growing more impatient by the day. The DHS was doing everything in their power to get information about active terrorist cells in the United States. Bits of information came in daily, analysts sifted through it to try and piece things together. He felt Steve Bradshaw was going in the right direction with his work at the NSA. Moe was sure there was a duplication of efforts, but he was fine with it to a point. Coming at their analysis from different angles could be a good thing and they fed off each organization's strengths. He still wanted autonomy as well, this allowed people to run with their ideas.

Moe was always working on ways to communicate with Chris. It was less than sporadic but not completely non-existent. Moe knew this cell was an important one and was kept in a vacuum. He wondered how long Chris would be able to mentally stand it? If Chris went off one day and killed the whole lot of them Moe would support him entirely. Matter of fact he had already worked up a couple of possible stories where a cell had imploded on itself with no survivors.

He had been involved personally in Chris' recruitment but had not been recruiting actively for months. It seemed like it was time to begin looking for another Chris. Maybe this time he'd look for someone with a Middle Eastern background. This would be much tougher to do and extremely dangerous for the person recruited. Bisma came to mind. She could keep her eyes open on her campus and the surrounding areas. He knew she wanted to get out more and learn more about the area. Bisma would be someone men would find attractive and intriguing. This could prove dreadfully dangerous for Bisma and he was not ready to send her out to recruit.

The more he got to know Bisma the more he respected her. She was very smart and felt fortunate to be able to work to realize her potential. Her thoughts on turning Chris to their side was extremely intuitive. Problem was, the man who ordered her murder was with Chris on a daily basis.

Indianapolis

Special Agent Tim Dailey felt he was spinning his wheels. When the Bureau had called off the overseas assignment of Nat Jackson, he was brushed back to his previous day to day duties. He saw Jackson's leaving as his chance to advance, but that had quickly stalled. He'd done his best to keep his hand in the investigation of the attack on the Purdue campus three months ago. They had exhausted all leads and had the forensic findings on every bit of evidence. Jackson was the lead investigator and required little of him.

Until they caught the people involved to give them the entire story, they knew explosives had been placed inside the horse. The C-4 explosives had been placed in more than one Trojan condom. The Trojan horse story had made its way around the Indianapolis office and all the way to D.C. Thoughts on Dr. Charley Summers as the target would always be bantered about. It seemed his connection as being part of the Boiler Club with Mike Baker were too much to be 'just' a coincidence.

It had taken two weeks before a terrorist organization had claimed responsibility for the Purdue attack. Funny thing was that two different factions claimed it was their plan. The Bureau gave much more credence to the group that had also been involved in two other central Indiana attacks in the previous twelve months. Tim had examined both videos numerous times. He looked at each hooded face and studied the eyes. The best signature was the voices.

Tim had spent six months stationed at Guantanamo Bay. He spent each day with the Middle Eastern population and got to know them well. Most of the prisoners were docile, they had quickly become resigned to their fate. A few remained extremely defiant and let everyone know the jihad burned inside them. They would have killed everyone there including their brothers who had given up information. In a few cases, they had killed their own. This chapter of his life had changed him.

Missouri

Janet had been thinking about the information she'd received from Roger and decided his real motive was to cause havoc from the grave. He had hatched this idea to cause Asis problems as well as maybe give a gift to her, albeit a very dangerous gift. She had information people would kill for and the first person they would kill would be her. The question she couldn't get out of her mind... would this Asis person consider her a loose end? It seemed he had kept himself sealed off from anyone besides his inner circle in England, at least according to what Roger seemed to know. Roger was the only person who had spent time with him one on one and knew what he looked like. Roger had given Janet two pictures of Asis. All of this led her to believe that Asis would be the number one suspect in his death. Had Roger's usefulness run its course for Asis? Roger had written her he had always worried about this. There was nothing he could do about it, but stay on Asis's good side if possible.

Roger had also written to Janet that he had never told Asis about her, but she knew that wouldn't be hard for Asis to find out about her. A simple search of his obituary would mention his sister, Janet Knight of St. Louis, Missouri. So, the chill again made its way down her spine as she contemplated this thought. If Roger was worried Asis might send someone to kill him at any time, Janet inherited the same worry. Roger never saw it coming. He had poured himself a bourbon and sat in a comfortable chair beside his beautiful pool and was then impaled to that chair. Death was brutal for him, this had to be a message sent by someone. The only communication she had received from local law enforcement was to inform her that she was a suspect. She had been questioned at length twice. She had never been told she was no longer a suspect. It was easy to see they weren't worried about letting her stew, they couldn't care less about her feelings. She felt strongly that FBI agent Natalie Jackson was the main person working this case. Janet had bumped into her on the day Roger's home was on the home tour. She also knew that Morris Keane with the Department of Homeland Security was involved. He was the person who had brought her to Washington for four days last year. It turned out many of his suspicions about her brother had been correct. The information she now possessed in the letter from her brother would be extremely valuable to Keane. Asis was the person Keane was ultimately after. Asis was the international tip of the iceberg for everything that had happened in the Midwest.

So, she was back to the question of how to use this information for the most good for her. Would it get her safety from Asis provided by Keane? Or would it get her more wealth in which she could buy her own safety? There was no question her safety was her primary concern, but she couldn't help thinking she might just play it both ways. Why not at least consider playing both ends against the middle? If she started with Keane, any chance of getting money from Asis was over. Keane would take the information and move full speed ahead to capture or kill Asis. No, she'd have to start with Asis to see what she could get before bringing Keane into the picture.

Chapter 8

London

Asis was pleased with the progress of Farid's recruitment over the summer. Farid looked up to what his older brother Babur had accomplished but was eager to make his own mark. What he didn't match in intelligence with Babur, was made up by his exuberance to kill infidels. As Asis reported the progress to his most inner circle they were thrilled and maybe a little chilled at what they heard. It seemed this boy didn't know fear. He was a full-bore 'put me in coach' player.

Farid's mother was treated poorly by her husband as was the custom with men like Asis and his brother, her husband. She knew her place. Her shining light was Farid. They shared a bond she cherished, this told her it was possible a man could treat a woman with respect. Farid's demeanor had begun to change over the summer months. His mother fully enjoyed when it was just the two of them and she could have a conversation with him.

"Farid have you enjoyed your summer?"

"Yes Mother, very much."

"You seem a little more withdrawn the last few weeks."

"I have a lot on my mind Mother."

"Like what," she asked.

"My future."

"And?"

"It's hard to say mother, I have many options."

"I'm so excited for you to make a bright future for yourself. I'm still heartbroken over your brother's choices."

This hit a nerve with Farid and she could see it. He didn't reply, but she knew he looked up to his older brother. She would make sure Farid did not go down the same path.

"I miss him as well Mother, he was a great man."

She looked down not wanting to say what she truly thought. Giving his life as a martyr for the jihad was more than suicide. Her older son was a mass murderer in her eyes. She trusted Farid but knew better than to verbalize these thoughts. Her husband and brother-in-law had planned and sent Babur down that path.

"It's been good to spend time with Uncle Asis this summer."

Now it was time for his mother to bristle. This is the exact scenario she did not want. She saw no good in Farid spending any time with Asis. He had proven he didn't care one bit about his family, he would send anyone but himself into harm's way. Her silence told Farid everything he already knew. His mother undoubtedly hated Asis. He understood this, even though the jihad burned in him. Asis and his father had taken her oldest son.

Missouri

Janet began the process of setting up her technology. Weeks of research led her to purchase this new laptop that would only be used for this plan of communication. She had set up an integrated routing system Russian hackers would be proud of. The system was set up to change at random times for increased levels of security. She had taken this as far as possible and had not spared any expense. She was still writing her script or game plan. It seemed too many switchbacks would give Asis more time and/or chances to find her, but she wanted enough layers to drive him crazy.

This plan was more than just to worry Asis, she wanted money from him. Not because she needed it, but who better to extort money from than an international terrorist. He had used her brother for money for years and Roger had willingly complied. She was sure Roger got a lot less from the arrangement than he gave over the years. Asis couldn't have cared less about her brother, she knew it but wasn't sure Roger had. He was only being used for money and ended up sponsoring international terrorism that got her hauled into a cell by the Department of Homeland Security. A few days with Mr. Keane had taught her a lot about what Roger was messing with, he had been in deep. Whether this part of his life or the Indiana farmland conspiracy had gotten him killed was a mystery.

Janet felt the best way to get at this Asis character was to threaten his exposure as well as the exposure of his network both in England and in the States. This was the world he'd built. He didn't care that much about money. Money was just a tool he needed to operate his network. He had no problem getting all the money he needed, her brother had just been one source.

Janet had started writing carefully worded emails to initially get his full attention, then quickly moved to her demands. Nothing would be traced to the United States. It would not be that far of a stretch for Asis to consider Roger's family in this extortion plan if there was a U.S. connection.

Fort Meade, Maryland

Steve had been making notes to come up with a reason to give Nat Jackson a call and not make it seem like he was calling just to talk to her. It was no problem talking shop with her since they both had security clearances to match. He knew Nat cared about her home and wanted to get to the bottom of the terrorist attacks.

"Hi, Steve, how you doin?"

"Doing good Nat, you?"

"Not making the progress I'd hoped, but then again it might be as close as the next email or internet search."

"That's part of what drives you crazy. You get to the end of your rope on a series of leads and know you need to give it up, but then you decide that since you've gone that far, and the answer could be around the corner."

"Exactly, it never ends. Giving up is never an option."

"So, you go a different way for a while, but keep every bit of info. I have had times when my focus was totally cold, and something comes up somewhere entirely different that pushes you back that way and it leads you right where you hoped. I will say I am still interested in our London assignment if Keane ever changes his mind.

"Me too, Steve. I felt we were up to that challenge. I wanted to work with their counterterrorism division. I was hoping to pick up something new that would help us here. I was also hoping to find something to get us hot on the trail of the London person."

Yeah, that would've been great. Doing something good that would also further our careers would be a plus. I know that sounds so self-serving but…"

"So be it, it's a win-win."

"That's how I see it, Nat."

"Well, for now, we search from the States."

Steve was ready for this conversation to take a more personal turn, but she never seemed to give him an opening. She was undoubtedly the most guarded person he'd ever met. He'd always wonder what was behind those eyes he liked so much. She maybe wasn't gorgeous to most, but to him she certainly was. A relationship with her probably wasn't possible, but he wanted to give it a try.

Western Hampton County

It still gave Gary the chills every time he entered the barn. This had been the scene where two Hampton County Sheriff Deputies had been murdered months earlier. The house had been leveled by the explosion and resulting fire, but the barn still stood after also being booby-trapped. There had been damage to the south end, but it was easily repaired. Gary had rented the farm for crops but also got the barn to use for storing his equipment as well as hay. He was raising a few beef steers around the barn and in the woods. What they didn't get foraging for grass he supplemented with hay that had been left in the barn. It was no doubt not as good as it once was, but it still gave them some extra nutrition.

He had a nice area of concrete next to the barn on the east side where he'd scatter a couple bales of hay each morning. Today he was working on the second bale when he heard something metallic hit the concrete and saw a small glint of something in the sunlight. He kicked around a couple sections of hay when he saw it on the concrete. He bent down to see a bullet. As he reached to pick it up it hit him this could be something valuable considering where it had been. His memory of watching dozens of police shows on TV kicked in and he reached in his pocket for his clean handkerchief. He carefully picked up the bullet and after giving it a look wrapped it carefully in the cotton bandana and stuffed it down in his pocket. He was going into town this afternoon for parts, so he would drop it off at the sheriff's office.

That afternoon he wheeled his truck into the sheriff's parking lot and headed inside. He walked up to the window and was buzzed in when he said he might have some evidence from the Hinkle farm west of town. Before he got fully seated in the waiting area he had a deputy coming out to meet him. They shook hands.

"What have you brought us?" the deputy asked.

"I'm renting the Hinkle farm and was feeding calves this morning. I'd opened two bales of hay and heard something hit the concrete as I was getting it scattered and I also noticed a glint in the sunlight. After a little searching, I found this."

Gary carefully opened the handkerchief to reveal the bullet. It was easy to see the bullet had been fired, it was slightly misshapen.

"Let me get an evidence bag," the deputy said. "Did you pick it up with your fingers?"

"Almost, but then thought I shouldn't touch it. I picked it up with my handkerchief."

"Good work sir, very intuitive."

"I've watched so many police shows I thought this seemed like a good idea."

"Yes, that's good work. I'd like to get your name and contact info."

Gary filled out a short form with his relevant info and again they shook hands. "I'm sure it's a long shot, but I hope this somehow helps."

"Yes, sir and thank you."

Gary headed out feeling he'd done the right thing.

A knock on the sheriff's door got the response it always got, "Yeah, come in."

The deputy explained everything that had just happened.

"You never know, do you Bob?"

"No sir Sheriff Hatfield, you don't"

"I know who to call. Thank you."

The sheriff dialed the number for Special Agent Nat Jackson. After a short wait, she was on the line.

"Agent Jackson I'll get right to it, I know you're busy. I'm holding a bullet that a local farmer just brought in that came from the Hinkle farm."

"Go on," Nat said.

"From the story he told this bullet was buried in a bale of hay from the barn. He was feeding calves this morning and just happened to see it and brought it to us."

"We realize this could be absolutely nothing. It will be easy to determine if it came from the gun of one of my fallen officers. Can I have one of my people bring it to your office?"

"Yes, please. Thank you, Sheriff Hatfield. Will you also bring the two firearms from your men?"

"Yes, it will all be together."

"Thanks again, Sheriff." Jackson clicked off.

Everything was assembled to preserve evidence and the chain of custody paperwork was filled out. One hour later it was at the FBI building on the north-east side of Indianapolis.

Chapter 9

Greenville

Harvest was now in full swing. Mike and all his farm friends were finishing beans and starting to shell corn. So far it appeared soybean yields were going to be decent this year. A couple of nice rains in August helped fill out the pods. He felt good about getting the use of the combine in a timelier fashion than he had when he got the equipment for spring planting. The White Oak Holding Company was under new leadership with Roger Knight being out of the picture, they were now under the guidance of a farm management firm that did business with common sense and not just greed. His mind wandered to Roger Knight, he didn't think of him much, but when he did his thoughts were never good. There was a time when the negative thoughts would have bothered him more, but with everything going on in the country a big callous seemed to have formed on his brain. The lack of civility was truly alarming as well as politicians saying anything to get elected.

He did wonder who had killed Knight. He didn't just get killed, he got killed good! Someone had sent a message. According to Nat Jackson, he would've had a couple minutes to think about that message before he left this world in agonizing fashion with an arrow through his neck. There'd been a time when he would've felt remorse for Roger Knight's terrible murder, it seemed that callous on his brain was not allowing any remorse for him. If there truly was a hell, Knight should be there.

Mike then let his thoughts wander over to Sandy. He'd never forgotten and told many people that when they got married she had told Mike she wanted them to be a family that attended church. Sandy had been raised in the church. Her family was active in their church and her faith was important to her. Mike's family had not attended church on a regular basis. He'd always felt there was faith in God in his family, even though they were not a church-going family. There was always the same prayer at each meal, but no church attendance. His father, Gordon, had shown a reverence for Mother Nature. They had talked about God as Mother Nature in Mike's mind. Sandy had never demanded anything but said she wanted them to be a family that attended church. Mike thought if this was important to Sandy, it was important to him and they'd always attended church.

His church attendance since she was now gone had grown a little sporadic, but he was still going. His church family as well as the entire community had been wonderful through everything that had happened. Everyone had been affected by the restaurant explosion and the town had pulled together.

The other thing that was hard to take was how he'd lost his optimistic attitude. He had always been the eternal optimist reciting the Optimist Creed to himself at times he needed a boost. Those days had passed. It was more practical to be a realist but a lot more depressing. Maybe it was time to turn on the radio. He'd gotten himself into a funk alone with his thoughts, and he knew music could get him back on track.

Indianapolis

A hunch had taken Nat Jackson back to her favorite shooting range to look at the video from many months prior. The video was unclear but showed a female who was proficient with a crossbow. The range owner was okay letting her see the video from that day, but when she asked to see the credit card receipts from that day he dug in his heels a little. A short conversation persuaded him when the thought of a team of FBI agents coming through his front door with a warrant to look at more records than that one particular day. Nat scanned his records and was relieved she didn't find the name she was looking for. In fact, there were no female names using the bow range that day.

"Some people pay cash no doubt?" Nat asked the owner.

"Yes."

"Any records of who pays cash?"

"No."

"That's why they're paying cash?'

"Maybe." Randy was shifting his weight from one foot to the other, his hands fidgeted on the counter.

"Okay Randy, cut the bullshit. You know me. You know I like this place and wish you no harm."

"I know Agent Jackson. I like seeing you come in here. You've probably helped my business. Many customers know who you are and respect what you've done here in central Indiana and yes it's true several customers just pay cash for whatever reason."

"And I can respect that Randy. I know you run a reputable business. I have one last question for you. I'd just like you to tell me if you have seen this person in here. At this point, the investigation is only for me."

Randy nodded his understanding. Nat pushed a picture across his desk. He stared for a few seconds, looked up at her and gave a slight nod. Nat pulled it back and put the picture into her binder.

"Thanks, Randy, see you soon." Nat headed for the door.

She didn't have enough evidence to approach the person, and she didn't think she would even if it were clear. There was no problem with motive if she did have the correct person. She knew the FBI was always looking for talented people, this person might be in the recruitment pipeline for Homeland Security or the FBI. She'd keep thinking on it and decide when she'd approach Sarah Baker to talk.

For now, she'd get in some range time to settle her nerves. Practicing was a good way for her to focus.

The FBI crime lab started work on matching the bullet from the Hampton County barn to the deputy's guns. This was standard procedure. Gun number one was quickly ruled out making it more than likely gun number two would be as well since both officers had the standard issue sidearm. Gun number two was also ruled out. The report hit Nat Jackson's desk and she was pleased with the findings. She didn't want this bullet to be from the gun of law enforcement, she wanted the possibilities it might give them down the road to lead to some answers.

Nat had not yet forwarded this information to Moe Keane and Steve Bradshaw. She wanted to know more, and she now had this much. She typed an email explaining all that had happened and the lack of finding a match thus far. It was not from the two deputies who had been gunned down that afternoon. The evidence had been safely preserved for another day. She hit send.

Columbus, Ohio

Chris and his two roommates had been living in Columbus for three weeks now. They had spent many hours on reconnaissance and getting to know the area. This was all Hazaq had given them to do, nothing more and no further information. They had driven all over the city but spent most of their time on foot around campus where it was easier to blend in. Chris was happy they were not hurting anybody, but he was getting tired of just hanging out. If he could get information on what was being planned, he'd do his best to help stop it. The trick would be for him to not get caught by the local police and not be discovered by Hazaq.

He had spent one day touring the local air force museum at Wright Patterson Air Force Base. He enjoyed this very much. He'd told the others he wanted to research the facility. If only they knew he just needed to get away from them. It had been years now and he fought depression by being around this group of jihadists. He fought the urge to just kill them all and be done with them. He knew the Department of Homeland Security and the Federal Bureau of Investigation could use all the intel they could get. So Chris had given himself the gift of a mental health day by just being alone with other normal Americans.

He arrived back at the apartment and fired up his laptop. He was almost relieved to see the email from Hazaq. He opened and began to read. There were no details, but he could read between the lines. The big picture was an attack during a college football game in Columbus. Chris was not surprised at the venue. There would be over 100,000 people at the game tailgating before and after.

Hazaq was sending two men with supplies from Chicago. More details would follow. Chris wondered if this was just Hazaq or if this plan came from up the terror chain in London. Hazaq was getting more dangerous over time and this plan had the audacity to go well over the top of what Chris could let happen.

Missouri

Kurtz arrived in the St. Louis area in the late afternoon. This was the only part of the plan that bothered him. The bank teller named Rachelle, was only guilty of greed if you can call $5,000 greed. Many people had died for much less. This girl would have no idea she was a loose end, but she was just that. She had no information other than the number she'd called, but that was enough to be a loose end.

He knew Rachelle followed the same route to and from work four and a half days a week. Friday evenings were reserved for social time with friends. Kurtz had followed her for two days to make sure of the route and to look for possibilities and traffic cameras. The days he was spending in St. Louis were not only for reconnaissance on Rachelle, he was also watching Janet Knight. It turned out that Knight, in spite of all her wealth, was not much more interesting than Rachelle. At least Rachelle had one night out each week, it seemed Janet Knight was most comfortable in the safety of home.

Kurtz had brought a Knight's Armament Mk 11 SWS sniper rifle. He was using 7.62 NATO ammunition and had it fitted with a suppressor that did little more than mute the subsonic round. This didn't matter since he'd be nearly a thousand yards away.

Rachelle and her two co-workers were the last ones to leave and lock up for the night.

"See you tomorrow," Rachelle said as she waved over her shoulder.

"Night, girl."

Rachelle fired up her Celica and turned out the side entrance. Fifteen minutes later she was pulling up to her apartment, traffic had been lighter than normal. As she opened the door juggling things in both hands she was met at the door. Her dog, Max, had nearly knocked her over. Max was ready to go outside. Rachelle pulled on a pair of old tennis shoes she kept by the door. She reached for her purse, put her phone in her back pocket and they headed north for the park.

Max had marked his territory on every fire hydrant during the six-minute walk along with one small flag the local gas company had left behind. Rachelle found that one amusing. They hit the park in full stride and made one lap around. On lap two Rachelle found her usual bench unoccupied and sat down to check texts. Plans were being made for a girl's night out Friday. Max laid down now content to also take a break. The phone screen made a slight glow on her face as she began to type her response of, *See you Friday*. Max growled as his owner's arm lurched tightly on the leash. Max looked up to see a face that was no longer there. Rachelle had a microsecond of intense realization that something happened. The 7.62 mm round hitting anywhere else would have given her pain in her moment of death. Kurtz had spared her any agony.

First responders were mostly not ready for this type of scene. Detectives were thankful she was carrying a small wallet in the cross-body purse she was wearing. Identification was now possible.

One news photographer got close enough for a dimly lit video of the scene. There was not enough detail to warrant the "disturbing images" disclaimer, but his station used it anyway.

Janet Knight was reading as the nightly news came on. She was on her second pour of bourbon and was looking forward to a good night's sleep. As the "Breaking News" flashed at the start of the broadcast her attention stayed on finishing the chapter. What did get her attention was the mention of a sniper. Something about a sniper is intriguing. Death from afar. As she raised her eyes over the book she saw a face flashed on the screen and listened to how this young woman was brutally killed while walking her dog after leaving the bank where she worked. Janet grabbed the remote and backed it up to listen again and pause the picture of this woman.

Through the haze of the bourbon, she realized she had seen this face. Janet pulled up the news story on her iPad to see this young woman worked at the bank with the safety deposit box and yes it was the person who helped her. She remembered treating her poorly and felt a pang of remorse for doing that. Remorse was not something she dwelled on a lot. The last thing that got her attention was the term "assassination" as the news anchor ended the story. Yes, sniper and assassination were two terms that got your attention. The local police were not saying much because they didn't know much, but there were no leads at this time and no clues why Rachelle Spillman would have been targeted. It's easy to just brush something off as a coincidence, but this left Janet feeling something in her gut.

Chapter 10

Columbus

Two days after Chris received the email from Hazaq he got a text saying two friends from Chicago would be arriving this afternoon. He told the other cell members two brothers from Chicago were coming and their time of destiny was drawing closer. He sensed the excitement in the others, they wanted jihad. They were trained and ready. Chris had seen it before and would never understand it, but sadly he had grown accustomed to being around men who had no other purpose in life but to kill infidels. No other cares or ambitions.

They'd picked an apartment where they could accommodate a few more brothers. They had also picked an area with a student population to blend in. This had worked well for the cell in Indianapolis. Student populations were diverse at larger universities, stuck to themselves, and didn't notice a couple extra people staying around for a few days. They went mostly unnoticed.

The brothers arrived, Chris and one other cell member greeted them and helped them carry in their bags. Chris knew there would be a lot more left in the trunk and hidden away under the seats. This group had traveled with more explosives than normal causing their potential exposure to rise. They normally used a specially designed area that housed airbags. This area was not perfectly free from detection by bomb-sniffing dogs but made it much tougher to be discovered.

Chris sat down on Thursday evening to talk to the other cell members. Everyone reported what they had learned about game day security. The two new arrivals had just arrived after spending time out and about to get the lay of the land, they brought pizza. This was their third day in Columbus.

"Did your day go as planned?" Chris asked them.

They both nodded.

"Care to share a little more?"

They both shook their heads no. Chris gave them a slight frown and said, "How are we to help each other?"

One said, "You have your job to do and we have ours."

Chris decided to leave it for now, but he wanted to know what their role was in this attack. Hazaq was awfully good at this type of game. He seemed to enjoy it, and Chris had to admit he was an effective leader. Hazaq's compartmentalizing in Indianapolis had prevented Chris from stopping the attack at the State Fairgrounds. At that time Chris was not sure if Hazaq was testing him or if that's just how he did business. This time he had to learn more to find a way to stop the attack.

Cell members shared information on what they had learned about local security. It all seemed to be standard for sports venues of this size. The first line of security checked bags before people got up to the gate. They were requiring anything carried into the stadium to be in a plastic see-through tote bag. No open liquids could be carried in, only unopened water bottles. Another line of security would be carefully observing everyone and then further inside the gates, plain clothes people were milling around. No dogs were being used as far as anyone knew.

Hazaq had not given any orders for Chris or the two others who came with him originally. He knew the two new arrivals had brought explosives, but he wasn't sure about weapons.

"There's a home game this Saturday. Hazaq hasn't told me yet, but I assume the attack happens then?" Chris posed as a question.

No one answered. He didn't expect anything from the two knotheads with him but was hoping for anything from the two new ones. They knew more than they were letting on, no question.

"Well okay, we sit tight and wait for instructions."

Another fun evening sitting around with jihadists. Their conversation was always in English and never got personal except for hoping to kill as many infidels as possible. Without Joel, Chris was the only one in the room who was not of Middle Eastern heritage and it felt like it.

Friday morning came, and the two new arrivals got up and were on their way without so much as a word. Chris wanted to press them for more information but knew it would be for naught. If the attack were scheduled for tomorrow, he was running out of time to alert local authorities. He checked his email hourly knowing this might get his two roommates ramped up, but he didn't care at this point. The damn suite was beginning to smell like his roommates and the only thing he seriously wanted to blow up was this room with these crazy terrorists still in it. He usually stayed razor sharp, didn't let himself drift off into thoughts of what they were doing here, but these thoughts of actual lucidity could drive him crazy within a short time. None of this made sense. These people didn't make sense.

That afternoon he had an email from Hazaq with instructions for his two roommates. He was to direct them into the middle of tailgate heaven each wearing a suicide vest. They were to detonate when the other explosion happened. What other explosion he wondered? It must be something planned by the two new arrivals. He had to get out to alert authorities. The other two were watching Dr. Phil or something in the other room. Chris went in to see two zombies sitting on the couch.

"Tomorrow is the day my brothers! Tomorrow you each drive a stake in the heart of the infidels. As they gather to eat and drink themselves to death you will speed them on their way to hell!"

Their looks told him all he wanted to know. They were ready to give their lives for this jihadist cause. Young men with all their lives ahead of them ready to die for jihad, kill infidels.

"I have to make further preparations, I'll be back later."

They spoke no words, just nodded their heads. Chris put on his jacket and headed for the door. Get me the hell out of here he thought to himself. He grabbed his keys and wallet and pulled the door closed behind him. Now, what is the best way to bring this all to an end without blowing his own cover? Chris would like the authorities to knock down the door and take them all into custody, but if that happened, how would he escape? If they let him go it would get back to Hazaq someway, somehow. He'd have to think this through quickly.

Indianapolis

The communication center at the Indianapolis FBI office was not busy this evening. The junior agent on duty answered on the second ring.

"Nat Jackson please, it's urgent."

"Special Agent Jackson is not in the office, I will transfer…"

"No, I must speak to Agent Jackson, patch me through to her cell."

"That's not possible."

"Sure, it is."

"No."

"Yes, it is. This is a matter of national security and she'll be extremely pissed if you don't patch me through."

"One moment."

One moment was about four minutes and Chris was getting plenty pissed. He assumed they were tracing the call, that was not a problem. Time was the problem, every minute meant something. He looked at the phone he was holding, he'd found it a few days ago while wandering around this mostly student hangout. These were places he and the others could blend into the crowd and get some decent coffee. It wasn't easy to find a pay phone nowadays and he didn't dare use his cell for what he was doing.

"This is Special Agent Tim Dailey, how may I help you?"

"You can't, I asked for Agent Jackson."

"She's not available. How can I help you?"

Chris clicked off and gave the phone a little extra effort as he placed it back on its hangar. Maybe she wasn't available, or they just wouldn't play ball with someone calling like this. He did not have contact information for Moe Keane, this would have to change. While at the Chicago cell location he never had a chance to be safely alone to make a contact. It was now late afternoon and he was running out of time and options. He was six blocks from the edge of the campus and decided to walk east to find the nearest library.

On campus, he asked two students to point him toward the library. One told him to go two buildings south and he'd see it to the right. He hurried that way and found it across an open grassy area. He kicked through the leaves as he made his way to the front steps. Inside, he gave a quick look to see a computer area that was hardly being used. He walked over and noticed ceiling cameras, the kind behind the little black half circles. This was not a problem for Chris. He sat down and Googled the Department of Homeland Security. There was generic contact information and that would have to do. He memorized the number, deleted the history for the day and headed for the front desk.

"Where can I find the nearest pay phone?" Chris asked the bored student behind the desk.

He got a look that was more quizzical than irritated. He could tell this kid was thinking about it and may well not have any idea.

"I'm not sure really."

"Where's the closest place I can buy a cheap phone?"

This got an immediate response. He directed Chris to a small strip mall on the edge of campus. Chris thanked him and headed down a side hallway to exit the library in that direction. The kid probably thinks I'm a drug dealer, he thought to himself.

The purchase at the strip mall took seventeen minutes. The phone he bought was what people called a burner phone and was exactly what he needed. He made his way to a small open area away from foot traffic and called the number. Three rings later he had a recorded message. That angered him more than it should have, but he knew it was the standard operating procedure. He began to calculate how many steps it would take to get the Director on the line.

Six minutes later he was getting closer. He was now talking to a person. He wasn't sure this person was ready to believe he needed to speak directly to Moe Keane, but he did his best to convince him without saying too much.

"May I have a number that Mr. Keane can use to return your call?" Chris gave the number and asked they please hurry.

Washington

Moe Keane was reading intelligence reports, as he often did when the knock came.

"Come in." he didn't look up.

"The switchboard sent this call to our floor. You have someone wanting to talk to you. They asked for you by name."

"Who is it?"

"We didn't get a name. Our people got the number and said they'd have you call back."

He reached for the paper more annoyed than intrigued.

"Thank you."

His assistant left, and he eyed the number. Moe picked up the office phone and dialed the number. Two rings later there was a connection.

"Keane?" the other party said.

"Yes."

There was a pause, "Chris Powell."

This time Keane paused, "You okay Chris?"

"I am for now. I need to give you information about an attack tomorrow in Columbus, Ohio."

"Go ahead." He had a yellow pad at the ready and hit the record button on his phone console.

Chris hurriedly laid out what he knew which honestly wasn't much. Keane listened more than he wrote.

"So, there will be two suicide bombers going into the crowd at the game tomorrow afternoon?"

"Yes, that's correct. There are two other cell members planning something that I've not been read in on. I have tried to ask questions but the cell leader in Chicago is especially careful to keep things compartmentalized. He's damn good at it actually."

"Thoughts on how we stop this?" Keane asked.

"I've been working on it with the idea to keep me operational in this cell. If the local boys come in and take us all into custody I don't see how I go forward. If you grab the two suicide threats after they leave tomorrow, they will already be armed to explode. It seems you should raid the apartment tonight while I'm not there."

"It's going to look pretty suspicious to your cell leader that you happened to be away."

"Agreed. We communicate by secure email. Usually, just one way, him to me. I could email and ask to message him late this evening. You could have the local FBI take down the internet in our area for an hour, so I would have to leave the apartment.

While I'm out you go in and take them down. I start to return but see police activity, so I get in my car and head back to Chicago."

"Is your phone secure?"

"I bought a burner today that would cost me my life if they knew I had it. It's strictly forbidden by the cell. I'm at a point where I want a cell number for you, a number I can memorize and count on."

Moe gave it to him.

Chris said, "I never know when the other two cell members are going to show up each evening. They've only been in Columbus for three days. I want to wait until they're all there this evening, it could be very late."

"That's no problem. We'll be ready. When you are out of the apartment give me a call at the number I just gave you and we'll raid the apartment. Anything else for now?"

"No sir."

"Good luck son."

Moe began formulating a plan before calling his contact at the FBI. The area internet outage would require some help and need to be verifiable to the Chicago cell leader. That part of the plan might save Chris' life.

With enough of the plan in his head, he made the call. A quick up to date briefing and his friend asked for his plan knowing he wouldn't have called without one. Moe laid out the details and hit send on the email. With a couple tweaks from his friend, they were in agreement.

"Thanks, Paul, talk to you later."

"Will do Moe."

Columbus

Chris stopped at the car on the way back to the apartment. He turned off the phone and hid it, locked the car and headed inside. The boys inside were as jacked up as he'd ever seen them. They were upset he'd been gone so long. They were ready for their destiny and the next 18 hours were not going to be easy for them. Chris let them berate him for about a minute and then told them everything was progressing as planned. He wouldn't match their intensity, instead he'd show them calm in the hopes he could settle them down for the evening. These guys loved pizza so Chris asked if they wanted to eat and he ordered two large pies for delivery. The two men picked their favorites. This seemed to make them happy.

Chris let himself enjoy the pizza, truth be known he needed some food in him and time to think. As the evening wore on the other two jihadists did not show. He asked the others when their brothers would be back to eat. Neither one knew and didn't seem concerned. Chris was not sure how long to wait, he decided to wait until midnight. He sat as they watched TV and worked on his laptop. As it turned 11:45 he told them he had to go out for a while, the internet connection was giving him trouble. He shut his laptop and put it in his backpack and headed out the door. He went to the car, got the phone and dialed Moe Keane as soon as he was out of any line of sight from their room.

"Keane."

"The other two are not back yet, we have no idea where they are or if they're coming back," Chris told Moe.

"Okay, Chris let's do this, I want these two. You get to a place where you can watch safely. Responding officers have seen your picture, but I don't want you caught up in this."

"Understood. There are explosives in the apartment, they've been trained to never be taken alive so make sure there's no hesitation. Knock the door off the hinges and take them. I want them to see our car parked where we left it when they are taken out."

"Good idea. Keep your eyes open for the other two." Moe clicked off.

Moe made the call to his contact.

Chris found a secluded spot and sat down to watch the action begin. In no more than four minutes he could see the perimeter start to form. He could see six agents at the front door, Hand signals were given, and the door was breached. Agents quickly entered guns drawn, Chris was pleased he heard no shots fired. Very quickly two hooded men were brought from the apartment and loaded into a police van. Chris was sure a local swat team would be watching for any potential threat. Chris decided to wait until he approached the car for the same reason, to make sure no one would be watching him leave. He had to consider the other two brothers could be watching the area. He realized while sitting there that he needed to provide Keane with possible lines of questioning they could use on the cell numbers. Chris knew that one of these men was involved with the school bus attack west of Greenville. For now, Chris would focus on how he wanted to handle things with Hazaq.

Forty-five minutes passed, and the activity was still happening in the apartment. He wished he could go in to get his belongings which weren't many. It made more sense for him to arrive back in Chicago with no more than the clothes on his back. He worked through every scenario in his mind of questions Hazaq might ask. He was also weighing the option of staying in Columbus to try and stop the other two cell members. Or would they also head back to Chicago? He decided to stay the night and keep watch in the area, he was the only person who could identify the other two jihadists. He would tell Hazaq he stayed to give them support and protection and if they never showed then he'd tell him that.

Chris found an area with Wi-Fi and sent Hazaq an email saying his two roommates were no longer available to work tomorrow. He hit send.

Chapter 11

Chicago

Hazaq heard the tone and turned to his laptop. The short email was enough for him to slam his fist down on the desk. What does this mean? Are they dead or captured? He googled Columbus to see what was showing on the local news stations. Nothing yet showing, no shootouts or explosions. He never wanted a cell member to be taken into custody. He trained them not to talk, but he knew everyone had their breaking point. It was interesting Chris was not part of it. He typed a return email, "Head home."

Columbus

Chris' laptop buzzed, and he saw the 'head home' response. He would not answer. He'd be seeing Hazaq soon enough.

Early Saturday morning Chris called Keane.

"Keane."

"It's Powell."

"How ya doin?"

"I have a lot running through my mind about what I should accomplish with you in the next few hours before I return to Chicago. I've been called back as you'd guess. I know I'll be interrogated and I'm running through all my answers."

"Anything I can do to help on that?" Keane asked.

"Nothing I've thought of. I do want to give you intel why we have the chance. You recording this?"

"Yes."

"One of the cell members in custody was involved with the school bus attack in Greenville. You can go at both of them on this, Roquan is the one."

"What about the other two that didn't show up last night?" Keane asked.

"I don't much about these two. Everyone is trained in the same way, so my assumption is they are suicide bombers. Hazaq keeps everyone in the dark with his planning. The two in custody have no idea what these other two have planned. Spend no time on this questioning."

"Understood. You can identify them. Any pictures on your phone?"

"That's strictly forbidden and would get me killed."

"Understood"

"I could walk around the area of the stadium today to look for them. I know what areas the two in custody were to target, those spots would be out. This would leave a lot of ground to cover."

"I don't think you should go against your orders. Get in your vehicle and head back to Chicago. You've got a six-hour drive. Is there any chance your vehicle could be wired for sound? Any way your cell could be listening to you in that car?"

"There's no way I can know for sure, but I'd say no."

"We can't chance it for your safety. No talking in that car. If I need you, I'll call. Stop the car and then call me. Since we never get this chance anyway and you'll be ditching this phone before you get back, stop and call when you're close to Chicago."

"Will do."

Chris logged off his laptop, shut it down and laid it in the front seat. He got in and fired it up. Interstate 70 was about a fifteen-minute drive and he'd be heading west, sun coming up in his rear-view mirror.

College football weekends in Columbus, Ohio were some-thing to behold. Tail-gating was an art. The Columbus police department had every person available in the area. The FBI was there along with the Department of Homeland Security. Local Sheriff Departments from adjoining counties had been called in. It was going to be a long day. They all knew there was a terror threat today on a different level than a normal weekend. They'd been trained and set out walking and watching. Most fans didn't notice their presence, some did. Some people felt a heightened presence and put up their own internal radars. This could be good and bad.

The morning wore on and the 1:00 PM kick-off grew closer. Law enforcement preferred a day game better than a night game anytime. The crowd began moving into the stadium as game time grew closer. Many opted for one more cold beer before heading in. Law enforcement puts the odds of an attack one hour before and one hour after the game due to the highest concentration of fans milling about. They felt the odds of a suicide bomber getting into the stadium were very low. They wished they could have a bomb-sniffing dog at every gate, the ones available were walking the lots.

Both teams took the field and pre-game rituals were happening. As the teams left the field for their sidelines the Ohio State band took the field. Colors were presented, and the National Anthem started. As the anthem ended the rumble started off to the west. It quickly grew louder as three huge Boeing C-17 Globemaster III troop carriers came into view over the edge of the stadium, the noise was enormous as was the cheering. Wright-Patterson Air Force Base was close by and pilots of the 445th Airlift Wing always enjoyed the flyovers.

Joe Barr and Carson Spurling had known each other since 8th grade. They were patrolling together and amazed at how many people were still outside the stadium.

"Why aren't these people inside watching?" Joe said.

"I'll bet some sold their tickets for a nice price and just decided to sit out and drink beer."

"Not a bad idea."

Both kept patrolling as trained, heads on a swivel and taking in everything. Joe heard the faint sound off in the distance. It was a whine instead of a rumble. He knew within seconds it was an aircraft and he knew seconds later what type of aircraft. He'd grown up on a farm out in the country. He looked at Carson.

"What is that?"

"Crop duster."

Carson stopped to look in the distance, "You sure?"

"Pretty damn sure. They have a distinct sound and I've always loved to watch them work a field. They're very powerful to carry heavy tanks and be able to pull up quickly at the end of a field to miss the power lines."

They both stood to watch as the small speck was coming fast. This was a single wing plane, not the old bi-planes people loved to watch.

"Is this part of today's game?" Joe asked.

"Never heard anything about this. What the hell?"

"I feel confident in these times an area like this would be a no-fly zone."

All they could do was stand and watch. The plane was coming fast and suddenly started to gain some altitude. It then began a slow dive and disappeared over the edge of the stadium. Fans in the stadium were surprised at a low flying plane suddenly over the stadium. Fans on the opposite side could see the spray coming from the plane. As soon as it appeared it was gone. Officials stopped play, and everyone stood stunned. Lower crowd noise made the plane easier to hear this time, it sounded like it was coming back. Three seconds later it again appeared and was coming back over the other side of the stadium. Fans again saw spray coming from the plane and this time it did not exit the stadium. The plane made a sudden dive and went down into the crowd. It seemed the crash lasted forever as it kept going through the crowd. The final impact resulted in a huge fireball and explosion. Survivors were experiencing hysteria, panic and shock.

A large part of what just happened was caught on video. This was a nationally televised game. Network commentators were stunned in disbelief with few words. Officials and coaches were getting their teams off the field and into locker rooms. This seemed the smart thing to do at this point. FBI authorities had already asked for air support to be scrambled from Wright-Patterson for other potential threats. Medical personnel were being called in from every hospital in central Ohio.

Chicago

Chris arrived back in Chicago by late afternoon. Hazaq began questioning him immediately.

"Where have you been? You should have been here before now? What have you been doing?"

Chris was just letting him get it out. Hazaq may be wanting to make a spectacle in front of the other cell members as much as wanting information.

"I stopped to eat and rest, I was up all night."

Hazaq continued but Chris was letting most go in one ear and out the other. He began giving Hazaq other intel versus what he was being asked. He knew he couldn't overstep his bounds too much but was damned tired of this arrogant prick of a terrorist. The national news they had on in the background went back to "Breaking News" and the attack in Columbus, Ohio. This deflected Hazaq's attention for now. Chris had been monitoring the radio for news and had learned of the attack while driving. He was taking this hard and knew Moe Keane was doing the same. Chris had called Keane about an hour south of Chicago and Keane told him as much as he knew at the time.

Hazaq turned back to Chris, "We will talk later."

Chris nodded and turned.

Columbus

Rescue and evidence gathering went on the rest of the day and into the night. Stadium lights allowed work to go on all night. Victims were put into body bags until the body bags ran out. Helicopters landed and took off from the playing field all day long. Ambulances also came in and out of the stadium continuously for hours. Hazmat teams also worked continuously to wash people down from the spray the crop duster had used on the crowd. Samples including clothing were taken to the university for testing. It was quickly determined the spray the terrorists had used was mostly an agricultural insecticide. They had mixed it with a herbicide. Officials were assuming this was done to make sure they had the tanks full at the time of the attack.

Forty miles away a local Sheriff Department found two bodies at a private airstrip. This was a father/son operation that owned the plane used in the attack. Time of death was placed early Saturday morning and it was apparent this was murder. This gave the terrorists time to get the aircraft ready for the attack. Phone records showed the two men had been called on Friday by an unknown number. One of them had made a note about a meeting scheduled for Saturday morning at 7:30 AM. No security cameras were in place at the rural business. It was an active crime scene with authorities looking for evidence but knowing the people involved had likely died in the attack.

No one was ready to give a numerical estimate for casualties yet even though the local news stations as well as the national news teams were pressing. Numbers began floating about with no confirmation. It seemed likely it would approach one thousand innocent souls who had gathered to watch a college football game. Thousands of others had been sprayed with the insecticide/herbicide mix that was not likely to cause death, but officials had no idea of the long-term effects. Initial worries centered on respiratory problems and damage to the eyes.

Indianapolis

There was a lot of talk at the Indianapolis FBI office on Monday morning. There was talk about the two cell members who were taken into custody on the Friday night before the Columbus attack on Saturday. Office administration had confirmed that they'd received a call from a man asking for Natalie Jackson. The caller had insisted on speaking to Agent Jackson but was referred to Agent Dailey. At that point, the caller hung up. The call lasted long enough for it to be traced to a campus phone at Ohio State University. So, there was speculation among staff as to why the caller had asked for special agent Jackson specifically. The call had of course been recorded and Agent Jackson had listened to it several times. She was not sure of the caller's identity and had forwarded the audio file to Moe Keane. He called her within the hour.

"Jackson."

"Morning Nat, this conversation between just us?'

"Yes sir."

"It was our man Chris, he was trying to stop it, but he couldn't locate the other two. He's back with the cell in Chicago and may be in more danger than ever."

"What a life."

"I think I need to get him out. Take down the entire Chicago cell and get him out."

"That's a tough call for you, he's been valuable."

"And he's been doing it a long time."

"Anything the Indianapolis office can do to help?"

"No, not right now"

"Chris's involvement means it's the same group as the other central Indiana attacks?

"Yes, same group. I'll be in touch Nat, take care."

"You too."

Chapter 12

Greenville

Mike had just hit send on an email that was going between the Boiler Club members. They'd learned from Charley Summers that he'd lost a good friend in the attack at Ohio State. He was good friends with a veterinarian from northeastern Indiana who was an Ohio State grad and was killed in the attack last weekend. Everyone had sent their condolences along with their outrage at the attack. They were all speculating if it was the same group involved with the attacks in Indiana. This was extremely personal to all of them, especially Mike.

Anything new like this fueled Mike's desire to want to help stop it. He always felt like the Federal agents could only do so much. He knew their hands were at least partially tied. He felt a headache coming on so he decided to fill up the kettle and make a fresh pot of coffee in his Chemex.

As more information became available about the attack in Columbus he thought it would be good to get the Boiler Club members together for lunch soon. They certainly shared a common bond. Their discussions usually ended up with more questions than answers. There were times when the questions this group postulated had proven to be helpful for law enforcement with lines of investigation and/or questions they had used on detainees.

Mike's thoughts also went to the man he'd met at the farm last winter. Moe Keane told him his name was Chris and he was an embedded agent with the DHS. He just couldn't imagine the life he was living and how dangerous it would be to coexist with terrorists and their hatred of Americans. He'd really like to meet him one day and shake his hand, hopefully at a time when Chris was safe and living a different life. Mike had signed a paper from the government promising he'd never talk about what he knew of Chris Powell. What would the life expectancy be for someone who had infiltrated an organization such as this? He'd seen this kind of thing in movies and television shows, this guy had given up his life to actually do it. He was a hero.

Missouri

Janet was editing the two-page letter for the hundredth time. This had to be perfect with no indication of who was sending it. It had to grab Asis by the balls and squeeze, had to plant enough worry for him to act on it and not just dismiss it. Roger had given her this gift. It wasn't so much a gift for Janet as a way for him to have the upper hand on his old acquaintance from the grave. Roger felt Asis saw himself as superior to him and any infidel. Asis seemed to show him friendship, but Roger knew Asis couldn't have cared less about him. Roger had left her a way to pay him back big time.

When she decided this was her final draft she slipped on a pair of latex gloves and opened the new package of paper. She lifted off the top half and fingered two sheets to put into her printer. She opened the file and hit the print icon and seconds later the letter was waiting. She carefully picked up the two sheets and placed them into the padded envelope. There was no signature on this letter.

Janet had done her research on the location where this letter was going. It was legit, this murderous terrorist was hiding in plain sight. She printed the address label, took it off the printer and attached it to the envelope. She carried the envelope over to the counter and took off her gloves. She'd get it on its way with no fingerprint of hers on it.

Roger realized years earlier he knew precious little about his old friend Asis. They used to meet at coffee houses and pubs. Asis had visited Roger while he attended Kingston University, but never the other way around. Roger learned later that everything Asis had told him was a lie. His occupation and business were all a lie. Asis had recruited him feeding off his need to feel important. As the years went by Roger had enough money to look deeper. He also had the feeling it might be a very good insurance policy to have this information on his old friend. As it turned out Asis was not his problem, he was the victim of a young lady who was incredibly proficient with a crossbow and bent on revenge for the death of her mother.

The next morning Janet dropped the letter in a mailbox after affixing extra postage. There was no denying the knot in her stomach with the storm she'd unleashed. Asis was undoubtedly responsible for the deaths of hundreds of innocent people in Ohio in the last week.

London

The parcel arrived at Asis' office mid-afternoon. His assistant knocked gently on the door.

"Come in," he said.

She entered and placed the package on his desk.

"Thank you," he said, and she left without a word.

He looked it over to see no return address and noticed the label was generated by a computer printer. He tore open the end and pulled out two sheets of paper. He began reading. Six minutes later he had read the two-page letter three times. He noticed a slight shake to his hands as he pulled out the top right desk drawer and put the letter inside. He slowly closed the drawer and sat back in his chair. His life had just changed.

As the afternoon turned into early evening Asis finished up some business emails and studied some marketing ideas a contact had sent him. He was trying to finish a normal day, but it was far from normal. He put some things into his briefcase and opened the top right drawer. He reached into the drawer like a man sticking his hand into a viper's nest and lifted the letter out and put it in his briefcase. He zipped it shut and walked over to get his coat.

"Have a nice evening," he said to his assistant. She returned a small nod and smile. Asis walked out for some cold London air. He had a four-minute walk to the Underground station and had timed it right for a short wait until the next train arrived. The twenty-minute ride to his flat gave him time to think. He'd prefer to be distracted by other thoughts but think he must. He was used to being in charge, in control. He'd grown complacent with the security measures that had served him perfectly up until now, but now someone knew his real identity.

Bethesda

The fall semester was half over, and classes were going well for Bisma. She was settling into college life and it was mostly everything she'd hoped it would be. This was not a normal university; all students were down to business. She'd never had a day in her life that wasn't down to business. One class was focused on current events going on domestically and abroad. One recent news story was coming from a St. Louis suburb involving a murder by a sniper. A local young lady was killed by a high-powered round from a distance. Not normal.

"Thoughts?" the professor asked.

"Professional," said one student.

"Ex-military?" said another.

"Target practice or making sure it was done right."

This remark turned heads.

Bisma said, "An assassination for hire."

"All possibilities," said the professor.

More discussion followed, but the consensus was what Bisma had said. Students thought law enforcement would want to investigate the victim's financial records, employment history and who would want her dead. No mention was made of terrorism, this was not how the cells worked.

Most of the day's discussion involved the attack in Columbus. This was a classic terrorist attack. This one made Bisma nauseous. She couldn't know for certain but felt it highly likely that

Hazaq would have been behind this. She wondered what part Chris might have played in this attack? He may be dead.

Bisma still had her mind on Chris and wondered if Moe Keane had given any thought to her idea of recruiting him. She'd like to do it herself but knew this was not a good idea for many reasons. She thought of people like Mike Baker and all his losses. She knew personally about his wife being killed in the attack on the restaurant in Greenville and had been told how his father had died. His brother had died in the submarine explosion by terrorism and his family's farm had been taken away by a man named Roger Knight. She had never met Knight but had been involved in getting communications set up for him and the London connection. Oh, how her life had changed in a year. She was extremely remorseful for her involvement and determined to make Hazaq pay. She'd do anything they needed to put him out of business and would love to put a bullet in him herself.

.

Chapter 13

Greenville

Mike received the letter he'd heard was coming. It was detailed and would take time to process. The Federal government was offering a plan for farm families to buy back their farm ground that had been purchased by the White Oak Holding Company. This farm ground was in Hampton County and several other counties around central Indiana.

Initially, at the request of Moe Keane, two separate agencies began looking at the possibility of trying to make this right with the farm community. The Justice system got involved and was able to seize the assets of White Oak. This would have taken much longer if there had been a larger ownership in the holding company, but White Oak was the now deceased Roger Knight and his sister, Janet Knight. Ms. Knight seemed to have the resources to fight this process and filed two separate injunctions to put a halt to it, she quickly softened after another conversation with Moe Keane. This conversation happened on her turf in St. Louis instead of Washington, D.C. and was in the presence of her counsel. The last time they'd spoken was in a small room at the Department of Homeland Security. Even though Janet felt more empowered this time it seemed she saw the light when it came to what Moe Keane had to tell her and quietly stepped aside from White Oak Holding to let it be unwound and parceled off.

Moe thought this was surprising for two reasons. One, he knew she shared the same greed as her brother, but she was more practical and not as reckless. Two, he was sure she hated him for the five days in her life when he had taken her into custody for questioning and asked her to turn against her brother. For Janet to agree to divest from all this farm ground told Moe she certainly had other assets, most likely on foreign soil and well hidden.

Mike was certain he wanted to get the farm back, if for no other reason than for Sandy and his parents. He also knew they'd want him to do it if the deal made sense for him. This would take time to think all the way through. He was able to determine the government was offering to sell the ground back to the farmers at a reasonable cost per acre, an amount per acre that should pay for itself, meaning the revenue would be enough to make the payments and not require the payment to be subsidized from other income sources. It was clear the government wanted this buyback plan to work. The government would be selling on contract, thus not requiring the farm families to seek financing at their banks or other local options. Loan servicing would be handled by agricultural lending co-operatives that would be in tune with the agricultural economy. Some farmers would want a more conventional route of financing. Knight's former bank was being overly cooperative with its former customers, they had written off debt and were offering extremely favorable interest rates. The bank desperately needed to rebuild its reputation. Mike was happy to see that several ag economic professors from Purdue had been involved with the formation of this plan along with professors from other ag universities.

He was also worried about the part of the plan that involved farm machinery the holding company had purchased. He would be able to buy back pieces of his own machinery that had been purchased by the holding company and the list was included with the letter. He saw several items were missing. These had surely been traded or sold by the holding company as they were depreciated out. This included the grain wagons that were probably never used by the holding company operators. All grain had been hauled away by semis. He felt confident any equipment he could buy back wouldn't have had the care he would've given it, thus making this a much less attractive alternative. This may be the time to go back to the old days when his father had started farming. In those days more than one farmer owned a piece of equipment, they shared ownership costs and had to work together to share the equipment. This wasn't necessarily easy but made a lot of horse sense.

This letter coming in late October seemed a little late. The first of September was the time landlords and tenants make decisions about the coming year. Mike had to make his decision by the end of the year, thus he had two months to decide. All previous owners were given first dibs on their own land and equipment. For any farmers who chose not to buy back their ground, the government would be looking for other tenants to farm it. It would be interesting to see how many actually wanted to participate in this plan. He knew of some families who had moved on with other career decisions and would not want anything to do with farming going forward. Alternatively, there would be some who wanted to expand their operations. Mike had no interest in that, he only wanted to get back what had been in the Baker family.

He'd like to discuss this with both David and Sarah, but that wouldn't happen any time soon, David was gone for an overseas deployment until early next year. Mike was sure they'd both support him in whatever he wanted to do. They'd been able to keep their family home and a few acres when the farm was sold at auction. This would allow them to re-establish what they had always had, all the farmland back with the house. It seemed he was possibly making up his mind a lot quicker than he thought he would. Another Chemex full of strong coffee and he'd be signing the contract.

As he imagined, thoughts of this decision consumed his day and night. He decided at one point in the middle of the night he had to tell the kids what was happening and would write an email to both of them. David had shared that communication was limited but there would be times he could check email. Mike liked the idea of putting his thoughts in an email

and began making notes of what he wanted to say.

He gave them a good overview of the deal that was being offered, told them a few of his misgivings and lastly asked for their thoughts after telling them he was leaning toward doing it. After reading it over two more times and letting it sit for forty minutes, he hit send.

Mike made himself not look at his computer for their responses until that evening. After dinner, he opened emails to see they had both answered and copied each other so all could see between them. As he imagined they both gave their support and thought it was the right thing to do. Sarah was in favor of renting it out, so he would not have to deal with the farm machinery issues. David thought he should farm the ground himself, buy any of their old equipment that was in good shape and then buy good used equipment to keep costs down. Mike smiled to himself as he began to type a thank you to both for their responses. They were both well-grounded young people with good heads on their shoulders. Their mother would have been so proud to have read their thoughts.

Greencastle, Indiana

Sarah was glad to have had this family conversation even by an email thread. It made her feel closer to David just reading what he'd written. The campus at DePauw was buzzing after the attack at Ohio State. She was happy to be at a smaller campus but still knew an attack could happen anywhere. Losing her mother in a restaurant attack in their hometown was proof enough. She frequently went back in her mind to that late afternoon last May. She had planned her attack and trained for it, cold-blooded, premeditated. She lived with the worry she'd be discovered at some point. She knew it would kill her dad, but it was over and revenge felt especially good. She'd saved the Hampton County taxpayers a lot of money for a trial.

Sarah also wondered if she could do it again. Maybe not, but who knows? David was either already in combat or getting very close to it. She wondered how he felt about killing bad guys? Stupid question, he was a trained Marine. Still, training was different. Sarah admired Special Agent Natalie Jackson. She was the right amount of tough with the right amount of empathy. Jackson had shown her family care and concern. She wondered if she could be a Nat Jackson and work for the FBI?

She had not seen or talked to Nat for several months. Maybe she should reach out to her. Part of her wondered if Nat would be able to read her face if the subject of Roger Knight came up. That felt like a risk that she shouldn't push at this point. If it was on her mind that meant something, probably guilt. Guilt was something people like Agent Jackson could smell.

Her classes were going well. She was focused and working toward her goal of education. She'd heard her dad say that being a college professor would be a great way to make a living in education. Her mother had been a student of Women's History and had studied the suffrage movement. As a family they'd visited Seneca Falls during the 150th anniversary of the first Women's Rights Convention. Sarah and her mom had dressed up like Susan B. Anthony and Elizabeth Cady Stanton and put on a skit her mom had written for her class in fifth grade. Sarah decided she would work toward a professorship to teach Women's History at DePauw or somewhere in the Midwest. She was also intrigued by military service David had chosen. She wouldn't go that direction mainly because of the worry it would cause her dad to have both of them in the military.

Her mind then went to Thanksgiving coming up in a few weeks. It would be hard not having David with them. For that reason, she would be looking forward to spending time with her dad and keeping him busy helping make persimmon pudding and sugar cream pie. At that moment she felt compelled to reach out to him and sent a text, '*Can't wait to see you Thanksgiving, Dad, love you!*' It wasn't two minutes for his response, '*Me too. I'll have persimmon pulp! Love you!!*'

London

Asis spent the next few days trying to decide what he wanted to do. It became clear to him that he had no one to help him, no one he trusted to share this extortion plan that had been delivered to him. He needed proof before he would consider meeting the demands. Whoever this person was, they threatened him with exposure and had given enough information for Asis to know this was a credible threat. He began making a list of who this might be. It was a short list and he wondered who he was missing. Most of those on the list were in London, three in Saudi Arabia and only one in the States. Two others in the States were now dead or supposed to be, Roger Knight and the woman, Bisma, who worked for Hazaq.

He must consider Hazaq. Asis had trusted him and trained him and felt good about his abilities. Like any good leader, he wanted more responsibility and had let Asis know he wanted to grow the network and plan more attacks. Could Hazaq be behind this? He couldn't imagine that, but at this point, it was still a possibility, everyone was a possibility. He was wondering if this would be a good time for an extended vacation. He had four days left to respond to the demands. He'd decided his initial response was to stall for more time. This person would have undoubtedly expected this response. He felt there was no way they'd "turn him in" this quick. They wanted money and should be willing to bargain longer for it.

He had to think long-term as well, not just short term. In any movie or book, a plot like this never ended with the pay-off, it was never over. If he did pay them off, they'd come back at some point and want more and then more again. The only way to possibly end this was to find them and turn the tables on them. Extinguish any intel they had on him and kill them. For this reason, he'd have to go on the offense, not on the defense like they wanted, he must draw them out. This thinking had now put him into attack mode. This is where he did his best work. He would dissect their demand letter for every detail they included along with the details they didn't mention.

Chapter 14

Rockton

Kurtz checked his account to make sure the deposit had been made. There'd been no need to inform his paymaster the job was done. This one had made national news. The big payday was next, this was the one he genuinely wanted. He'd made plans for how to approach the investigation. He had the computer skills to hack into about anywhere he wanted and ways to get past other obstacles. He had theories of who might be involved, he'd let the authorities lead for now.

Roger Knight's murder seldom made its way into the news at this point. It had been five months since his gruesome death, there was no love loss for Roger Knight by anyone as far as he could tell. His murder only came up when the newspaper reported on the business of agriculture. Farmers were now getting a chance to buy back some or all the ground they'd lost to Knight. The government had only made part of the story official which made the public like him even less. "Good riddance" was the consensus from the public. Kurtz's searching showed that state and federal authorities were not doing much if anything on this case.

There was a local reporter in Indianapolis Kurtz was following. This person had shown more interest than anyone on

Knight's murder. He decided to feed her information along the way and let her dog the police. So far intel from this reporter had been as good as the police reports. She must have someone else feeding her enough information to put her on the right track to question people. Maybe she also had some unholy alliances she was beholden to for whatever reason. Kurtz had been approached in a market one morning while stationed in Iraq eighteen years ago. He'd always wondered if he'd been specifically targeted or just in the right/wrong place at the right/wrong time.

The two men who approached him that morning had offered him a great deal of money when he returned to the states to use his skills as a Marine. This was at a time in his deployment when he felt like listening and told them he would talk. He was still considering their proposal when they let him know a few days later their initial meeting had been video recorded including audio. He knew this would look very bad if they turned it over to the Marines. Two years went by with no further contact from these Iraqis, in that time he'd been discharged and was back home in Indiana. One day out of the blue he received a parcel at work showing pictures of his wife and family including a picture of his home. The letter was clear, he was to do what he was told, or his family was not safe. He would be paid well for his work and his full discretion was expected. He was extremely upset but saw no way out.

One assignment was no more than to meet a banker named Roger Knight in Indianapolis. The expectation was he'd be available to do an occasional assignment for Mr. Knight. His compensation was a few acres of land in western Indiana with a nice older farmhouse and a barn. Kurtz loved it, just what he'd always wanted. As it turned out he never had an assignment from Mr. Knight until this one which he received after his death. If Knight lost his life by foul play, make sure his murderer was brought to justice by any means.

Lafayette

Tom Sutherlin was researching the attack at Ohio State. He was particularly interested in the spray that had been used from the crop duster before it crashed. That was an intentional part of the attack, not just them flipping a switch as they came over the stadium. The authorities were not saying much yet, but he had acquaintances at Ohio State he'd asked. Interestingly the spray was a concoction of insecticide and herbicide that, thank goodness, was not going to be lethal for the people involved. There was speculation the spray might be related to the poison that infected the Red Tanager birds a few years ago in Brazil. That caused many problems for the livestock industry in the Midwest and some loss of human life as well.

Tom sent a short email to his Boiler Club friends to update them on his findings. Later that day the other three men had answered and set up a breakfast meeting for the coming Saturday in Lafayette.

Saturday morning arrived, and they met as scheduled. Handshakes happened all around, and they were seated at a large booth. All wanted coffee and orders were taken without the need for menus.

"Can you believe they used a crop duster"? Doc Summers asked.

"They seem to be especially innovative in their planning. As you mentioned in the email, Tom, they were trying to do more harm with the spray." Brian Miller added.

Tom said, "Thank goodness there should be no long-term effects for the people who were sprayed. There have been reports of flu-like symptoms for some, many had headaches and respiratory distress that day. This keeps pulling me back to the Alberto Mulina thug, poisoning birds to kill livestock and people when they migrated back to the States from Brazil."

"Yeah we have firsthand knowledge of that guy," Brian said.

Tom shook his head.

Mike Baker just listened. This attack affected him like every other one. "What the hell do these people want with us?"

No one answered because no one had any idea either. Coffee was being poured and Mike was asking for cream which he got in a small pitcher that had hopefully been washed a time or two since the Cold War. It was one of those little metal pitchers with the top on a hinge. Mike was deciding whether or not to look inside or just pour. Brian was watching him and looked in himself.

"Go ahead, nothing growing that shouldn't be or that'll kill you."

Mike gave him a half smile and half snarl and poured away.

"Might help the taste of their crappy coffee if I'm lucky," Mike said.

"Yes, you're the coffee snob, I forgot," Tom said.

Mike shrugged, "I know what's good."

"Cheers Boiler Club," Doc Summers said.

They all clinked mugs. Mike told the group he'd received a letter from the government about buying the farm back. He gave them few details, but they all agreed it was good that things were being handled with a semblance of common sense.

"You made a decision?" Tom asked.

"Yeah, I'm going to do it. My kids are in favor. One thinks I should farm it myself and the other thinks I should rent it out, but we're in agreement to bring it back into the family."

"Good deal Mike."

Breakfast plates hit the table and they got down to what they do best, breakfast talk centered around Purdue sports, football and basketball and how it was all on the upswing. Basketball turned to birding and Brian offered stories on three new entries on his life list, two that he went in search of and one just happened. They could all tell the one that just happened out of nowhere was a lot of fun for a guy like Brian. Those were extremely rare when you had a life list number like he had.

"Any trips out of the states planned?" Tom asked.

"I'm looking close at a trip to Cuba. I had this in my sights years ago when our first child was on the way, decided I shouldn't go then but I'm thinking strongly about it now."

"I've always been interested in going there. I guess it just seemed mysterious to me. It was out of reach for political reasons my entire life, now it seems like a possibility," Mike said.

"More coffee gentlemen?" the waitress asked.

Mike initially had his hand over his cup but said, "I'll take a warm up please."

"Like that coffee Mike?" Brian grinned.

"Pretty sure they ran this through an old paper placemat."

"So flavorful and yet musky with a hint of bathroom ceiling mold!"

"Exactly," Mike said.

That comment had two of the four pushing mugs away from them and calling for their checks. Handshakes were exchanged and they were all on their way. Brian rode up with Mike but was meeting Pam at the mall to do some shopping afterward. Mike dropped him at the north end of the mall and went in the bookstore to look around. He still couldn't pass up a bookstore.

"See you at home buddy."

"Thanks for the ride Mike, see you soon," Brian waved.

Mike looked in his favorite section, fiction. He had his favorite authors and looked for new offerings. Some would have a new title come out the same time each year, same month. He always looked for Sandy's favorites as well. This would always be hard for him. She had always looked forward to the latest in a series as much as anyone. He wished she were here to be excited seeing the new book on the shelf. He could still see her eyes light up when she found it. He could see her pick it up and hold it like it was a treasure. He could hear her say and see her thinking that she should not buy it yet, but instead keep it as a Christmas idea for David or Sarah. And like the true partners they were, he'd do the same exact thing.

He spent some time walking the store and liked the smell of coffee near the magazine section. He enjoyed the thirty-minute drive home on U.S. 52 which was not nearly as busy as the interstate. He enjoyed seeing farms along the way and had one he always admired and wished he owned. This farm had a small guest house on the same property which always fascinated him. It had an old concrete stave silo back by a big barn that seemed to stay in pretty good shape. Many barns of that vintage had gone downhill, roofs had been blown off in heavy winds and some had begun to collapse altogether. Always made him sad to see it. He'd told David and Sarah to look for old barns and think of the time when they were the centerpiece of the farmstead. They were used for livestock of all kinds, hay and straw storage and smaller machinery was stored in them as well.

Before long he'd crossed into Hampton County and was approaching the Dairy Queen, a favorite stopping place. He'd skip the milkshake this time, but it sounded good any time of day. Milkshakes were a dairy product and could be enjoyed at breakfast, lunch or dinner. He made his turn on the country road that took him home. He was glad he'd be getting the farm back, it was his family's home.

Fort Meade

Steve Bradshaw spent his days brainstorming. His searches had turned up little, but little things could be enough to pull you along further. He came upon a piece of information that he didn't know. He learned the Navy had DNA samples on all crewmembers who were aboard the USS South Carolina. DNA was available. He felt confident it would be no easy task to get to a point where they could use this in an investigation, but Moe Keane had a way of making things like this happen. If this were the case, it was also a strong possibility the government was cataloging the DNA of prisoners. His first thought went to

Guantanamo Bay. Why not cross-check the DNA of his five suspected crewmembers with prisoner DNA? How much good intel would this yield?

His mind turned to Nat Jackson and he decided to come up with a couple questions to warrant a call to her. Not his best use of NSA time, but he could use some distraction conversing with an extremely nice-looking FBI agent. He sent her a text, '*time for a call?*' His phone buzzed about three minutes later.

"How you doin' Nat?"

"Not bad, how about you?"

"Not much progress on the London terrorist. Have they involved you in the Columbus attack?"

"Not like I'd hoped. There's always an underlying turf war when anyone else is called in from another region."

"Were you called in?" Steve asked.

"Not really. Someone called asking for me saying he had information the night before the attack, but I was not available, so when they sent the call to another agent, the caller hung up."

"Any idea who that was?"

Nat knew Steve would have an idea of who the caller was if she told him the truth, but she was not at liberty to say so she just deflected, "No there was not enough information. The call did last long enough to determine it came from the Columbus, Ohio area, but that's it."

"Very interesting for sure. Someone trying to warn the authorities and they called for you. You must have another admirer besides me."

"Someone needs to warn me about you," Nat said.

"I'm needing some time in Indianapolis for research."

"Research for what?"

"Research on how much more effective FBI agents would be if they had a more fulfilling personal life with someone who made them happy," Steve said.

"How long did it take you to come up with that line?"

"Not that long, I'd like to see you."

"Your wife would not be happy about that."

"She's not my wife much longer. She's gone back to North Carolina and has taken the kids. She's near her folks and they get to enjoy their grandchildren. I can't blame her, I work all the time, I'm never home."

"I'm sorry Steve."

"You know I'm not that sorry. I do miss my kids very much, but they're all better off back where we grew up in North Carolina."

This led to a few seconds of silence from both sides. It dragged on until the awkward stage, which didn't take long.

"Take care, Steve, and keep in touch."

"You too, Nat, stay safe. Call me sometime."

"Okay."

Chapter 15

Afghanistan

David Baker had found his way into the thick of it. His platoon of Marines was two months into a proposed seven-month deployment. He learned there was no such thing as a routine patrol even though they tried hard to believe it. They'd leave the base for a routine patrol mission and be out two to three hours. Last week an Afghani patrol was hit by a roadside bomb killing four of their men. Truth was, there was not much you could do to avoid it. If you hit one there was an explosion. Their troop carriers were well protected, but not completely. For this reason, your stomach stayed tied in a knot while you were out.

Opportunities to communicate with family at home were intermittent while you were deployed. They'd allow some email and occasional facetime if someone had a real need, otherwise you could always sit down and write a letter. He had gotten mail from his dad and his sister along with a few other friends. He couldn't tell anyone much, which he understood. They didn't want anything revealed that could put them all in more danger than they were already experiencing.

"You hear from home, Baker?"

"No, rereading a letter from my dad."

"Your folks doing okay?"

"It's just my dad and my sister, my mom was killed in a terrorist attack in my hometown in Indiana."

"I'm sorry man."

"Yeah, me too."

"I guess this is personal for all of us in different ways, I'm really sorry."

"Thanks. There's got to be a way to turn the jihadists back."

"Yeah, I sure as hell hope so for everyone. I'm not sure though."

"Me either," David said.

David's buddy left, leaving him to his thoughts. They'd gotten the news of the attack at Ohio State. Some days he wondered why they were fighting in Afghanistan and not deployed on American soil. The terrorists wanted to bring the fight to the heartland of the States and he'd seen it firsthand. No one wanted to see troops patrolling the streets of Indianapolis or Greenville, but he wasn't sure if it wouldn't come to that.

Washington

Moe Keane had been successful in getting the two prisoners moved from Columbus, Ohio to the Department of Homeland Security. A few local lawyers in Ohio had pitched a fit centering on their rights, but more than one judge in Ohio saw fit to get them on their way to Washington. National security overshadowed their rights at the moment. If the attack had not happened, it may have been a different story. But it did happen and they were prime suspects.

Keane would first concentrate on making a link between these two and the two suicide bombers in the plane. He knew from Chris this would not be easy. They were trained not to talk, but every operative in every branch of service around the world was trained not to talk. Everyone eventually talked. He also knew from Chris these two didn't know about the attack with the crop duster plane, they'd been kept in the dark like Chris.

He questioned them separately, then together and again separately. Keane had no intention of letting these two free anytime soon but he also knew a good lawyer would argue there was not a lot to hold them on. He knew what they were planning. Suicide vests were found in the apartment.

After being questioned by several different agents over a few days they'd put them through the wringer. Keane had them moved to a new area with several other prisoners. It was easy to see this gave the two prisoners new hope, they must have felt they were back in with their cell. Keane would see what they might get now. All of their new cellmates were his agents.

It had now been two weeks since the attack at Ohio State. The cell number he'd given Chris was always close at hand. He knew Chris would hardly have any chance for communication but was glad it was now possible. He also knew if that number was dialed, he'd have to act quickly. Moe also felt in his bones it had been long enough. Chris had been embedded with this group for many months. They were at a point they could raid the Chicago cell and take them down. He still wanted the London connection. This is the man who had engineered all the attacks costing many lives as well as causing much harm to the agricultural sector of the economy.

The Chicago leader was named Hazaq. Keane had no background information on this man. Chris didn't know how much Hazaq knew about the London connection. Hazaq answered to him but had probably never met him. Their technology would most likely be the main way to get to the person in London. When the Chicago cell was out of business the London connection might go underground and who knew for how long. For this reason, he still needed people in London searching for him or them. Nat Jackson should have been there six months ago, but he'd pulled the plug on that deployment.

His thoughts went to Bisma. She was not a trained operative, but she had been an operative for the jihadists. He fully trusted her loyalties at this time and he knew she wanted this type of work. It seemed time to talk. He sent her a text and got a reply back within two minutes. He'd make the forty-five-minute drive to Bethesda this evening.

When she walked into the small restaurant she immediately saw him sitting at a booth in a back corner. He had the seat looking at the door and saw her. Good spy craft she thought. She moved past the hostess and found her way through the tables. Moe stood and extended his hand, she reached and placed her hand in his. She smiled up at this big bear of a man. At six-foot-three he stood about a foot taller than Bisma. She was thinking his next shirt needed to be an inch bigger in the neck, it appeared his tie was cutting off some blood flow.

"How you doin'?" Moe asked.

"I'm doing well, Mr. Keane."

"Let's order dinner."

They both declined the waiter's offer of drinks and asked for ice water with lemon. They made small talk about her classes and their food came quickly. Moe told the waiter they were good after a water refill and they were left alone. The restaurant was nearly empty on a weekend and for a later dinner.

"I was so sorry to hear about the attack at Ohio State. Any leads?"

"Yes, we have two in custody."

This perked Bisma up, she was not expecting to hear that.

"That is very good sir. They don't like to be captured."

"Why's that?" he asked already knowing the answer.

"It doesn't fit in with their plans in paradise."

Moe shook his head.

"Yes, I know. Forty virgins," Moe said.

Moe had already decided he was not ready to talk to her about Chris.

"How did you get them?"

"Good police work," he answered with a smile.

"Okay you don't want to say, I understand."

"I will tell you they've not been helpful. I'm not sure they actually know much."

"Any idea if they are connected to Hazaq?"

"That's what I'd like to know," as he slid two pictures over to her side.

She looked at each one carefully and pointed to one.

"He's been with the Chicago cell, I've seen him. He was involved with the bus attack on the school and was in the barn the night the deputies were killed."

This was new information to Moe. Chris had confirmed that one of the two had been involved with the school bus attack but had not shared information about the barn.

"Did he kill one or both of the deputies?"

"I'm not sure, but I know he was in the barn. I heard him talking."

This was information Moe could feed his cellmates and see if he felt like doing any bragging about killing an infidel sheriff deputy. That would keep him in custody for a long time.

"That is a help."

"Mr. Keane, can I ask, was Chris involved with this attack?"

"Not that we know of."

She gave him a look he couldn't read but thought it might mean a hundred things.

"Have you given any more thought to recruiting him? It's my idea you know. It's a good idea, Mr. Keane."

He smiled at her, "I admire your tenacity, Bisma. You've settled on this idea of recruiting a terrorist, a home-grown terrorist. Some people think that's worse than a jihadist coming from another country."

"I can see why. It does make him a traitor, but maybe he's ready to atone for his sins. Maybe he'd like out, I can sure understand that feeling."

"I know you can. I need to ask you a question."

She gave a quick nod, brown eyes bright.

"I am thinking of sending you to London for some study abroad. While there you'd track leads on the London connection."

"Put me in coach."

That actually made Moe smile, "Where'd you get that?"

"Americans say stuff like that, right?"

"Yes."

"Then I'm learning."

"Yes, you are. Okay, I'd like for you to finish the semester. How many weeks left?"

"About six I think."

"That's good, finish strong and we'll send you to London."

"I'll be ready."

"Bisma, one last question. Do you have feelings for Chris?"

Her eyes answered first he thought, now let's see what her mouth says.

"I could have if he weren't a jihadist. We spent two days together and like I've told you in the past I felt he was different. He's smart, and he's tough. He also seemed to have another side that I'm sure he didn't want to show me. I felt his guard was not up nearly as much as it would be sitting in the Chicago cell. He grew up in Iowa. I've looked up Iowa. It's a nice place. Not a place for people who want to blow up women and children and innocent people. So yes, I'll be honest, he seems like the kind of guy I might like to know more if he were one of the good guys."

"Thank you."

"That's it?" she said.

"I asked, you answered. I care about you, Bisma. You're working for us and I care about my people. You risked a lot and gave up a lot in your life. I'm still getting to know you and you have my respect."

With that, she smiled and gave a slight nod. Moe got up from the table and waved the waiter over for the check. He handed him two twenties and headed for the door. Bisma watched him go out, then gathered up her things and followed. He was across the street and in his car as she came out the door. As she walked the short distance to her apartment she thought to herself he was more of a father figure than she'd ever had. She remembered loving her father as a little girl but losing him in the war against the Russians was a long time ago. Mr. Keane was always down to business, but the last two minutes of their conversation showed her a new side. It was not like he gave her much, but it meant a lot to her. Fathers in other parts of the world didn't show a lot of affection to their daughters. Far from it. This seemed like the way it should be.

It was late enough Moe decided to head on home. He thought about his family and his daughters. His middle child, a daughter, was Bisma's age. He knew enough of Bisma's background to want better for her with her life moving forward. She was special and he'd do his best to make sure she was protected.

London

Tonight at midnight was his deadline to answer the person demanding money. Farid had worked to reverse engineer the email he was given to respond. He'd reported to Asis the email was set up with many different points of contact. He had made it through a few of them but was still not close. Asis had crafted his reply which was nothing more than a stall message to give Farid more time. He would play the game and set it to send at 11:55 London time. His overnight bag was packed, and he was heading north for a couple days in the country. No need to take a chance on Scotland Yard banging on the door to his flat in the middle of the night. He had people watching just in case it did happen.

He let himself enjoy the three-hour drive as much as possible that afternoon. He checked in and made his way to the bar for a stout. A light dinner with pint number two along with a spirited football match on the screen behind the bar made for a relaxing evening. The bar was mostly empty with no one to bother him. He finished and made his way up to his room, twenty minutes later he was in bed.

Missouri

The email popped on her screen at 5:21 AM. It had been sent at 11:55, thus it took twenty-six minutes to get through all the twists and turns she had set up around the world. The pattern was completely random and would change with each transmission. The email was nearly exactly what she imagined, and more formal than she expected. He had given respect. That might not be good but now her mind was playing with her a little. She reread the response she had written days ago, it was appropriate for what he had said. She set it to send at 6:00 AM London time. She wanted him to consider this was coming from his own part of the world.

London

He was mostly still asleep when he heard his laptop buzz. His man watching the flat was to have alerted him by text if anyone had shown up at his door last night. That phone showed no activity. He checked the laptop to see he had a new email that appeared to be the one he was expecting. He read quickly and then went back to read slower. Short and to the point.

"You'll not get another stall tactic. You have forty-eight hours to make the transfer.

Deadline: Tuesday, November 3rd, 1800 hours London time."

This felt real to Asis and did not allow time for Farid to find the person or group. He had already made calls to the Middle East and was met with some pushback when they heard the number. A constant flow of oil made it possible and he was told it would happen. Asis knew he'd now be indebted to this group more than he ever wanted, but what choice did he have? He also would have their help tracking down this person. They wanted their money back.

6:00 PM London time on November 3rd was noon in the United States, middle of the day on Election Day. The presidential race was as contentious as everyone had guessed it would be. One hundred million U.S. dollars flowing around the world that day would not be noticed for a couple of days. The money laundering maze was incredible. Pay-offs had to happen with each link on the chain amounting to about twenty million of it on day one. By the end of the first two weeks, the total would be another twenty million leaving about sixty million dollars for Janet Knight. She couldn't imagine the price she'd have on her head.

Chapter 16

Jakarta, Indonesia

Chimera was up early as usual. Her workout involved a kettlebell as well as a run on the beach. She couldn't think of a better place to spend her days. Anyone else who lived here made their living from tourism. People from all over the world would come and go, no one stayed forever. She did. Her business was all based on technology. She saw transmissions come from one direction and go out another. Everything based on algorithms she had developed on her own experience and years of studying failures by others. She moved money for people, and it was all based on legitimate businesses from around the world. It looked like money market or Treasury Bill type investments. Gains based on fractions of a percent, but gains were not her goal. Laundering funds were her goal and she made a percentage for the risk.

The Russians were her biggest clients. Every type of organized crime one could imagine was alive and well in that part of the world. They were incredibly good at it. The occasional indictment was rarely prosecuted. The highly unlikely prosecution was habitually overturned. There was always a steady flow of money coming through her portal. She would have a large amount hit the pipeline from time to time. That had just happened. This one was unusual, she rarely knew the client, didn't want to know them. This client had taken precautions to a new level, using more twists, turns, and switchbacks than ever before. Most transactions had some type of signature albeit slight, kind of like a fingerprint on a human. This transaction had something she noticed that she'd not seen for a while. What made it interesting was the fact it was going the wrong direction. She'd seen something similar but not in this fashion. This had the feel of a client she had based in London. She didn't like working with terrorists, but the pay was just as good.

The client in London always seemed to be the one in charge. This time it felt like he was taking a hit. She was not worried about it, but intuition in her business meant safety. She could follow part of the money as it left her control. The only way she caught this nuance was the fact she was either the third or fourth cog in the process from the London jihadist. She decided to give this a little time and then consider contacting him. He had certainly appreciated her expertise in the past. He'd been kind to her after the tsunami in 2004. Her area was devastated but was able to come back with help from Middle Eastern oil money.

Two days later she typed a short email and hit send. She had not used this code name for a long time and assumed she'd never use it again. The code name referred to a Brazilian named Alberto Mulina. He had been captured by the American CIA and then killed in an attack on a safe house in the states. She used to be part of the line that funneled money from London to Mulina in Brazil. If her London connection wanted to talk more he'd reroute the transmission and give her the protocol to use. This happened within twenty minutes, this told her he was motivated in some way. She gave him a brief description of what she'd noticed in the transmissions. He came back with more detail than she liked, they kept any communication as generic as possible even though they felt it secure. He did let her know he was out a large amount of money and any help finding it would be greatly appreciated. She gave him what she had which wasn't much. He thanked her and let her know he'd repay the favor.

Asis read what she'd sent. This may have been the break he needed. He sent the information to Farid and let him do his magic.

Indianapolis

Tim Dailey was still following leads from the Roger Knight murder. There'd never been many leads and they all led nowhere. At this point, he was just going on gut instinct. The murder scene had always made him feel revenge was involved. The bad part of this thinking was coming up with the list of people who might want revenge, that list was long. With the violent and targeted death of Sandy Baker at the request of Knight, Mike Baker was always on the list. Agent Nat Jackson had dismissed that idea quickly and had enough influence to convince everyone else, but not Dailey. Why couldn't Mike Baker have shot an arrow through his neck? Hell, he wouldn't blame him.

There was no forensic evidence ever found. The bolt that had been shot presumably from a crossbow could be purchased by anyone at any major sporting goods retailer. There were no fingerprints on anything. He also thought of the Baker children.

Son, David, was now in the Marines, maybe he needed a major change in his life to cover up something like murder. Daughter, Sarah, was a college student at DePauw University. A source said she was doing well in college while fighting depression over her mother's death.

Their best bet for a lead might well be someone talking at some point. Maybe a witness or someone who knew something about a person with a crossbow would come forward. If someone had been hired to do this as an assassin, then more than one person knew the truth. If this were someone acting on their own, then the case might go unsolved. Tim himself had fired a crossbow while growing up. A buddy of his had a Barnett Crossbow and they'd taken it out one fall afternoon for target practice. Up until then, he'd only seen them on television. He had to admit the pistol grip had a nice feel. This was a very lethal weapon. He also had the sense someone who was adept at sighting in a high-powered rifle and lining up a shot would be good with a crossbow. The controlled breathing required would be the same. Wind and environmental factors would not be the same due to the proximity needed for a lethal crossbow shot. This also told him the shooter would have extraordinary skills of being able to get close undetected. Not the same for a human target versus an animal with a great sense of smell though, humans would be much easier.

Every report he'd seen detailed Janet Knight's skills with a crossbow. She'd been a successful archer in college. She'd won competitions and set records. Her brother's death at the hands of someone using a crossbow just pointed in her direction. Neighbors had seen her leave his place in a hurry, even squealed her tires a little. But evidence had been uncovered to show she was not there at the time of death. They had a video of Ms. Knight filling her car with gasoline before the murder had been committed.

Rockton

The assassin was growing more impatient all the time. Information flow had dried up. There was nothing to feed to the reporter. This had progressed to the point he'd imagined which was dead end after dead end. He didn't have forever so he was ready to put his plan into action. Somebody had to pay for this murder for him to get paid. The big break in the case would come right out of the blue. One piece of evidence no one saw coming. It had to be one of those things that people would say was hiding in plain sight for this to work as he planned. It was going to be controversial which made it good.

Constance Tremblay had given her life to the banking business. She started her career during a time when women were just getting opportunities for management positions. She worked hard at her first bank branch and seven years later got the chance to be the branch manager. A good record of consumer lending with low default rates had her moving downtown to the main office of a major regional bank while she was in her mid-thirties. It was not as exciting as she initially hoped when she learned she'd be an assistant to Roger Knight. He was not talked about as being a tyrant but he deserved to be called whatever a close second was. With few problems early on, their working relationship began better than she imagined.

Things began to change when Mr. Knight showed more interest in her than she was comfortable with. Constance began feeling the effects of sexual harassment. It was small things early on and then began to ramp upward. Knight wasn't married and was about fifteen years her senior. Constance was also not married but she was in a relationship with a man who wanted her to put a stop to his bullshit. This was happening at a time when it was still better for a woman's career to put up with harassment and keep quiet than say anything. Constance only shared things with her boyfriend who was growing more upset.

Things hit the fan one day when Knight touched Constance in his office and delivered an ultimatum about what needed to happen between them in order for her career to advance. Constance pushed him away and headed straight for the HR department. She insisted on filing a formal complaint after being warned against doing so by two female employees which made it hurt all the more. She filed the complaint and went back to a hostile work environment. In the next few days, threats from her boyfriend became public in social media and all over the bank. Three days later Constance was escorted out of her office as she carried a box of personal belongings and her career with Indiana Constellation National Bank was over.

The restraining order that soon followed along with other filings by bank attorneys had squarely placed all blame on Constance and her jealous boyfriend as the bad guys. As it turned out for Constance, the jealous boyfriend turned out to be abusive towards her as well and soon found himself the subject of another restraining order from Constance.

The assassin had done ample research on Tyler Harper to learn he did get out of hand. Constance was a professional woman who happened to be beautiful. She was the best thing that had happened to Tyler and a real loss when she left him behind. Tyler had a lot of reason to hate 'ole Roger Knight including having an aunt and cousin who'd been killed in the restaurant attack in Greenville. When Kurtz made sure the proper evidence finally happened to show up it would lead any reasonable person to believe Tyler had taken his crossbow, laid in wait for Knight to appear for his evening drink by the pool and put a lethal crossbow bolt through his neck pinning him to the chair.

Depending on how his reporter friend spun the story over the next few weeks, people would begin to see how these pieces fit together. Tyler had a job working maintenance at a local hospital and was keeping himself down the straight and narrow to keep his parole officer happy with each visit. He'd keep an eye on Tyler to make sure he wasn't a flight risk. News articles mentioned Tim Dailey from the FBI was on the case, the lead investigator was Special Agent Natalie Jackson also out of the Indianapolis office.

Kurtz knew these agents would want an arrest and a conviction for the crime. His contract didn't specify a conviction was better than a hit by him. He'd let law enforcement do the dirty work for him. This would save him from covering up another murder and he'd still get his big payday.

Chapter 17

Greenville

Sarah was home for Thanksgiving. Just she and Dad this year. David had been home last year, the first year Mom was not there. Their emotions were all over the place last year, and this year they were both worried about David. They shared stories about David and did more laughing than crying. They made more food than they needed but enjoyed every bit of the time cooking together.

"Did you get persimmon pulp this year, Dad?"

"Sure did, I bought it though."

"That's okay, but how will you determine our winter weather."

Mike smiled, he knew what she meant with that question.

"I'll do my best to find a persimmon seed from this year."

"Okay, tell me again."

"Split the seed in half. If you see a knife shape inside, it means the winter will be cutting cold. If you see a spoon shape, it means lots of snow to shovel and I can never remember what a fork means. Something good I'll bet."

"Like a winter with lots of BBQ!"

"Exactly," Mike said.

The turkey got carved, the gravy got thickened, the potatoes got smashed and the persimmon pudding sat out to cool next to a big container of whipped topping. They said their family prayer holding hands and then each added prayers for David, Mom, and Grandparents who had made wonderful memories of this day. Mike took a big drink of sweet tea and they started passing bowls back and forth. The turkey platter sat close enough so that it didn't need to be passed. Mike thought they'd be eating turkey for days which was not a problem.

"Did you ever think of planting persimmon trees, Dad?"

"No, but David has mentioned it. He wanted to plant some more trees back in the woods."

"That's a good idea."

"I agree. I did some research to learn you must have a female and male tree to get persimmon fruit."

"Really?"

"Yes," Mike said. "I've been told you should buy ten persimmon trees to make sure you'll have enough to bear fruit. A friend of mine told me that some of the earliest golf clubs used persimmon wood for the club head. Persimmon wood is very hard, that's what's needed for golf clubs."

"Then you need to plant some persimmon trees. Mom would've liked that."

"Yes, she would have. I can see her sharing pulp with her friends if we had plenty each year."

Talk turned to school, and Mike learned that Sarah was doing great as always. She was a dedicated student and was enjoying her college experience. He also knew she battled some depression. He probably did as well if he were honest with himself, why wouldn't they?

"Have you started to narrow down your plans after school?"

"I'd like to teach at the college level, and I'd like to teach history with an emphasis on Women's History."

This brought a smile to Mike's face. Sandy loved learning about history and women's history in particular.

"That sounds great to me Sarah. I've always thought being a college professor would be the best job ever."

"I've heard you say that over the years. I always knew it came from your experience at Purdue and how you felt about your professors. I also know how much you enjoyed the college campus experience. I'm having a great one too."

"Colleges bring cultural things to the community along with sports and educational opportunities for all ages."

"I totally agree, that's all part of my thinking."

"Well I'm excited and David will like that."

"I'd like to stay fairly close, but I'll look around this part of the country for opportunities. If DePauw has that opportunity, all the better."

"Understood."

With that, they were clearing dishes and finding dessert plates for sugar cream pie and persimmon pudding. Mike poured himself a cup of coffee from the Chemex and Sarah put on the kettle for hot water to make tea. He was glad she was home for the weekend. They'd watch the Old Oaken Bucket game on Saturday and decide how to eat leftover turkey. They might be to turkey manhattan's by Saturday.

Chicago

Thanksgiving and Christmas hit hard for Chris Powell. Several years spent in a jihadist terrorist cell did not lend itself to watching the Macy's parade. If they did turn on the television to see the parade, it would've been to plan where they could bring death and destruction, the more women and children, the better. It was so sickening, and he had to play along. If Hazaq had noticed any part of him acting the wrong way he'd be in big trouble. He'd gotten good at showing no emotion, and he'd also gotten very good at retreating fully into himself and remembering times with his family. He could relive wonderful family meals with cousins and grandparents. He always felt sorry for the other men living here. They did not have these times to remember. If they did have any good memories, any mention of them was always guarded.

He couldn't help but wonder if he'd ever have a normal life again. There'd been times he'd resigned himself to the fact that he'd die with this bunch of terrorists in an event he wasn't able to stop. His greatest fear was that he'd be thought of as a terrorist and not someone who'd given his life to stop them. Only Moe Keane could make it right if that ever happened. He even thought about writing this out to make sure people would know the truth, but if he got caught with it, he knew there were things worse than death and they'd make sure he'd experience terrible things.

The cell had been laying low since the attack in Ohio, this was usually the case. Chris knew Hazaq was always planning something. He never knew how much came from Hazaq and how much came from London. Recruitment was always a focus and this seemed to happen entirely by the internet. It seemed a steady stream of young men from any part of the world were always looking to join this cause. He wondered how many potential recruits the FBI and Homeland Security caught each year or put on watch lists. It seemed when some lone wolf did something in the United States they'd say he was on some watch list. Chris figured the size of the watch list far outweighed the manpower available to oversee it.

Whenever new recruits showed up in Chicago they always arrived in pairs. They usually came from the east coast and were ninety percent Middle Eastern descent. He felt sure Hazaq didn't want or trust Caucasians to come into their cells. The jihadists were happy for any American to become that lone wolf terrorist who shot up a county music concert or ran his pickup truck into a group of innocent women and children.

The phone he used to talk to Moe Keane from Columbus, Ohio was long gone, but Keane's number was burned into his memory. Being able to stop the two suicide bombers felt good, but the attack by the crop duster plane still stung. Hazaq had kept the attacks completely separate leaving Chris no way to keep either event from happening. He told Keane exactly where the Chicago cell was based which made him feel they could be taken down at any time. Keane must have other plans if he were leaving them operational. Chris knew they were being watched, that was a given. Maybe Keane was waiting for the next group to be sent out for an attack.

Chris knew Hazaq and the Middle Eastern cell members didn't like cold weather. Cold weather was in full swing in Chicago as the first of December had arrived. Hazaq did like the extra cover their winter coats provided if he wanted to use a suicide bomber or have a concealed weapon available. Hazaq had never run an operation in the Chicago area as far as Chris knew. He had basically hidden this cell in plain sight for months and months. Chris didn't see how this could happen in a place that wasn't urban or a college town. Those melting pot places where everyone blended in were prime areas to live and recruit.

Missouri

Janet realized it was Thanksgiving because her office was going to be closed on Thursday. At least they'd be open for business on Friday, she made money when the markets were open. She was a little surprised when she let herself feel sentimental about missing Roger. That was funny because she didn't usually see him at Thanksgiving anyway, now he was gone. Janet was also letting herself daydream a little about retiring from her job as a registered representative.

She could turn over her book of business to other associates in the firm, they'd pay her part of ongoing commissions for a couple years and she'd just live in a warm place much closer to the equator. She would make her decision by the end of the year.

She knew her plan to get money from Asis had upset some extremely dangerous people. They killed for a lot less and if they knew they'd been had by a woman. She had enough money to last a few lifetimes hidden away in offshore accounts. This might be a good time to disappear, get off the grid as people say.

Janet poured herself a glass of wine and began to walk through her home. She walked slowly from room to room looking at what she would take with her when she made a huge move like this. She had spent her life working hard and living in the middle part of the country. The last thirty years had been in St. Louis after growing up in central Indiana. The winters were less enjoyable year by year. If she did this, it was all or none. If she kept this home and came back from time to time she'd be an easy target. She could keep it for a while and have it watched to see if anyone else was waiting for her to return. This seemed like a waste of money and would not guarantee anything.

She saw things in her house she'd have to take with her. She didn't have lots of happy memories which was mostly her fault. She'd not tried to make many memories with anyone and Roger had followed the same path. They were cut from the same cloth even though she wanted to think differently.

Fort Meade

Steve sat his third cup of coffee on a desk that was cleaner than normal. He liked piles of paper but was printing less and less all the time because he liked trees and realized how much paper went through the shredder each week. He'd also developed his own way of filing paperwork digitally that made it quicker for him to do research and pull things together in a meaningful manner. No sorting through piles, his digital filing system had excellent sort qualities.

He opened his email to find what he was looking for, an early morning communique from Moe Keane. He smiled when he saw the length of the email, Keane was succinct and to the point.

Bradshaw,

'You have permission to use the DNA information on the five crew members. It is attached. If you screw this up, it'll be your ass.'

Keane

He smiled to himself. Keane was like your dad, your coach and your boss all rolled into one salty bastard. He also knew Keane would have his back if he ever needed it. Steve opened the attachments and realized he basically knew nothing about DNA results. He knew part of what Keane meant about not screwing this up involved the families of the sailors. All families had lost a loved one in the line of duty. Speculation that their loved one was a murderous, treasonous traitor wouldn't sit well. If one of these sailors were the traitor, he'd have to get it right. It might be possible the family would never need to know. There was plenty of information buried no one would ever see again. His mind went to the warehouse at the end of the first Indiana Jones movie.

Steve made the initial contact with the British Security Service or M15 months ago when he and Nat Jackson were to have traveled to London. His contact in London he knew as Fiona. He was still wondering if that was her real name. He didn't mind, he liked Fiona. They usually emailed but had skyped twice and she was intriguing. He thought Nat Jackson was drop-dead gorgeous and now this woman was the same with a British accent. There must be some reason they needed to meet in person.

Steve worked for ninety minutes getting his email worded correctly and all the information laid out. He told Fiona about the five crew members and included the DNA information on each. He sent her birth dates on all five men and apologized he didn't have more information. He then forced himself to not get cutesy with anything else. He got up to go to the bathroom, came back to reread it twice before hitting send. He'd learned the hard way this was a good idea.

Fiona saw the email from the NSA pop-up at 4:18 PM. She opened it and read with interest. She loved digging into these types of things and enjoyed being known as a bulldog. They desperately wanted to track down anyone with terrorist ties in their country and put them out of business. The number of attacks in the London area had grown over the last four years including lone wolf incidents of driving vehicles into crowds of pedestrians. Their Middle Eastern population was extensive and had grown over the years due to immigration.

About 15 minutes after Steve hit send on the email his Skype icon was flashing on his screen. He clicked on it and there was Fiona.

"Hi, Steve."

"Fiona."

"I'll get working on this, it looks very interesting."

"Yeah, that's several months of research plus some serious arm-twisting of the Department of the Navy."

"Don't tell me anymore," she said.

"I can't anyway but it took help way above my pay grade. How're things in London, Fiona?"

"Same old, same old. Why do you ask?"

"Just interested."

"Why don't you come over to London and see for yourself."

"I'd love that, I've never been there."

"Well then put in for some vacation time or whatever kinda time and come on over. I'd better get to work on this so I can get back to you as soon as possible."

"It's time for you to go home for the day," Steve said.

"That's for people with normal hours, that's not us."

"Understood, you take care."

"You too."

Steve clicked off and sat there thinking to himself. Her idea sounded like a great one. He hadn't had any vacation for a long time. Since his wife left and took the kids, he'd been a workaholic to keep his mind off things. Maybe a trip overseas would be just what he needed.

If this information turned into something, he'd talk to Moe Keane about going to London himself to follow up. This was supposed to happen with Nat Jackson last summer, so why not now? It seemed Keane had a lot of pull with his superiors, he must have a friend in the NSA. Keane probably knew he was interested in Jackson. Hell, Keane probably knew before he knew himself.

Chapter 18

Chicago

The Ohio State attack had mostly worked as planned. The secondary attack on the crowd had been stopped by the local authorities. Two cell members had been arrested while Chris was able to avoid the raid. Chris had made it back safely and the story he told Hazaq of how it all happened seemed convincing, anything less would have cost Chris his life. Hazaq had given a lot of thought to all of this and decided to reward Chris by launching an attack in his honor. Chris had never disclosed much about his background. Hazaq had picked up bits and pieces along the way including finding out he had been an accomplished wrestler.

Hazaq spent considerable time on the internet before learning more about his past. Chris' real last name was Powell and he was raised in Iowa earning a scholarship to a small school to wrestle. He'd left the school abruptly after Christmas break his Sophomore year and several months later showed up as part of this cell. Chris had been recruited by a cell on the east coast and after thorough vetting ended up here in Chicago. Hazaq always found him capable of handling himself and very smart but Hazaq had never fully trusted him. Chris and Joel had proved valuable since they could blend in like other cell members could not. Two Caucasian men to run errands was a good thing.

He'd already decided on the site of the attack. He hadn't decided if Chris should know about it ahead of time. Hazaq could have him be a part of it, oversee it or just let him be surprised after the fact. Each one had its positives and each one had the potential to make sure of his loyalties once and for all. Other cell members would never question Hazaq, he'd made sure of that months ago by splattering the brains of one young man over the dining room table one night. The others had cleaned up the mess and he was sure the story was still being told to new recruits. Chris was the only one who'd ever asked to talk to him alone. He had asked for more responsibilities and more of a leadership role. Hazaq had used this in sending him out to set up bases of operations for other cell members.

Greenville

Cold weather meant chili and Mike had what he needed to make a big pot. This recipe had been refined and tweaked over the years. Mike went to the basement to get a quart of tomato juice and it made him sad as he knew it would. Three quarts left from the last time Sandy had canned or as he liked to say "put up" tomato juice. These would normally have been long gone but he'd carefully rationed them. He'd never use the last one. She'd labeled them like his mom used to do it. "CO" on the lid meant celery and onion had been added and "P" was plain. All three left were "CO".

Mike did not add spaghetti like his mom always did, he liked spaghetti well enough but usually ended up flipping chili on his shirt if spaghetti was involved. He also never made chili without thinking about his childhood dog, Betsy. She was a good friend on the farm even though she was mostly a house dog. Mom always said she would be their only house dog and that had been the case. Mom would give Betsy chili which he didn't think much about as a kid, but it made him laugh now. The best story was when they checked on Betsy after his Mom had put chili in her bowl. Betsy would pick out the beans, lick them clean, and leave them in a pile next to her bowl. He had examined the beans more than once to not find a single tooth mark on the soft red kidney beans. Betsy obviously wanted nothing to do with the beans. He remembered telling his Mom that Betsy had washed them off and she could use them again in the next pot of chili.

He put things together as he fried the ground beef and twenty minutes later all was in the pot and ready to do its thing for about ninety minutes. He timed it right to have a bowl for dinner at the start of tonight's Purdue game. This was an easy meal and the best part was leftovers for about three or four days. His biggest decision now was whether to bake some cornbread or just have a PBJ with it tonight. He decided on the PBJ.

While eating he decided it was time for a breakfast meeting with Brian Miller, it had been a while. He sent a text and heard back within five minutes, '*Tomorrow morning usual time*?' He answered '*yes*' and got a '*see you then*'.

He enjoyed the chili and mostly enjoyed the game that Purdue ended up making closer than it should have been, but still won.

The next morning he parked the truck and saw The Birdman walking in to the diner, they'd been coming to this place for years. He wondered what the town would do without this place.

He was also pleased to see it had made it after new ownership, which sometimes could be the kiss of death. He was also happy to find the coffee had improved. The old stuff was not good which was not good for a diner. The new owner must like good coffee.

"How you doin' buddy?" Brian asked.

"I'm good, you?"

"Good, trying to stay out of the way while Pam gets ready for Christmas."

Mike nodded and appreciated how Brian treated him. Brian was himself and didn't treat Mike with kid gloves. He knew the holidays were hard for Mike, but he didn't try to dodge the subject. Mike would have seen that kind of treatment a mile away.

"You an Amazon shopper like me?" Mike asked.

"Pretty much, we're a family who likes books and that's what I like to give."

"Same here."

Breakfast was ordered and came quickly to the table. These two never had to fill every minute with conversation which they both appreciated. Mike was almost through two cups of coffee when his plate arrived. He could do this every morning but was glad he didn't. He could never get his hash browns as crispy as they did, it must be that big griddle surface. He also didn't need the two pancakes that came on the side, but they'd be gone when she took their plates.

"Hey, why don't you go with Pam and me to the Christmas Cantata, think you'd feel like it?"

"Truth is I've been thinking about it and I want to go. I know Sandy would tell me to go."

"That she would. She loved to go."

Mike shook his head as he looked down and took a long sip of coffee. Checks were dropped off and they got up to pay.

"Let's go to Barney's for dinner after the Cantata, think Pam would like that?"

"Definitely."

Bethesda

Bisma finished her finals and was happy with her first semester. She felt like she was living in a dream most days when she remembered her past. It was just ten months ago she was left for dead bleeding out in her bathtub. Now she was finishing her first semester at college and being treated as more of an equal than she'd ever imagined. She lifted a finger to touch her neck and lightly moved it along the entire length of the scar. She would work as hard as possible to become one of the good guys. She'd seen things in the United States that made her understand why other parts of the world disliked them, but the hate that made someone put on a suicide vest and walk into a small-town restaurant, she'd never understand. The jihad was out of control.

She'd been doing research on London and was looking forward to the mission. She was looking forward to this new experience and would miss Bethesda. She was more intrigued by the idea of following leads.

Bisma had too much at stake to ever go around Moe Keane, but she felt strongly he was missing the boat on going after Chris Powell. She knew it was on his radar because she'd mentioned it twice, they'd discussed it briefly both times and she'd been dismissed both times.

Fort Meade

Steve was at a point where he needed time out of the office, it felt more like a fortress. For as much as he liked working for the NSA, it could become a prison. Fiona had contacted him to say the DNA information he'd sent yielded virtually nothing. She was still exploring every avenue she knew to explore. There were several hits on the birth dates he'd sent, more than he would have guessed. This would take time to try to locate any family members still in the United Kingdom. Boys born in the area could be from any of the four countries of this island nation.

He knew Keane liked short emails to the point, this is exactly what he drafted. He looked at it again in twenty minutes and decided to hit send.

Keane opened the email and had an idea. He picked up the phone and called Bradshaw's boss. They agreed a two-week trip to London could be good for all involved including Steve's work psyche. They agreed to split the costs from each of their budgets, send him for two weeks with a departure date the following Sunday.

"I'll make arrangements and get the tickets."

"I'll go tell Steve right now. Thanks, Moe."

"Thanks, Grant."

Steve heard the knock on his door and looked up to see his boss.

"Steve I just got off the phone with Moe Keane at DHS."

"Yes."

"We've decided to send you to London for two weeks with one of Keane's people. You'll leave next Sunday. Keane is making arrangements and will send information to you."

"Thank you, sir."

He walked out, and Steve sat back. This would be an adventure out of the office. His thoughts went immediately to Fiona. Wonder what that would bring? He fired off a quick email. *'I'll be in London next Monday morning, see you then.'*

Keane fired off two quick emails after his assistant gave him flight info. He briefly introduced Steve to Bisma in her email and just had to remind Steve who Bisma was in his email. Steve knew of Bisma after events in Indianapolis ten months ago in February.

Both were surprised to learn they would be traveling with a companion. They both trusted Moe Keane, he told them they could get to know each other on the way to London.

Missouri

Janet was realizing she couldn't get this off her mind. Her gut was telling her to get away. She intended to make her decision by Christmas, but something was telling her to make it quicker. Some people called it women's intuition, she knew her gut was telling her something. She usually listened when it involved an investment decision, this instinct had served her well. She felt it was years of experience and not intuition, but she wasn't above thinking this all worked together in some way she didn't understand, and not paying attention might be at your own peril.

Her succession plan was fully written and would not be hard to implement with other representatives in her office. Her clients would be surprised for sure. The new reps would have to come up with creative ways to explain her sudden retirement. They could give her some terrible illness. That's what she would do if she were them, something to amuse herself while she was telling it.

The real question would be getting personal items she wanted to keep transported to her new place without leaving a trail. She realized anything she had to move would put her at risk.

Chapter 19

Chicago

Mike had always wanted to take the train to Chicago. He drove thirty minutes west, parked his car and boarded the train after buying his ticket online the morning before. He enjoyed the four-hour journey watching the farm ground roll past his window. He had fraternity brothers in this part of the state, he smiled to himself as he thought about them. When they rolled into Chicago he grabbed his bag and decided to walk around. He'd studied maps to put together his plan of where he wanted to go. The room he booked was in a marginal neighborhood, but close to the area he wanted to surveil.

Mike made his way by the L train to the area he saw on the map in Natalie Jackson's office. He was going to walk the streets and keep his head down and his eyes open. He picked out a neighborhood grocery store he thought would be promising for lots of local foot traffic. A nearby park offered some benches and a place he could spend time watching the grocery store. It seemed like a likely spot to begin his search for Chris. He pulled a novel out of his backpack and sipped on his stainless-steel Purdue coffee mug. He immediately missed his Chemex, but this coffee was not half bad. He watched patrons coming and going from the store and was struggling with recon and getting into this new book. He was not good at doing both which made him think of the time he and David watched Bisma's apartment in Indianapolis. It was amazing this woman had turned into someone who was helping Moe Keane and Homeland Security. Only thirty-five minutes had passed, and he was wondering if he could do this type of work. Who knew how long it might be before Chris Powell walked past him. He wondered what he should do if other cell members were with him and he couldn't get his attention for a conversation. He'd wait a while longer and try again tomorrow.

He made his way back to his hotel and went back up to his room. He changed into a pair of khakis from his jeans, pulled on a sweater and grabbed a yellow notepad to take with him to the restaurant. He'd picked out a BBQ/Steakhouse five blocks away. The walk there helped his appetite and he was ushered to a booth with a good view of two TVs showing sports. Baseball fever always burned in Chicago, the hope for another Cubs World Series title ever present. He was happy they'd won one but would be happier to see the Braves get back on top. Atlanta had built up around the new stadium over the last four years making it a nice venue. Winter always brought on the thoughts of another opening day.

Mike went about the same routine for the next two days. He picked different spots and varied the timing of his surveillance. He did his best to blend in and learn the neighborhood better by walking. He couldn't stay here forever. He'd not booked a return ticket but was now thinking of the morning after tomorrow. He'd give it one more full day and then head home.

Hazaq had taken lots of precautions over time to protect his cell and more so himself. He truly didn't care much about the recruits under his control. They were tools for his jihadist plans, he couldn't let himself become friends with young men he'd send to their deaths. He was good at making them think he cared about them. Even though he was not that much older than most of them he'd acted as a father-type figure. Few of them had a father figure growing up. Their actual fathers had most likely been killed in the jihad by the infidels.

Cell members had been trained in counter-surveillance and were always practicing. They'd debrief at the evening meal and quiz each other on things they'd seen or picked up on. This evening the conversation caught Hazaq's attention. It seemed three different brothers had noticed the same man in the area by their local grocery for the third day now. Two days didn't mean much, three days in a row caught their attention.

"What did he look like?" Hazaq asked.

"White man with a medium build, near fifty years old. Mustache. Baseball cap with a P on it one day, Cubs hat another day. Sunglasses each day and coffee mug."

"He was always by himself?"

They all nodded yes.

"Any photographs?"

"No."

He knew that answer, he didn't allow cell phones and would never allow them outside of the apartment.

"Anything else?" Hazaq asked.

"He's on his phone a lot."

"Talking?"

"No, maybe taking pictures or videos. I don't know."

Hazaq nodded. This store was three blocks from the apartment. It was in all probability nothing, but his gut was telling him to give this some credence.

Chris had listened to the entire conversation without saying a word. Thoughts began swirling though. Was this the time when Keane would take down the Chicago cell? What should he do? They knew he was here, but he sure as hell didn't want to go down in a hail of bullets with a bunch of terrorists. He'd told Keane the apartment had cameras with someone always at the monitor, day and night. They never ordered any take-out food, never had anyone else come to the door. If someone did, they were closely watched. This was a neighborhood where the Girl Scouts didn't sell cookies door to door.

He did his best to let Hazaq see him showing the correct amount of interest, no more no less. He felt he was always under scrutiny.

The next morning Hazaq told Chris, Joel and one of the brothers who had noticed this man to meet in his office.

"I want more information on this man. If he is back for the fourth day, then he is up to something. Probably not with us, but let's be sure. Hadid you take the lead and find him. Joel, you get close and get his attention. Ask him for directions to somewhere close. Listen carefully to see if he's local or not. Chris, you get pictures while this is happening and send them back here immediately. Joel and Hadid stay close enough to watch him. If he leaves, go ahead and follow as you've been taught. Everybody takes a phone. They grabbed coats and phones and headed for the door.

Mike had a good breakfast and was enjoying his second cup of coffee. He thought to himself he'd better watch it, or he would need to find a place to take a leak over by the park. He paid his check and put his yellow pad into his backpack. He'd booked the late train south which meant he'd leave this area by 3:00 PM at the latest. The twelve-minute walk to his spot got him good and awake with a little more "Windy City" breeze happening this morning. He found a different bench this morning that had less of a view but a welcome wind block. He began seeing some of the same folks he'd seen the other days which struck him as good and bad. Good in his power of observation, bad in that someone else may be doing the same for him.

Hadid approached the area first. Chris and Joel lagged behind. Hadid went to the bench where they'd been seeing this man. Not finding him, he proceeded to make a lap in the park and was about to give up when he spotted him farther to the west. He was partially hidden behind some bushes, but Hadid knew it was the same person. He passed about twenty feet from him on the path and headed back to Chris and Joel.

"He's moved, but it's him."

"Where?" Joel asked.

Hadid told them making sure he was out of any line of sight.

"Dark brown coat, Cubs hat, and no sunglasses. Backpack setting next to him. Chris your best view will be east of him with the morning light."

"I'll go first to get into position. Follow me by fifty yards and go past after I start my phone conversation. I'll act like I'm on the speaker to get ready to take pictures."

Joel nodded, and Chris took off. They'd have a three-minute walk to get into position.

Chris stopped making sure he was out of earshot. It just had to look like he was having a conversation. Joel passed him also acting like he was searching for something on his phone. As Joel approached their target he came to a stop.

"Shit," he said to no one in particular.

Mike raised his eyes from the magazine he was reading.

Joel looked over at Mike, "Can you help me with some directions? I'm having no luck with this phone."

"I would if I could, but I'm not from here," Mike said.

"Me either, I live in a small town. Can you help with my bearings though? North, south, east and west."

"That I can do with some sun this morning. Sun to the east, opposite west. Downtown over there is north and opposite south."

Mike had stood to do his pointing, this gave Chris some really nice shots. It also gave Joel a sense that he'd seen this guy somewhere. He couldn't put his finger on it, but he was familiar. How could that be?

"Thanks man."

Mike nodded as he walked away. He saw another man finishing a phone call and turning. He quickly lifted his phone and clicked off two pictures but only got a partial profile. He sat back down and opened the pictures. He began to make the image bigger and soon had the biggest image he could. Was this him? The more he looked the more he thought that could be Chris Powell.

Mike thought to himself, now what do I do? He stuffed the magazine into his backpack and stood. The man was walking away and he'd quickly lose him if he didn't follow.

Chris had five decent pictures of the man and couldn't believe his eyes. As he looked closer he was seeing Mike Baker. What the hell was Mike Baker from Greenville, Indiana doing in this part of Chicago for the last four days? He knew Baker had balls. He'd driven right up to the barn to check them out last winter. He took a huge risk doing that and probably got a huge ass chewing from Moe Keane. Now he was here in Chicago. Chris forwarded the pictures to Hazaq as he'd been instructed and said a silent prayer that Hazaq would not know this man. He also realized Joel might remember him. Thank God Joel was not the sharpest tool in the shed, but he had his moments. Hopefully, this wouldn't be one.

Chris' phone vibrated with a text from Hadid, '*He's on the move, maybe following you?*'

'*Okay,*' is all Chris wanted to say.

Joel texted both, '*Think he's following. He looks like someone I've seen before.*'

Shit, Chris thought to himself. Baker is walking himself right into a bad situation. Hazaq would kill him without thinking. He would have to convince Hazaq that Baker was more valuable alive. First of all, he was not going to lead him back to the cell, he'd get him away from the cell. It was the best for Baker and he could defend this action with Hazaq.

Ten minutes later they'd made it to a retail area with more people. Chris ducked into a convenience store and headed for the restroom.

Mike thought he was keeping up and staying back far enough not to be spotted. He had no idea there were two others following him. Chris had gone into a convenience store which seemed like a good place for a conversation, off the street. He went in and looked around. Not seeing him had to mean he was in the restroom. What to do? He decided to stand by the magazines and wait for him to come out. He'd come this far, why not talk to him unless it seemed like there was someone else in here with him.

Chris took the opportunity to relieve himself and washed his hands. That should be enough time for Baker to catch up. He'd see if he came in the store. He would not confront him if Joel or Hadid were also in the store. Chris walked out and within seconds spotted Mike Baker. Baker looked at him then looked around the store. Chris did the same and didn't see anyone. He knew they'd have staged somewhere close outside the store.

Mike approached and held out his hand, "Mike Baker."

"I know who you are, what the hell are you doing here? You're in more danger than you know."

Mike gestured with both hands, turning his palms up and giving a slight shrug.

"You've been spotted by cell members and we were sent to check you out."

"What should I do? I know you're a good guy."

"I'm not sure. I think we need to get you out the back door and you need to disappear quickly. I'll get the two guys with me off your trail and you need to get out of Chicago immediately."

Chris had noticed an employee area in the back that would surely have a back door. He stepped to the counter and asked for a lottery ticket. When the young lady approached, Chris leaned in with a low voice.

"This man is in danger. Please let him leave through the back."

As she began to shake her head no Chris said," This is a matter of Homeland Security and no harm will come to anyone here if you help, please hurry."

With that, she motioned for Mike to follow and they headed to the back. Less than a minute later she was back and he paid for his lottery ticket.

"Thank you," Chris said as he turned to leave.

She said nothing looking a little shaken. Chris made his way out the front door and turned left to head up the sidewalk. Joel was easy to spot and Chris crossed at the next corner to join him.

"He followed you in," Joel said.

"And I confronted him."

"Did he look familiar to you?"

"Not really."

"He did to me. What did you talk about?"

"Not here, let's get back. Where's Hadid?"

"I'm not sure, he went his own way."

"All right, let's head back."

Mike exited the store to find himself in an alley that was pretty tight. He guessed cars belonged to employees of stores along this street. The only activity was a box truck fifty yards to the north unloading produce. He decided to walk that way to get back to pick up his bags and then get to the train station.

Hadid had been checking for cameras and was finding none. He stopped to wait by a dumpster and wondered how long he could hold his breath. Even in cold weather things could get pretty ripe. No more than three minutes later a door swung open and he saw the man they'd followed. He pushed back a little further to make sure he would not be easy to see and waited.

Mike heard a faint scrape as he turned his head to the left. He was barely able to raise his left arm to deflect some of the blow. His world went black before he crumpled to the ground.

Hadid threw the pipe into the dumpster and immediately began dragging his victim into the area where he'd been waiting. He was looking for anyone who may have seen what happened but saw no motion anywhere. He peered into the dumpster to find a dirty cloth napkin he'd use to tie his mouth and a piece of wire for his hands behind his back. He reached into Mike's jacket pocket and pulled out his phone. He dropped it on the ground and smashed it with his heel. They wouldn't track this phone any further than right here. Hadid left him there as he began to walk down the street and look into cars. The seventh car he passed was unlocked with keys hanging in the ignition. He jumped in and it started with a little cough. He pulled into the alley and carefully backed up to the dumpster. He popped open the trunk and with a lot of effort got his prey into the trunk. Giving a quick look again for witnesses he jumped in and started down the street. He turned left at his first opportunity and made his way down another alley onto a busy street.

Chapter 20

Chicago

Chris sent Hadid a text and got no response. He shrugged his shoulders as Joel looked at him. They were one block from the apartment and doubled back to the left looking for Hadid.

"You think he's in trouble?" Joel asked.

"Nah, he's probably just enjoying being out by himself for a while. Let's wait a few minutes before going in."

Hazaq was getting impatient. He'd not heard from any of them for forty minutes. He looked down to see a text. He checked his sheet of numbers to see it was from the phone he'd given Hadid.

'I'm alone at the garage with a special package. You might want to come see.'

He texted back, *'Be there in twenty minutes. Where are your friends?'*

'We were separated.'

'Sit tight.'

Hazaq put the phone in his pocket and grabbed his coat and keys. He fired up the car and gave it a minute to warm up. Cold weather was another thing he hated about this country. As he started to pull away from the curb he saw Chris and Joel walking toward him a block away. He put it in park and waited.

Chris saw the brake lights and knew Hazaq was in the car.

"C'mon let's see what going on," Chris said to Joel.

As they approached the car they could see Hazaq waving for them to get in. Joel opened the front door and Chris got in the back.

"What's happening?" Joel asked.

"I just got a text from Hadid, he's at the garage with a special package. Wanted me to come see. What's happening?"

"We got separated on the way back from the park. Not sure. Did you have time to look at the pictures I sent?" Chris asked.

"I saw them but didn't have time to try to figure out who he is," Hazaq said.

"Man I'm sure I've seen that dude somewhere," Joel said.

Hazaq was driving with traffic and obeying the law. He was even using his turn signal to change lanes, not something most people did in the big city.

They pulled up to the door of the garage and hit the opener. No one was around which is why Hazaq had picked this spot originally. Hadid had left plenty of room for them to pull in behind him, they put the door down and got out. Hadid was waiting at the opened trunk of his car and seemed as anxious as one might suspect. Chris knew he would be nervous about Hazaq's reaction. Mike Baker was laying in the trunk, Hadid had replaced the dirty rag with a piece of duct tape over his mouth.

"What should we do now?" Hadid asked.

"Get him out of there," Hazaq said.

They weren't too careful as they drug him out by the arms. They half pulled, and he half walked to a nearby wooden straight back chair, they sat him down hard. Hazaq pulled his arms behind the chair and Chris duct-taped his hands.

"You goin' to be quiet?" Hazaq asked.

Mike nodded yes and Hadid pulled the duct tape off his mouth. He fought off the urge to tell them what they could do to themselves. He also did his best to not let his face show any recognition of Chris, but he was sure as hell glad to see him. The next thing he realized was the fact he was seeing all of them, none of them were wearing masks. This would not be good for his future, they didn't intend for him to be leaving here alive.

"You get his phone?" Chris asked.

"Smashed it in the alley. Figured it would lead anyone looking for him right here."

"Good thinking Hadid," Hazaq said.

Mike was relieved. If they had his phone they'd see a photograph of Chris and photos and notes he'd emailed to himself over the last few days. He wasn't sure he'd be in any more trouble than he already was, but it wouldn't have been good for Chris. The throbbing in the back of his head was growing into a wicked headache. He assumed he had at least a mild concussion, maybe worse. He felt wet on the back right side of his head and upper neck, no doubt blood from being hit. He'd like to return the favor.

Hazaq nodded his head to have Hadid, Chris, and Joel to follow him. They went in the small office to talk. Hazaq turned Mike's chair so he wouldn't be able to see them. Mike gave a look that got him a back-hand across the face. He immediately noticed that metallic taste of blood in the mouth.

The four men sat around a table.

"What do we know about him?" Hazaq asked.

"I know I've seen him before. You remember him, Chris?"

"I've been thinking, but no I don't recognize him."

"I checked for a wallet, but he had nothing more than his phone and some cash," Hadid added.

"Not normal for the average citizen, he was working on something. Let's go ask him."

With that Hazaq pushed his chair back and stood. They all followed Hazaq out of the office. Chris wondered how Baker would do. If he talked or just gave up Chris looking to be saved, they'd both be dead.

Greenville

Pam and Brian had finished dinner and were loading the dishwasher.

"Let's make our final plans with Mike for Saturday evening," Pam said.

"Will do, I'll send him a text. Betcha I hear back within five minutes and he'll be thinking breakfast in the morning."

"No way I'll take that bet. That's exactly what he'll say."

Brian smiled and sat down to click out a quick text. He hit send and put down his phone. He looked at the clock on the stove and made a mental note. Pam had just finished wiping down the counter and they went in and flipped on the Nightly Business Report on the local PBS channel. Fifteen minutes later, Pam looked up from the Greenville Reporter and said, "I should have bet you."

Brian shook his head. "Not like him, is it?

"No, he's pretty good especially if he thinks biscuits and gravy are involved."

"If I haven't heard by morning, I'll touch base again."

Brian stirred at his normal time of 6:20 and after taking care of business pulled his phone off the charger and headed for the kitchen to start coffee. He put some extra in the filter this morning, it felt like a strong coffee day, stronger than normal. He checked his phone to see nothing from Mike, which was very unusual since Mike was up before now as a rule. Thoughts began rolling through his mind. Maybe he's sick, he's hardly ever sick. Maybe he had a date and stayed over? Not Mike. Maybe he was neck-deep in a real page-turner and turned off his phone? That was possible, but not likely. He'd not want to be out of touch if Sarah needed him. He hit send on another text.

Chicago

It had been a rough night for Mike Baker. He expected nothing less and was just happy to still be alive. His only hope would be Chris. He knew Chris had to be extremely careful or they'd both be in trouble. He decided to trust him. If he could survive in this life he is not just tough but capable on many levels.

He figured questioning would start again soon. He'd told them mostly the truth. He'd told them how he got to Chicago from central Indiana, took the train which was something he'd always wanted to do. He told them he'd always lived in the country and just wanted to look around Chicago. The person who appeared to be the asshole in charge had hit him a few times. This seemed a lot less than he would have expected, but this wasn't over yet. He also decided they weren't well trained in interrogation, they'd not even asked his name. He was still deciding on what to say if they did.

His thoughts went to Brian and Tom Sutherlin being taken in Brazil. The only way that turned out good was Tom having the chip implanted in his shoulder. He sure as hell wished he had one of those chips. The idea crossed his mind that he might tell them he had a GPS tracking device and the FBI would be on top of them at any moment. He then had the thought of them trying to dig it out of him with one of the knives he'd seen on a workbench.

Greenville

It was now noon and Brian had not heard a thing from Mike. Pam was out running errands, Brian sent her a text saying he was heading out to Mike's house to check on him. He put on his heavy coat to hold off the cutting wind and headed out of town. Fifteen minutes later he was in Mike's driveway and pulling up to the house. He wished there was some snow cover so he could look for truck tracks. He walked up to the back door and knocked. He waited a few seconds and rapped harder this time. Thirty seconds later he was heading over to the corner of the house to find the key hidden by the downspout. It was where it should be and he let himself in.

"Hey, Mike....Mike!" Nothing.

"Baker you takin' a mid-day nap?" he said in a raised voice. Nothing.

With that, he went into the kitchen. Counters were clean and things were put away. There was a sheet from a yellow pad laying by a picture of David and Sarah. He picked it up to see a date and time at the top.

'I'm driving to Crawfordsville to catch the train to Chicago. I'll be there this afternoon. I'm staying at the Kent hotel on 87th street. I plan to do some looking around to see if I might spot Chris Powell. I saw his picture in Natalie Jackson's office a few weeks ago along with a map of Chicago. I took a picture with my phone. I know this is out of my league, but maybe I can do something to help put these murderers out of business. My plan is to be home and destroy this page, but if someone is reading it, I may need help. You should call me first but if I don't answer you might want to call Natalie Jackson at 800-555-6833.'

Brian immediately called the FBI. Four minutes later he'd been patched through to Special Agent Jackson.

"Jackson."

"Agent Jackson this is Brian Miller from Greenville."

"Good afternoon Brian, what can I do for you?"

"I tried to contact Mike Baker last evening with no answer. I tried again early this morning with no result, so I'm at his house."

Natalie's internal radar was going off, this kind of call was never good. "Go ahead," she said.

"He's left a handwritten note."

"Read it to me."

Brian read the entire note in 38 seconds.

"Read it again."

Brian did as she asked and was met with a few seconds of silence, "Are you...?"

"I'm thinking."

Brian respected her enough to stay quiet.

"Brian, please leave the note where you found it. Give a quick look around to make sure nothing looks out of place, lock up and head back home. You comfortable doing that?"

"Yes. Will do."

"I'll ask you to tell no one about this. Is the number you're using now the best one to get back to you?"

"Yes."

"Then wish me good luck and say a prayer for your buddy. He's someone I respect very much, but he may be in deep shit."

"Good luck," she was gone.

"Dammit!" Brian hit the counter and slid the page back to where he found it. He did a quick walk-through and then did the steps upstairs two at a time. Nothing out of place up here as far as he knew. He came back downstairs and headed for the back door. He grabbed the key off the dryer, locked the door and put the key back in its place. He made his mind up on the way home he'd tell Pam about this, she'd keep it quiet and would be able to add more prayers to this situation.

Indianapolis

Natalie let out a short string of obscenities before making the call to the Chicago office. She had a contact there who she respected. He picked up and she told the story. She ended by telling him that DHS is monitoring this cell, and would no doubt want to take the lead. He ended the call with, "Shit."

Washington

"Keane. What's happening Agent Jackson?"

Natalie told Moe Keane the same story she had just told her contact in Chicago including the information that she'd just told the Chicago FBI office to get someone on the scene quickly.

"When we get his ass out of there I may lock him up. Who's your contact at Chicago?"

She gave him the name and number, "How can I help?"

"I have a small team in the city and we'll coordinate with the FBI. It's time to take down this cell. I've been planning this for months."

"Good luck," she said.

"I'll be in touch."

Chicago

The morning seemed to be more of the same. The violence got more pronounced which seemed to be more of a reflection of their hatred for Americans than his answers. He was doing the best he could to seem like a guy who was at the wrong damn place at the wrong damn time. They removed the duct tape from his wrists and let him eat part of a Subway sandwich with a cup of water. As he pulled his arms from behind the chair he experienced the worst pain he'd had thus far. It took him a few minutes to get enough feeling to pick up the sandwich. He felt sure it was Chris who'd made this happen for him. His four captors had been smart enough to not call each other by name as this had progressed. The one in charge had held a gun to his head as Chris had pulled the tape off his wrists.

"If you do anything to try to escape or just look at me wrong, I'll put a bullet in your head."

Mike gave him a mental, "I'll gladly do the same to you the first chance I get," and kept quiet. He figured they smelled the fear on him, he smelled it. He was looking around and studying oil stains on the floor, anything to keep his mind occupied with anything else than this. It wasn't working. Not the place you'd imagine you were going to end your life, a damp and dark garage smelling of diesel fuel.

Hazaq nodded to Chris, Joel, and Hadid to follow him to the office. He closed the door behind them as they watched their prisoner through the window.

"I'm going back to the apartment to take care of some business. Do as you wish with this man. Practice a new torture technique you've always wanted to try. See how long he can go with his head in a bucket of water. Have fun brothers, but make sure he's dead by evening and get back to the apartment. Call me when you're leaving here and make sure the body is secure."

With that, he stood and walked out the office door. Hazaq said something in Arabic and spit on him as he passed Mike Baker. Mike watched him walk out.

Chris reached over and closed the office door. Joel knew what was coming. Chris assumed he was in charge when Hazaq was not around and Joel had resented this for a long time. He knew Chris was smarter than he was but he was tired of it.

"Ideas?" Chris asked.

"Let's waterboard him. It looks pretty cool when I've seen it," Joel said.

Chris just looked at him and thought he sincerely meant it. He looked at Hadid.

"I'd probably use a car battery and jumper cables if I had to get something from a prisoner. I've seen it done in the movies."

"Do you think this man has any useful information for us?" Chris asked.

"Not really," Joel said. Hadid shook his head.

"Why don't you both go out and see what you can find in the shop to have some fun."

They both stood and headed out the door. Chris knew this was it. Hazaq had given Baker a death sentence to be carried out in the next few hours. He'd been running plans in his head since they got here, Hazaq being gone had improved his chances.

Chicago

Hazaq got back to the cell and called them together. Seven young men sat down around the table.

"Events have moved up our timetable. Three of you are leaving for your mission in Iowa. You are prepared and ready. You are taking the jihad into the heart of the infidels. I know you will receive your rewards in heaven. You can never let the devils take you as a prisoner. This is the worst thing that could ever happen to you. If this is possible make sure you send as many of them to their hell as possible."

Heads were nodding with their understanding around the table.

"The rest of you will travel south immediately. I have loaded your itinerary on this iPad as he pushed it across the table. There are rooms booked for you. Everything you need is packed and ready. Everyone be prepared to leave in ninety minutes."

With that, they all stood. Hazaq greeted each of them with a few words of encouragement and farewell. He gave each a hug and kiss on the cheek.

Hazaq went to his office and began expunging his technology. He intended to leave nothing behind. He knew the authorities could still recover data that seemed to be gone forever. For this reason, hard drives would be destroyed. He would take two external hard drives and three flash drives and one laptop with him; the rest would stay behind.

Joel and Hadid were enjoying themselves looking for items to be used for torture. Chris let himself begin feeling the joy of knowing he was not going to be spending time with these morons much longer. He'd spent time thinking about any useful intelligence either of them might possess or if there was anything of value from either one. This was an easy answer, nothing.

The Beretta was still where he'd left it months before. He ejected the magazine to make sure no one had found it and left him a big surprise. He quietly pushed the magazine back into place, pulled back the slide to chamber a round and slid it into his belt. He pulled his sweatshirt down and walked out into the garage. He'd already decided he take care of Hadid first since Joel posed much less of a threat.

Joel was standing in front of Mike Baker smiling in a way that gave Mike a chill. Here we go he thought to himself. Chris is not going to help and I'm going to die in a garage in Chicago. Not what I'd planned. He thought of Sandy and his kids, he thought of his dad and his brother. He was hoping some kind of calm resignation would wash over him, there are things worse than death he thought. At least Chris could make sure this didn't linger.

Joel bent down and reached for his right leg. Mike kicked at him with all the strength he had left and connected with Joel's right shoulder. He reached for his shoulder and a flash of instant anger went through him. As he reached back to deliver a punch he and Baker both jumped as the gunshot broke the silence of the garage behind them. As Joel turned to see Hadid slump to the floor, Chris was on top of him. He struggled to fight back, but Chris had him pinned and was tying his hands.

"What are you doin'?" Joel got out.

"Shut up."

Joel's face showed it all. Total misunderstanding. Chris used the hunk of duct tape he'd torn off earlier to make sure he'd stay quiet. Joel just sat there looking up at Chris and then felt something on his hands behind him. He rolled over to see Hadid's blood pooling on the dirty concrete floor.

Chris untied Baker and helped him stand. He reached down to pull Joel up and Mike helped him. They sat Joel in the same chair and duct taped each leg to a chair leg. Mike looked at Chris and was about to ask something when Chris gave him a look and slight nod to not speak. Chris headed for the office as he turned Joel away. He closed the door behind Mike.

"You okay?" Chris asked.

"I'll be fine. Thank you for saving my ass."

"I've got to call Keane."

Chris handed Mike a bottle of water and two energy bars. Mike nodded and started tearing off a wrapper. Chris sat down and punched in his number from memory.

Moe looked over as the phone on his desk buzzed to life. Only three people have this number. He grabbed it.

"Keane."

"We have to take down the Chicago cell. It's a longer story, but we need to move."

"I know that Mike Baker has gone missing. I assume you know this."

"He's going to be fine, sitting right here."

"You both safe?"

"For now. Hazaq left me here with two other cell members. He's gone back to the apartment to finish some business. I shot one man and have the other tied up."

"Does the man you shot need medical attention?'

"No."

"Illinois FBI will assist us in taking the apartment. Can I call you back on the phone you are using right now?"

"Yes."

"Give me your address and we'll get you and Baker out."

Chris gave him the address of the garage. Keane clicked off.

Hazaq watched the first four men leave. Their journey south would be a long drive. These four recruits were young men who had the least promise. They knew little about the cell and had always been expendable as far as he was concerned. They had enough explosives with them to blow up the car if they were stopped by the police and anyone who was close. He waited a few minutes before sending the three men leaving for Iowa. They'd have a five-hour drive ahead of them. These brothers would bring terror to the state of Iowa. "Allah Akbar," he said as they left through a side entrance into an alley behind the apartment.

Hazaq picked up his last bag and backpack and closed the door behind him. He got in the car and took off. This was not as he had planned. He'd always planned it would be on his terms but always knew this might happen. Even with all of his security and cameras he always figured they'd be raided in the middle of the night.

Chicago had been a good base of operations for the cell, they'd staged several successful attacks out of this part of the country. Hazaq for sure was not going to miss the cold weather.

Washington

Keane made the call to the FBI and began relaying information. He was not happy with the first response being how understaffed they were at the present.

"How many agents do you have at the apartment?" Keane asked.

"None, the two who were watching left a few minutes ago to follow four men who came out carrying bags and left in a car. We have a camera watching the apartment though."

"Shit."

"I told you we're understaffed."

"You should've told me before now. If we missed the cell leader there'll be hell to pay."

Silence on the other end told Keane the cooperation between DHS and the FBI in Chicago was waning.

"Keep me updated," Keane said and the line went dead.

Chicago

Hazaq was getting near the garage and began seeing the police presence. He turned off and hardly even looked back. He had to believe they were tipped off. They had kept this place a well-guarded secret, he intended on taking several things with him. There was a large cache of weapons and explosives. Asis would be dreadfully upset over this loss of weaponry that had taken years to build. He wondered if he should wait a while and then double back to make sure but decided he needed to keep moving and put miles between himself and this area.

Chris walked over and put up the large door to the garage. He was asked to get down and put his hands behind his head, he carefully obeyed.

"You'll find two more men inside who are unarmed. One is tied to a chair, the other has been held hostage here for the last two days."

They entered and asked the same of Mike Baker. He followed Chris' lead as he was quickly searched. Officers were comparing photos and quickly identified Chris Powell and Mike Baker. EMT personnel were called in to look at Mike Baker. He looked worse for the wear but would be fine. They cleaned up a busted lip and a cut eye. Bruises were beginning to turn purple and he was told he'd look worse before he looked better. This got a smile out of Mike, he was happy to be alive.

Chris was giving information to a forensics team and asking to be taken to the cell. They loaded Chris and Mike in an SUV and hurried off towards the apartment.

The FBI and local SWAT Teams were in place and ready to go. Everyone had been briefed on the possibility of booby-traps. Everyone knew this cell had killed law enforcement officers in central Indiana when a farmhouse had been filled with explosives. There was a front entrance, a side entrance to an alley and a back entrance to an alley. They had all entrances covered and then some. The news Moe Keane received about being understaffed had been dealt with. An armored vehicle pulled up in front, drove up on the sidewalk and stopped about fifteen feet from the front door. Two minutes later a robot named Rocky who looked like he was out of a Star Wars movie had been dispatched from a back door of the vehicle and was making his way around the vehicle and to the front door.

Everyone felt sure that this was being watched by inhabitants inside the apartment house. The robot placed two charges on either side of the door and rolled back a couple feet. Five seconds later an explosion rocked the door and Rocky rolled up to the door, pushed it into the room and entered. He immediately began to fill the room with the newest version of tear gas which should render everyone inside into the fetal position within seconds. Operators in the armored vehicle were looking at the cameras mounted on Rocky to see every direction including real-time video, heat signatures and night vision capabilities. Nothing was showing on this floor.

While this was all happening, an arm had been extending from the vehicle. This arm also had tear gas and the same camera capabilities. It was extended through all three of the second-floor windows, tear gas deployed and once again no one was found. This left the basement. Chris had told them where to find each of two entrances to the basement. Rocky was sent to each door and had no problem breaching each. Tear gas canisters were shot down each time and the stairs were monitored. Still nothing.

They all knew there could still be cell members hiding in the basement, they felt as sure as they could there was no one on the main and second floors.

Rocky made his way around each room on the main floor looking for trip wires or any type of laser sensor that might set off explosives as well as any pressure plates in the floor. Assured the main floor was safe, officers in full bomb gear were deployed to look around. A device best described as a slinky in reverse was sent up each staircase. This device put weight on each step to approximate a human. The hope was to make sure the steps were not wired to explode when weight was applied to them. With the staircases cleared, agents carried up smaller robots that looked like Roombas on steroids to cover all areas of the floors. These robots not only had cameras but had sensors to determine smells. They were as close as technology had come to bomb-sniffing dogs. Make no mistake, bomb-sniffing dogs were far superior, but these little devils did a pretty good initial sweep.

After clearing the upper floor, the same procedure happened in the basement. The robots did detect explosives in the lower floor which slowed the process to a crawl. Cameras finally determined this was coming from one room. Chris confirmed this room was always off limits and locked, he'd never been in it. Two Special Agents with military experience decided instead of trying to breach the door from the lower floor they'd drill a hole through the main floor area about the room and lower a camera in to look around. Chris was brought in to look at the video and it was determined this room was below the room Hazaq had used as his office. Chris had been in this room a couple times.

They had a drill in their equipment bags and long bits for things like this. Chris accompanied two agents to the office and they began looking for the best place to drill. They used a stud finder to look for joists and electrical wires. There was an area rug close to his desk. Rex looked at Chris and pointed.

"He used this for his prayer rug, but never put it away."

Rex grabbed the corner and gave it a pull. He was on his knees and ran his hand over the floor.

"Look at this."

The other two knelt to see, Rex traced a rectangle in the floor with his finger. He pulled out a pocket knife and pushed it into a crack that was barely noticeable and began to pry. He moved the blade along one side and then another. The piece came up with some effort to reveal an open space between the joists down to the ceiling below. There was a handle on this piece and he reached down to give it a tug.

"Careful," his partner said.

Rex pulled and the piece came loose revealing darkness below. He grabbed his flashlight and let it shine into the hole. They all stretched to look.

"I'll go," Chris said.

"The hell you will. Some guy named Moe Keane threatened us all with keeping you safe."

Rex sat and put his legs into the hole. There was a crude homemade ladder and he got a foot on the second rung down. He went down with the flashlight in his mouth. It took a few seconds to find the light switch next to the door. He gave the room a quick sweep and felt all was safe. He unlocked the door from the inside and opened it to see the basement. He got a whiff of tear gas and pushed the door shut.

"Whadda ya think?"

"Lots of shit down here, this will take a while. I see handguns, rifles, and ammunition. I'd like the dogs to check some of these boxes before we start tearing them open to see if they hit on anything."

"Good idea."

"I'm coming up."

With that Rex climbed out and they all headed for the door. The story was related to the Commander. Satisfied there was no one in the apartment he told them to lock it down and let forensics see what they could get.

Chris walked off to call Keane. He gave a quick rundown.

"How many were in the house without you and the others in the garage?"

"Seven and Hazaq."

"How many cars at their disposal?"

"Just one that I knew of. They didn't all fit in that. Others may have left on foot."

"Doubtful," Keane said. "The FBI had one team on sight and followed one car."

That's the first Chris had heard of that. "Okay, that's a start."

Later that morning came word about the cell members heading down I65. The two FBI agents were following them at a safe distance. There was some disagreement in the Chicago office as to how long this should go on. That was decided for them when they all came upon a big backup in northern Indiana due to a three-vehicle pileup. After watching for about twenty minutes the agents decided to approach the car. Their fear was the cell members would leave their vehicle on foot or go to another vehicle to take hostages. One agent approached the driver's side window while the other stayed one car back to cover him.

Jasim was the one Hazaq had put in charge of this group of four men all under twenty-four years old. When the driver told him someone was walking up to the window he had his hand on the switch. Kill as many as possible and never be taken prisoner he remembered hearing on several occasions from Hazaq.

He told the driver to put down his window and as the agent bent down he pushed the button. Most of the explosives were in the trunk. There was also C-4 packed into the upper part of each front fender. Besides the four cell members, the FBI agent and people in two cars were killed instantly. The agent who stood behind was badly burned and injured such that he wasn't expected to survive. A man in the car next to them was killed and three of four family members in the car behind were killed.

Emergency personnel working the accident came back to help and more ambulances were sent to the scene. The interstate was shut down for hours as cleanup turned into crime scene processing.

Chapter 22

Greenville

Brian Miller received the call he was hoping for. Mike Baker was safe and going to be okay. It sounded like he'd endured a similar experience he and Tom Sutherlin had in Brazil. Another saga to add to the adventures of the Boiler Club. Looks like another meeting will need to be planned for an update from Mike. Pam was relieved to hear the news. Both of them turned their thoughts to Sarah. As far as they knew she didn't know he was missing. If she had come home she would have seen the note from her father and called them or Nat Jackson.

Brian tried to call Mike, but it went directly to voicemail. They were most likely doing a time of debriefing. The authorities who deal with this type of situation were extremely good at gleaning everything possible from any situation. He'd seen this first hand after Brazil. He respected this even though it was exhausting.

Iowa

The three young men pulled into Greensburg at 7:30 AM after spending the night in the parking lot of a truck stop one hour east. The small town was coming to life as usual. One small diner on the edge of town was feeding townsfolk and farmers alike. The parking lot filled to overflowing. Shop owners were getting tidied up before unlocking doors at 9:00 AM. Like everywhere else more and more of their usual customers were shopping online for Christmas and any other occasion. Thank goodness they still had people who wanted to browse, touch things and pay with cash. Christmas was around the corner and this should be a good day.

The local college was ready to close for Christmas break. Finals ended two days from now, and the student union was packed with last-minute cramming and coffee drinking. No one noticed the two young men enter at opposite sides of the commons area. Both took their time looking for the best place to cause the largest loss of life. Their only contact was watching each other. One hand in a coat pocket on the detonator, the other hand to wave when they were each ready. There was not a lot of exact planning where they would stand with the exception of studying online pictures of the room and hoping they could also cause structural damage, maybe even cave in the second floor to the main floor and then on into the basement floor.

Nasheem was ready, his partner not as much, but here they were. More terror to the infidels in the heartland. Nasheem looked across the room. He met the eyes of his partner and lifted his arm. Nasheem screamed something no one understood but seemed to freeze the room. He then yelled, "Allah Akbar," and pushed the plunger on his detonator.

Windows were blown out, a fireball seemed to cross into the kitchen and screams filled what was left of the room. Yadier felt the rumble two blocks away as he slowly left town. He was next, he had a fifty-minute drive to his destination of Mays, Iowa.

Emergency vehicles were coming from everywhere close including Ames. The local campus and city police were overwhelmed. It was a war scene and even with all kinds of training, they still needed help.

Yadier had a lot going through his mind during his last hour on earth. He hoped it was worth it. He'd never admit any misgivings to his cellmates, but his short time on earth would be ending in the little town of Mays, Iowa. Would anyone care? Yes, the family members of the infidels he took with him would care, but no one would miss him. Which just showed he sure didn't have much to lose. Not much to see this time of year, field after field of harvested corn and soybean fields. He kept to the map Hazaq had programmed into his phone. Not speeding had him coming up to Mays at the exact time they'd planned.

Even though Mays was little more than a burg, it was the county seat of this rural county. This morning the monthly meeting of the county commissioners was held in the courthouse which was old and not protected by bollards as many city buildings are now. Bollards had been a point of discussion at two meetings. Two of the three commissioners said these concrete posts would have been handy if people still rode horses to the courthouse and tied them up in front. Needless to say, they tabled the bollard proposal.

Yadier would look for his best place to make the attack. He drove around the courthouse square and then drove to the other end of town. He pulled into an empty lot and got out to inspect his trunk. The smell of fertilizer would have gotten the attention from anyone close. The two tanks of diesel fuel were intact, he removed the caps and swished one of them around to wet the fertilizer bags. He got back in the car and bowed his head to ask for the favor of Allah. He put it into drive and seeing no traffic pulled back on to the two-lane highway. He looked ahead to see nothing had changed with the parking spots that gave him access to the front of the building. He pushed the accelerator to the floor and began to gain speed. All of the extra weight sure made a difference but he was getting there.

Kurt Jefferson, nickname Jingles Jefferson, didn't own the town but drove as if he did. When he backed out of a parking spot the whole town stopped including school buses. Jingles had just had a spirited conversation with the County Treasurer over his tax bill that he claimed was paid on November 9th, one day ahead of the due date. He'd never found it laying under the candy dish on his kitchen table. He started to back out of his spot across from the courthouse and took his normal extra wide berth. It was just quick enough and far enough to catch the right front fender of Yadier's Nissan Sentra. The resulting fireball left nothing of Yadier's Sentra and Jingles' Olds Cutlass. Windows were blown out of every business on Main St. including the Courthouse. A fire broke out in the Recorder's office that was quickly extinguished by the town's volunteer fire department.

Residents were coming downtown to see what happened. Any good possibility of forensic or bomb residue evidence was going to disappear. Witnesses from a block away had been knocked off their feet but were able to identify that Jingles Jefferson had been involved.

After an investigation by Federal ATF agents, it was determined a huge disaster for this town had been averted. This was an Oklahoma City style attack on a smaller scale. They'd also tried this with the Hampton County, Indiana school bus attempt. Using fertilizer and diesel fuel was easier to come by than military grade C-4. Jingles Jefferson had been recognized as a town hero and the Commissioners were proud of their new steel reinforced concrete bollards erected in his honor.

Washington

Chris Powell had spent three days with Moe Keane. He had to learn how to act. Spending time with normal people was a huge treat even if it was under the stress of trying to relive and unwind the last four and a half years of his life. He understood the need to learn everything possible about how a working terrorist cell operated. As far as anyone knew he'd been embedded longer than any agent in any agency. He was now ready to operate with other good guys.

News of the Iowa attacks hit him hard. Anger wasn't sufficient to describe his feelings. He had no trouble understanding this was directly pointed at hurting him. He wondered how long Hazaq had planned this operation. His mother had been spared, if only by a strange coincidence. He was sure Hazaq knew where she worked, this was an attempt on her life. The other attack at his college was also directed at him, no doubt in his mind.

Chris worked with a sketch artist to get the best rendition of Hazaq they could get. There were no pictures of him surprisingly, none good enough to use. The best help came from one photograph that Mike Baker had taken one day in the park across from the grocery store. Baker had emailed it to himself along with other photographs he'd taken, some of which were of other cell members. These would have all been destroyed with his crushed phone had he not emailed them, again proving Baker had instincts they could appreciate.

Chris had not been happy with Keane when he'd been called back to Washington. Chris argued he should immediately be on Hazaq's trail. Moe understood his thoughts and halfway agreed but decided to bring him in to debrief. Chris argued Hazaq was not that many hours from the Canadian border. Moe put the Canadian authorities on notice and they now had the sketch, with and without facial hair that could well be gone at this time. He was still deciding where to deploy Chris next. As of now, he was waiting on any possible hit on the sketch, Chris had a bug out bag ready to go and a DHS jet to take him.

Greenville

Mike was home and so was Sarah. She finished finals and was home for Christmas break. Mike picked his time and told her about what happened. She was very relieved that he was okay, but she gave him a stern talking to he had expected and deserved. They agreed to not tell David about this until later. Their communications with him were short and Mike didn't want to take this time to tell him something that would worry him. He wanted to focus his time on how David was doing. They got in two conversations with him, one on Christmas Day when they learned he'd get a month furlough sometime next year.

"Yes, that is what we've been told, one month."

"Wonderful news!" Sarah agreed. "Any idea on when?"

"No, not at this time. It depends on several things as you'd imagine."

"Understood."

"I did receive the package you both sent me, that means more than you know."

This brought emotion to Mike. The box contained not much more than essentials to them, but to David they were items that meant a lot in a battle zone. Mike had an idea percolating in the back of his mind, especially if David was coming home for a month.

Lafayette

The email had originated from Dr. Tom Sutherlin. He invited everyone to dinner in Lafayette and offered tickets to see a Purdue basketball game. Yes responses came back in record time and they set a time and place for dinner.

"Well Mike, I'd like to toast your safe return," Tom said.

Four frosty glasses clinked together, and everyone took a long pull.

"Thanks guys, I know I'm very lucky."

"What can you tell us?"

"Not much, but you know I was in Chicago. I can't say how I knew where to go. I have always wanted to take the train to Chicago, so I rode up and made my way to my room. I went each day to a park where I was watching a grocery store."

"Why a grocery?"

"I figured they'd have to come there for supplies and it was the only one close to the area I was staking out."

"You're watching too many movies or reading too many books, Mike. You're getting good at this." Charley said.

"Common sense, especially after I studied a map of the area. I just knew an area, not an exact location. Law enforcement said I must have stayed too long. The cell members figured out I was out of place."

"So how did they get you?" Brian asked.

"I can't talk about anything else. Moe Keane was pissed enough that I was there so I won't take a chance."

"Okay, understood," Tom said. "Okay, change the subject, this should be a great game tonight, the Boilers are playing great."

"Can't wait," Mike said.

The conversation stayed mainly on basketball until they left to head for the game. Purdue got a nice lead but then let it get close before pulling out the win. Handshakes all around before everyone said their good byes.

Chapter 23

London

Asis was still trying to get confirmation on the Chicago cell. He was careful not to do anything that would allow the FBI to track his position. If they had taken down the cell then they'd have their technology, so he couldn't take that chance. There had been protocol set up for this and he knew Hazaq was trustworthy. Hazaq would make contact with him as soon as he was safely in a new location. He had invested a lot of money in Hazaq and might have trained him too well if that's possible.

He'd spent the last few months looking over his shoulder. He grew more agitated each day. He was used to being the hunter, not the hunted. The extortion committed against him cost a lot more than one hundred million dollars. He'd lost credibility with his Saudi paymasters as well as the personal toll it had taken on him. The Saudis now seemed to be distancing themselves from him. If someone was able to get to him the Saudis didn't want to be next. As irritating as it was, he understood it. He'd done his best to keep this information from his circle of friends here in London. This group seemed to be distancing themselves from him just as the Saudis were doing. So be it, only two of them had ever shared his fervor for the jihad. The rest of them had settled into western ways as far as he could see.

Farid had gone as far as he could go with locating the perpetrator. The best potential break came from his acquaintance Chimera in Jakarta. What she'd given Farid was only marginally helpful in going further in either direction of the money laundering chain. This meant the process they used to launder money had done its job against him as it had worked for him many times before. Part of the sting of all this was lessened knowing it was the Saudis' money and not his own. They had more money from oil than they could ever spend anyway. But the real punch in the gut was that someone had gotten to him in the first place and could do so again. This was honestly the first time he did not feel safe in London. Maybe he'd just sell the family business and disappear to somewhere new. Maybe he'd find a place that wasn't as rainy and blustery as London for the rest of his life, somewhere he'd feel safe again.

Washington

Chris Powell was as ready as he'd ever been to make the call. Moe Keane had given him the go-ahead before Christmas, but Chris decided to wait. He could not imagine the reaction he'd get. Would his family ever forgive him? Would they be happy he was still alive? He'd know soon enough. Moe Keane was going to make the call and turn the phone over to Chris. He'd grease the skids as best he could.

"Mrs. Powell?"

"Yes."

"This is Moe Keane with the Department of Homeland Security."

"I remember you."

"I'm calling about Chris." He thought he could sense or hear the fear in her voice. He immediately went into his planned introduction.

"Mrs. Powell, Chris is fine and healthy."

"Thank God."

"I want you to know your son is an American hero. He has served his country beyond anything you could imagine. His service has been such that it must stay classified for many reasons including his personal safety and the safety of others. Mrs. Powell I would like to talk longer, but I've got someone here who wants to talk to you."

They could both hear her begin to cry.

"Hello Mom." Moe quietly shut the door behind him as he left his office. Their conversation lasted fifteen minutes. Against his best judgment on giving Hazaq more time to get farther away, Chris had agreed to take a week to go home and see his family. The attack on his hometown had made this decision easier.

"I'll be home tomorrow, Mom." He hung up.

The next day he flew into Ames and made the one-hour drive to Mays. This was a day he was convinced he'd never see, but here he was, pulling into the driveway. That afternoon he met two new nephews and a niece. He had the best meal he'd had in years. It was hard for the family not to know more than he could tell them, but they understood this was the way it had to be.

The week went fast as he knew it would. His mother knew he was going back to work for the DHS but was relieved to know his life as an undercover agent was supposed to be over. He would be able to keep in touch with his family. He said goodbye and headed for Ames.

Lexington, Kentucky

Hazaq reached the new cell location ahead of schedule. He was sure they'd be hunting him after the attacks in Iowa. He'd traveled a route that made no sense to anyone who'd be tracking him. There were times he spent a day heading due south, then turned around and headed back north before turning and heading at a ninety-degree angle to the west. He had arrived at his new location and wasn't going to show his face anywhere for a while. Two local students who'd been recruited months before had gathered everything on his list including new technology and a new identity including a passport. He'd not had a valid passport in many years, this one might save his life. He was going to hunker down and blend in with the local college crowd. They had his apartment ready for him to move in.

Hazaq was struggling with his connection to Asis, partly due to the fact he wanted to run things on his own, and partly because of the risk in contacting him again. He also struggled because he needed money from Asis. If he could find a link to the Saudis, he could be on his own to recruit and further the jihad as he saw fit.

Most of his beard was gone. He kept the mustache and goatee to blend in easier with American men. Any time he spent out would still be pretty close to a college campus and areas with younger citizens. Hazaq was thirty-nine but could pass for twenty-five with his youthful face and easy smile. He had put a plan into place leaving vague clues to hopefully point the authorities towards the northern states and Canada.

Washington

Moe Keane had taken great care in scheduling office time while Chris had been there debriefing. Chris had plenty on his mind in dealing with the debriefing as well as seeing his family for the first time in years. Moe thought a chance meeting with Bisma walking down the hall would be something neither needed right now. Chris and Bisma still thought the other was an enemy combatant. They'd both been part of the Chicago and Indianapolis cells and most importantly, Chris thought she was dead. Moe knew Bisma was interested in Chris for more than one reason. He didn't know Chris had been interested in her even though he thought she was a terrorist. Chris never felt she fit the mold of a jihadist. He'd be incredibly glad to know she was alive and well and now on the same team as him.

Bisma was prepared to travel to London with Steve. They were leaving in two days, which was two weeks later than Keane had planned. The Chicago cell takedown had changed things. Word had gotten around the agency much quicker than he intended but to no surprise. Bisma had heard and asked to meet, he was pondering how much to tell her.

"Mr. Keane?" Bisma stuck her head in the door.

"Come in Bisma. Have a seat."

"I've made final preparations and I'm ready to go."

"Very good. You and Steve have a plan of attack?"

"Yes. We spend day one with Steve's contact, Fiona. That fresh intel will tell us which way we go from there. As you suggested Steve will spend more time in-house working with their technology while I'm out and about."

"I know you're ready. Be careful how much you push and where. Make sure you stay in contact with Steve."

"Understood."

"Anything else?" Moe asked.

Bisma hesitated, "Do I have to ask?"

"Chris Powell was not injured."

"Is he in custody?" she asked.

"No, but he's under our watch. That's all I can say."

She gave her best inquisitive and annoyed stare and stood to leave.

"Hazaq?" she asked.

"He was gone, we're hunting him but no leads as of now."

"He's extremely dangerous Mr. Keane, no regard for any human life including his own people."

Moe shook his head, "Good luck, Bisma. I'm glad you're on my team."

She smiled with a slight nod and walked out of his office. Moe wondered to himself what Bisma would do if she ever confronted Hazaq. He had told his people to kill her and they'd almost gotten the job done. He guessed if she could return the favor Hazaq would not be so lucky.

London

Asis put the finishing touches on a plan that would put him back on the world stage. This attack would rival 911. His Saudi backers would once again be impressed at his ability to advance the jihad globally. His thoughts at first had gone to using a submarine. He knew all the difficulties and then luck they'd had to get his nephew Babur on the submarine a few years ago. That plan worked perfectly, but he didn't have the time to get someone in place for this type of operation. Getting control of a jet airliner was also a lot of work. This worked before, but he didn't feel it was necessary for this operation.

He stepped into his favorite coffee shop and was met with the usual smell of coffee and whatever was today's special in the bakery.

"Make me a double espresso this morning, Nathan."

Nathan gave him a smile. "Tough day coming up?"

"A lot on my mind today."

"Anything to eat?"

"Toast me a bagel please with cinnamon butter on the side."

"Coming right up, sir."

Asis sat down at a table by the front window and began to look through the morning paper. He looked out the window at another dreary day in London. They came one after the other. Three minutes later Nathan was at his side putting a double espresso and bagel in front of him. Asis gave him a nod of thanks. He ate in silence as he scoured the financial pages but couldn't get his mind off the task at hand. He caught Nathan's eye and waved him over.

"Yes, sir?"

"Nathan please make me another double to take with me."

Nathan chuckled, "You are having a rough day, coming right up, sir."

Asis left him a more generous tip than normal and was on his way.

The stroll pace turned into a walk that turned into a brisk walk as the wind came biting. Before leaving the bistro, he'd pulled up his collar and tightened his scarf, little good that seemed to do, it was going right through him today. Maybe it was time to look for a different place to live. He had all the money he'd ever need already invested around the world.

Asis chuckled to himself as he thought about Alberto Mulina. Mulina was as rough as they come, but he was fond of talking about Brazil. Asis had never traveled there but enjoyed seeing pictures of Rio and other points along the beaches of Brazil. He'd leave Brazil in the running for now. He'd also thought of points along the Mediterranean Sea, Italy, Greece, and of course France. All had their good and bad points.

The flight from Washington D.C. landed at London's Heathrow Airport at 10:25 AM local. They'd left at 7:20 PM last evening and enjoyed an uneventful flight. Steve had gotten a decent night's sleep on the way over, Bisma not at all. She had read the biggest portion of a novel she'd been wanting to dig into. Steve stirred within fifteen minutes of the final descent.

"Are you feeling rested?" Bisma asked.

"Yeah, feel great. You?"

"Dozed a little, read a lot."

208 · TERRY BARNETT

"Sorry. You want to get some sleep when we check in?"

"No time for that. You know we have a briefing scheduled for 1:30 with your contact Fiona."

The mention of Fiona seemed to brighten his eyes. It was subtle but Bisma noticed, this wasn't the first time. She felt he was all on board with their mission but felt he was also on board with getting to know Fiona better. Seemed like a win-win for Steve.

"Let's get our early check-in, I want to get freshened up a bit before the meeting and get some breakfast or lunch or both, I can't decide," Bisma said.

"Good ideas, let's find our luggage."

Thirty minutes later they were checking in and their bags were on the way to their rooms. Bisma made a beeline to the hotel restaurant, along with Steve who asked for a cup of coffee and wheat toast dry. Bisma looked at him and wondered what his mother had done wrong. She sat down and ordered a traditional London breakfast including a fried egg, bacon and sausage, black pudding and grilled tomatoes. She passed on the baked beans. The coffee was excellent, she ate like she'd never had food before. She wrote her room number on the check and headed for the stairs. Having a room on the sixth floor would be a nice workout and a quick shower would be even better. By 12:50 she felt like a whole new woman. She locked her door, walked the entire sixth-floor memorizing exits and looking for anything else she'd need to know. She pushed for the lift and then pushed for the main floor.

She made her way across a conservative lobby with tall ceilings and a patterned carpet that would make your head hurt if you had to look at it all day. It was kind of a labyrinth laid out with a spirograph. Made it hard to walk a straight line. She was wondering if there were secret cameras watching to see if people walked in circles or in arcs. She found an over-stuffed chair close to a window to minimize her view of the carpet. Their ride to the Thames House was to be outside at 1:05 and she was annoyed when Steve was not in the lobby at that time. Not being on time was a sign of disrespect as far as she was concerned along with a few other things depending on the person. He showed up two minutes late and they walked out to their waiting car. It was all she could do not to ask why he was late, but she decided not to pick this battle on day one. She also decided it was more than fine for Steve to work with Fiona at her base of operations while she was out doing her thing.

The fifteen-minute ride took them past both old and new parts of the city. They pulled through the heavy gates of the Thames House and were dropped off at a rear entrance. Fiona was waiting for them. She shook Bisma's hand and welcomed her to London. Bisma thanked her and said, "We are looking forward to a successful mission."

Fiona turned to Steve and extended her hand, "Welcome to London, Mr. Bradshaw."

"Thank you and please, it's Steve."

"As you wish. Follow me."

Bisma enjoyed that introduction nearly as much as Steve had. Steve noticed her slight grin and felt his face warm a bit. You can be taught to hide some things, embarrassment is not one of them. Fiona wore a blue jacket over a white blouse that was buttoned up just enough. Bisma noticed the slight bulge on her left hip under the jacket. It would be the standard issue sidearm for her agency.

Fiona led them into a conference room and offered coffee.

"Yes please," Steve said a little too quickly.

"Is it too early for tea?" Bisma asked.

"Not for me," Fiona said. She ordered two teas and a coffee and shut the door.

The three of them spent the afternoon going over reports, looking at photos and studying maps. When they decided they'd all had enough for the day, Fiona said, "I'd like to take you both to dinner."

"Thank you, but another night for me, Fiona. I didn't sleep on the plane."

"I understand, how about you, Steve?"

"Dinner sounds great."

"I'll call for your car Bisma, see you in the morning."

"Thank you," Bisma said. She stood up and headed for the door.

"Exit the same way as we came in?"

"Yes," Fiona said.

"I'll find my way then, see you both in the morning."

Bisma walked out and took her time making her way to the rear entrance. She was just taking it all in. It reminded her a little of Homeland Security and more like an office layout with mostly individual offices and a few cubicle set-ups.

As she climbed in the car she asked the same driver, "Can you take a different route back? I'd like to see more streets."

"Certainly," was his reply and they pulled into early evening traffic.

Bisma watched London pass by and wondered how the evening would go for Steve and Fiona. Her mind immediately went to Chris. She hoped he was being treated well by Keane's people.

Chapter 24

Greenville

It had been a cold day, but the sun was out with little wind. He could take any January day with the sun out. After coming home from Chicago, bruised but alive, everything looked like a blessing. He pulled on his favorite Purdue sweatshirt and grabbed his Braves hat and went out the back door. Mike liked to spend time in the tool shed like his dad used to. He saw the stack of cigar boxes he'd kept after Dad passed. Dad had used these to keep small machine parts, fuses, small seed corn books full of his notes, and just about anything else you could think of that would fit in a cigar box. Mike was using one by his side of the bed to keep notes of stories he'd remembered over time about Sandy, the kids, and his parents. The story he was remembering right now involved science. The science of germination.

When Mike was a boy his dad would keep back enough soybeans each fall to plant the next spring. No one does this anymore, it's more than likely not legal. It's definitely not legal to hold back corn for planting due to patents and genetic breeding. Seed companies want to protect their research. Dad would send Mike out to get some good black soil each spring to put into a cigar box. Dad would then give him enough of the soybeans he had kept back to plant three rows the length of the cigar box. He told Mike not to plant them too deep, but make sure they were covered well. He kept track of the exact number of seeds planted in each row. Mike would follow his instructions and then add a little bit of water to the soil, then he'd put the box in a window sill to get sunlight and the warmth of the sun you'd get through the window and wait.

Mike would check the cigar box every day, morning and evening, to see his results. Late in week one the soil would begin showing cracks along each row. Sometime early in week two, there would be the first signs of life springing forth. By the end of week two, he'd clearly see the soybean plant pushing its curved neck out and upward. Mike would keep the soil moist and keep watching this miracle of mother nature for at least another week.

Dad would ask Mike to write up some notes of the results. Since he had kept track of the number of seeds planted he was able to tell Dad the percentage of seeds that had germinated. Dad had explained to Mike why this was important to them for their farming operation and he'd always felt good about being able to help his dad. Of all the years Dad had him do this only one time did Mike have a crop failure. He remembered being sad about telling his dad that only half of the seed had germinated. Dad told him this was exactly why they did it and he called his seed dealer to buy new seed for that spring.

Mike smiled to himself as he remembered his parents. Dad had truly wanted to see how the seed was going to germinate and knew it was not the most scientific way to do it, but a little cigar box of black dirt and soybeans did more than give him germination results. He'd taught Mike responsibility, science and the wonder of Mother Nature. Even though Mike now always bought new seed for planting season, he felt like planting some in one of those cigar boxes stacked on the workbench.

Indianapolis

Natalie Jackson sent an email to Tim Dailey asking if he had time to meet later this afternoon. He responded yes and suggested 3:00 PM.

At five til three Special Agent Tim Dailey was standing at her door.

"C'mon in Tim, have a seat."

Tim sat down and put his coffee mug on the corner of her desk. He opened his yellow pad and took out a pen.

"What's up, Natalie?"

"You've got everything I have on the Roger Knight murder. I'm ready to arrest and charge Tyler Harper for first-degree murder. He laid in wait and executed him. Between us, I've lost no sleep not having Knight around, but justice deserves to be served."

"Agreed. Shall I go bring him in?"

"I was thinking we'd have the Hampton County Sheriff's Department do it. You know as well as I do we were tasked to lead up the investigation, but they've helped in every way we asked."

"That's correct. Send them out and put him in the Hampton County jail."

"Will do. I fully expect a change of venue to another jurisdiction, but let's start where it happened."

"Sounds fine to me. Our evidence may be a little sketchy, but this is the guy."

"You have reservations?" she asked.

He gave her a small smile, "Let's hope the Prosecutor doesn't spend a lot of time on his cross-bow skills."

"Why do you say that?"

"You know as well as I there are other more capable killers with a crossbow practicing their craft at local shooting ranges and behind their barns."

This set Nat back a little, she didn't see it coming, "You have more to say?"

"No, do you?"

"The Hampton County Prosecutor is fully on board with us, she'd like to nail this down. Of course, she'll never argue the case after a change of venue and then a Special Prosecutor is appointed," she said.

"But she'll be the one who charges him at his arraignment and starts the process."

"Exactly," Nat said.

"Anything else?" Tim asked.

"Yes. I'm wondering if there is anything new on the Purdue Vet School attack? Have you heard anything from the Chicago office since that cell was taken down?"

"Nothing new. They left behind nothing worthwhile in technology. They did leave behind a room full of other things including some explosives that are still being tested. I'm confident they were the ones behind that attack, aren't you?"

"Absolutely. I'm convinced they were trying to kill Charley Summers along with as many staff and students as possible. Hopefully, there'll be something to tie them to that officially."

"It never brings anyone back, but it'd be nice to say we cleared the case," Tim said.

Nat shook her head in agreement. Tim stood and reached out to shake her hand. That made Nat stand and she took his hand with a firm handshake. Tim turned to leave.

"Don't forget to take your Cabela's coffee mug with you," Nat said.

He smiled and grabbed his cup.

When he was gone she stared into her computer screen and tried to decide what the hell he was up to with his comments. That was on purpose. It was like he was staring through her and her thoughts of Sarah Baker were flashing like a Scarlet Letter on her chest. Her gut told her something was different with Tim Dailey. Maybe he didn't like working with women or maybe he had his own skeletons. She'd read his military record and knew he'd spent time serving in Guantanamo Bay. His interest was counterterrorism which was probably a result of that assignment. She'd never discussed it with him, maybe she should.

London

Bisma crossed the lobby trying not to look down at the carpet. She decided if she were to design cells for prisoners who were being interrogated, she'd have this carpet installed, it would drive them insane. Steve appeared at her side as she stood watching for their morning ride. She was pleased he was a few minutes early.

"Did you have a nice dinner?" she asked.

"Very nice, it's good to be with someone who knows the area and can show you around."

Their black government SUV pulled up and Steve held the door for Bisma. She thanked him and got in, he walked around and got in beside her.

"Ready for another day?" he asked.

"Yes."

"I've been looking forward to some field work for a long time. I'm comfortable working at the NSA but I wanted to get out some. I know I'm spending most of my time sitting at another computer in another office, but it feels different, I like it."

"Who knows, it might be a big change of life for you, Steve."

"I think I've pigeon-holed myself behind a desk, but who knows?"

They rode the rest of the way in silence, each thinking about their upcoming days. Bisma was ready to get out. She had studied the maps and planned her course of action. Questions raced in her mind and she had to tell herself to calm down, not overdo it with people, not press too hard.

Greenville

The arrest of Tyler Harper was uneventful. They came to get him at 5:15 AM and he had nothing to say except that this was a big mistake.

"Big mistake alright," one deputy said. "Put your hands behind your back."

News got around town and the county pretty quickly on social media. Ten months after the murder they had the killer in custody. Kurtz smiled when he received the alert on his phone. This was the news story he'd hoped for. A quick and speedy trial was the only thing between him and a huge transfer into his special account.

That evening one more person got the news on her laptop. She read the local news story carefully then searched to find the story on the Indianapolis television stations. Video showed the prisoner being taken into the jail, then they cut to the County Prosecutor congratulating local law enforcement and the FBI for untiring work.

"We will bring justice to the community of Elm Grove from this cold-blooded murder. Thank you."

Questions were shouted as the Prosecutor walked off. Sarah Baker didn't feel as relieved as she thought she'd feel. She'd always hoped this would just go unsolved, she didn't want to see an innocent man convicted and put in jail for life or worse. If this became a death penalty case, she was not sure what she would do. Could she live with herself? She couldn't let it go to the death penalty.

Nat was as sure as she could be that Sarah Baker had killed Roger Knight. She was reminiscent of the fact that some bad men deserve swift justice. She had to mete out this type of justice herself, but this was different, this was lying in wait, pre-meditated murder. She wanted to protect her and couldn't imagine how this would be taking a toll on Sarah.

Mike watched the eleven o'clock news as usual. Sometimes he used the mute button on the initial stories to get to weather and sports, but tonight he wanted to hear about the arrest of a local man for the murder of Roger Knight. It had been nearly ten months since the murder and here they were taking this guy in handcuffs into the county jail. He knew he should be feeling glad, but he just felt numb about all of it. Roger Knight had planned so many bad things and was partially responsible for Sandy's death. He'd brought death and destruction to Hampton County as well as several other Indiana counties.

London

Bisma was tired after a day of mostly spinning her wheels. She didn't feel too bad about it since she'd learned a thing or two, including never to put milk in her tea again. She knew better but wanted to give it a go. The five crew members Steve had focused on last September were going to be harder to locate than she imagined, but it had only been one day. She received a text from Steve saying he and Fiona were having dinner again and she was welcome to join them. She could feel his feet dragging as he punched in that text under the watchful eye of Fiona. She politely declined and said she see him tomorrow in the lobby.

Asis had spent the day on the internet researching places to live. He saw no reason to look too far from the tropics. There were absolutely stunning places in the outer longitudes with breathtaking vistas but cold and rainy was not a tradeoff he wanted. He kept thinking about Jakarta where Chimera set up her base of operations. He spent a lot of time studying everything he could find until he found Cirebon, a coastal city on the Indonesian island of West Java and fell in love. Less commercial than Jakarta but commercial enough for him with 300,000 people. It was located on the western edge of the ring of fire and had its share of earthquakes in the area. This decision was easier than he would have imagined. He'd nearly made up his mind before heading for home.

With no children of his own, his mind went to Farid as he walked to the Tube for his ride home. He was in the process of grooming Farid for future attacks. Maybe Farid could take the place of Hazaq in the United States. He was already studying there and doing well as far as Asis could tell. He felt confident Farid would not be satisfied coming back to London to run the business.

Asis was amazed how little sentiment he felt about the family business. He'd spent his entire adult life there. Learning from a father who cared more about the business than he did his wife or Asis and his younger brother. Taking over when his father died at age 47, when Asis was 23. His mother died four years later, and he'd been alone ever since. He was not close to his brother but had very much admired his nephew Babur and now Farid. His brother had raised intelligent boys who felt the fire of jihad much more than their father. This led them both to their uncle Asis and Asis had always given his younger brother more credit than he deserved. This praise had made it much easier to bring the boys into his plans.

At age 49 he realized he was now two years older than his father had been when he died of the stroke. He had worked himself to death and never showed enjoyment with anything Asis could remember. He asked himself how he was different and decided he didn't show much enjoyment in anything either. His passion came from planning terrorist attacks and seeing infidels killed. He had no feelings for people who worked at his office and he was sure those few employees felt the same way about him. He smiled to himself that his most treasured friend was Nathan at the coffee shop. This young man treated him well and would actually joke with him. He made a note on his phone to remember to reward Nathan in some way before he left.

Chapter 25

London

One week was complete and Bisma had made progress. Out of five families to investigate she had ruled out three. The two remaining families were interesting. She would be traveling north by train to a small town in the morning. As she guessed she had little access to any of the females in the families she had visited. She was talking to only the men and it appeared it would stay that way with the last two families.

The last family in the London area was small. Father, mother and one son overseas studying in the United States. The son they lost on the submarine was an excellent student, had attended the Naval Academy and was well liked by his crew members. All looked good with these folks as well. Maybe they were entirely on the wrong track. Maybe the submarine had just suffered a catastrophic engine failure and exploded, not an inside job at all. The Pentagon would have nothing of that, it had to have been a deliberate act.

Bisma had dinner alone and made her way to her room. She reread her notes for the week looking for something she missed. She found nothing unusual. She kicked off her shoes and sat back on the bed propping herself up with a couple of pillows and turned on the local news. Becoming fully relaxed, her thoughts went to Chris. She let this happen on a regular basis. She hoped he was being treated well and hoped he was cooperating with the authorities. Maybe they would turn him to their side. Things were going well for Bisma thus far, actually better than she ever imagined. She was making a habit of counting her blessings as people say, it seemed she was blessed.

She was startled by the knock on her door. She walked across the room and looked out the peephole to see a steward with her laundry over his shoulder. She opened the door and handed him the standard gratuity. He handed her the hangars and was on his way. She locked and bolted the door and was ready to brush her teeth before bed.

She was up early the next morning and headed down for another filling breakfast. She realized this was getting to be a habit. She didn't eat like this at home and figured she'd probably picked up a couple pounds. Ready to meet her driver after the second cup of coffee, she slipped on her coat and headed out the front door. He deposited her at the rail station and she checked in for the two-hour trip north. The scenery was mostly countryside with beautiful pastures and thick woods and the occasional old church.

She arrived at her destination and walked five blocks to the old downtown area with a few shops and an ornate old tavern that looked like the town lunch spot. She made her way inside, found a booth and ordered. Her order was out quickly and again she was eating as if she hadn't had food in a month. This cool clean air must have enhanced her appetite. She asked the waitress about the family she was here to see. The waitress pointed to a picture on the wall and a framed newspaper article next to it. Then she pointed to a crest on another wall and a cabinet of beer mugs with the families mugs lined up altogether. The son killed on the U.S. submarine still had his mug in the place he left it. He was a local hero in every way possible.

The waitress shared a couple stories before asking the tavern's owner to came over, Bisma invited him to sit down and he shared more stories of this young man. He finally asked why she was here and she made up a story that she was an American tourist and just wanted to know more about this town's favorite son. That pleased him, and he went on with more stories. Forty minutes later she told him she had a train to catch which was only partially true. She was not due to leave for three more hours but she'd heard enough. This young man had not blown up the submarine he was on. He was training on the USS South Carolina and would have come home, perhaps ending up as an Admiral in the Royal Navy.

She paid her check and wandered onto the street to look around the shops. She bought herself some dark chocolate, stopped for a spot of tea and had a wonderful afternoon. She walked back to the station for the evening ride south to London. She allowed herself a generous two-finger pour of a nice Scotch and sipped it as the British countryside rolled past.

Once they were pulling into the station, Bisma texted her driver to pick her up. He dropped her at the front door of the hotel and she made her way through the lobby again trying not to look down at the horrid carpet. She knew she'd soon never see it again and secretly smiled as she realized she'd miss it a little.

Chicago

The Chicago FBI personnel were finishing an exhaustive investigation of the apartment where the cell had lived for five years. Everyone was amazed they'd stayed in the same location that long without incident. Seems they were model citizens and kept their heads down. Nobody ever questioned them or their comings and goings. Their landlord had nothing bad to say, he was unhappy they were gone. They'd not told him they were moving out and had paid the last month's rent on time plus a little. He was going to keep their initial deposit since he didn't know where to send it. It was determined the room under Hazaq's office was a safe room for him as well as some onsite storage of materials.

The cell had the off-site garage where a lot of their work was accomplished. Suicide vests were made there, explosives were stored there, and recruits were trained there. It was in an area where all buildings were commercial properties. Agents wondered what else happened behind the closed doors on this block?

Chris traveled to Chicago for two days to show them where they shopped and did some recruiting. They were always looking at any college campus for students exhibiting any type of fringe behavior. Social media was an excellent way to be on the lookout for recruits. Chris had spoken to Moe Keane about this as well. Hazaq knew that if a student posted some radical stuff it wouldn't just be on his radar, it would also be on the Fed's. Hazaq would try to get to them quickly and tell them to cool off with the postings so they wouldn't be on a Federal watch list. Many times that worked and he would have someone else meet with them to determine their level of jihadism.

As Chris walked into the house the first time his skin began to crawl. He couldn't help but wonder if Hazaq was having the house watched. He could not think of a reason why he wouldn't be hundreds of miles away by now, but who knows.

"Have you had any of your people walk the neighborhood to look for surveillance?"

"No, but we've canvassed local stores to see what we could learn. We've talked to every neighbor in a three-block area."

Chris began to think about the last few years. Hazaq had kept his thumb on cell members, no one was ever allowed to go out alone, sometimes two and mostly three at a time depending on the task would venture out into the neighborhood. Hazaq would sometimes have other "teams" out to teach everyone surveillance, kind of a terrorist hide and seek which made Chris chuckle to himself. Why wouldn't Hazaq have cultivated people in the community to be another set of eyes for him? It had crossed his mind once when a recruit had been killed by Hazaq one evening at the dinner table in front of everyone. Chris knew he was making a statement to show his authority but was there something else. Hazaq had questioned the young man about something and purposefully pushed him too far, the recruit said the wrong thing which got him a bullet to the forehead.

"Hey, Powell, let's get a beer. There's a place down the street."

"Sound good, but not there. Let's get away from this area."

"Bad memories?"

"Something like that."

Chris was going through every shop on the street in his mind, every owner in his head, one by one. They got out of the neighborhood and five agents sat down to wash away some of the day. Chris enjoyed the camaraderie but was narrowing down his plans for one more day in Chicago. He'd call Keane to let him know he needed more time.

The next morning Chris got a ride down to the old neighborhood and began walking by himself. He'd told the rest of the crew he had some stops to make. He got a cup of coffee and started to work his line of questioning in his head. He wanted to see how this went before going to the three shops that he felt were most likely to yield results. As he guessed, word had gotten around the occupants of the one certain apartment house had all moved out at the same time. The last three shop owners would recognize him for sure. He was interested to see if they showed any surprise when he entered their stores. He knew he risked the possibility that someone would tip off someone else when he was wandering around. It was nearing the lunch hour when he walked into the cell phone store.

"May I help you?" the owner said looking up.

Chris caught his eye and got the ever so slight look of surprise he was hoping for, "I hope so."

The owner was Pakistani and had done well for himself with this store. He was known for his confidentiality and sometimes kept unusual hours. Chris stood at the counter and let enough time pass to make it awkward for both of them.

"I would like to buy a phone," he finally said.

Rostam turned and pointed to a call minute and data plan spreadsheet on the wall. "We have many choices depending on your needs."

"I'm needing to talk to someone. We were separated, and I've found myself alone here in the city."

"I don't see how I can help you with that, Sir. Again, here are your choices."

Chris let another long pause get uncomfortable, "It's extremely important. I'm sure my friend would be very indebted to you if he and I could talk on one of your phones. Would it be possible for me to come back tomorrow morning to pick up the phone?"

Rostam could now be risking everything. He needed time to think and assess the situation. This man looked familiar to him and he had him clearly on his security camera. "Pick a plan and your phone will be ready in the morning sir."

Chris picked a plan and paid for half of it in cash. "I'll see you in the morning." He walked out.

He had one more business to try but decided the cell phone store would be his best bet and he didn't want people to talk. Chris made his way a few blocks east and called Moe Keane. He filled him in on his plan and told him how it had gone.

"Okay, let's see how it plays out. Talk to you tomorrow."

Keane was a man of few words. Chris spent the rest of the day running scenarios in his head thinking of how the next morning might play out.

The next morning, he was standing at the door of the cell phone store as Rostam unlocked it. It actually, unnerved Rostam a little and that wasn't easy to do. Chris followed him through the small store and Rostam got himself behind the counter.

"Do you have a phone for me?" Chris asked.

Rostam wanted to gain control of this situation but felt he'd already lost that somehow. "I have it as he reached under the counter."

Chris didn't like seeing Rostam reaching somewhere he couldn't see. He was not armed so a gun in his face would be a problem. Rostam came out with a phone and charger in a Ziploc bag. He took the phone out and powered it up. His nervous eyes shifted back and forth from Chris to the phone.

"There is one number programmed in the phone. Please don't call it from here and please don't come back."

Without a word, Chris dropped the rest of the cash on the counter, picked up the phone and charger and was gone. After walking a few blocks from the store he pulled the phone out of his pocket and punched in contacts. One number showed up with no name. He played this over and over in his head several times but he still hesitated before making the call. How could this go wrong he wondered? He punched call. Three rings and he got a generic voice mail.

"This is Chris. I need help, please call."

London

Steve rolled out of bed ready for another day. He gave his head a quick shake to make sure it was all real. He'd never felt so energized. This time spent with Fiona was hitting on all cylinders both professionally and personally. He called room service, ordered breakfast and jumped in the shower. His mind was racing about how to modify their investigation and search engines for today. They were doing the "follow the money" thing and making progress. Money laundering had gotten sophisticated with the internet. No more cash in briefcases being passed around by guys in trench coats. Now it just moved around the world effortlessly. Casinos and horse tracks were good places for it to start or pass through. It could even be grocery store chains or big box retail. They were looking for choke points, places where big transfers happened, and local authorities were inclined to look the other way.

He toweled off and was dressed when his breakfast arrived. He ate and half-heartedly watched a London morning news show. It seemed much the same as in the States. He was not missing his home but he always missed his kids. Having his children move away was his biggest regret. They bore the brunt of his work. His wife had not missed one opportunity to make him the villain. He downed his first cup of coffee and poured the next cup in his UNC stainless steel travel mug and was out the door.

"Morning Bisma, are we sharing a ride this morning?"

"Yes, I'm going to the office first today. I need time to plan my route today."

Steve nodded and opened the door for her. He definitely seemed like a different man to her. He was smiling and animated. She knew he and Fiona were focused on all the financial aspects of terrorism. They were tracking anything they could find out of the Middle East to anywhere in Great Britain and points beyond looking for clues. She also felt confident Steve was focused on Fiona. So be it, he was a free man, but this would be turning into a long-distance relationship in about two weeks. That might be tough for him.

Chapter 26

Washington

Moe Keane thought he must be going soft. His mind was going over and over thoughts about his people more than the tasks at hand. His wife knew long ago she was married to a man who never left his job, not unlike a soldier or law enforcement officers. This lifestyle had been hard on marriages and caused many to fail. He understood it, he didn't have to like it though. As he got older it was harder to take. It wasn't up to him to play God, but he'd been doing just that when it came to Bisma and Chris. He'd made his mind up to let each of them know about the other and let whatever happened, happen. They'd both given more in their young years than should have been asked of them.

Bisma would be back in a week and at that time he'd reintroduce them to each other. They'd sure have a lot to talk about.

At this point, he was content in not sending Chris out to chase dead-ends. They vetted leads carefully before sending him. Moe spent little time worrying about budgetary constraints but was fiscally conservative enough not to spend money wastefully. He'd never believed in doing that but had sure seen others not worry about it and it pissed him off. He had Chris spend time each day with two individuals who knew how to ask the right questions to drill down deeper into his memories. They were trying to get at the smallest day to day workings of a cell. The DHS was continuing to develop algorithms that included any type of nuances dealing with the cells. They would use these algorithms to work at determining where cells might be forming or were likely to form.

Moe was still a boots on the ground soldier who believed there was no better way than to keep a keen eye and use old-fashioned common sense but he was also realizing that if the tech guys could help point them in the right direction, then why not use their help. Law enforcement had applied similar thinking to looking for patterns of crime by serial killers. He saw how this applied common sense theory into the process but sometimes the common sense of it didn't come out until the whole picture was known.

London

Bisma had set the time and place to meet with the last family. She would only be seeing the father. She had asked to meet at his home, but he politely refused and offered a quiet coffee shop after the morning rush of patrons. She arrived five minutes early to find him already finishing a pastry and a cup of coffee. She got herself a cup and walked over. He gave her a pained smile and she sat across the booth. His demeanor made an already cool morning, cooler.

"Thank you for meeting with me Mr. el-Tariq."

"You're welcome. Please get along with your questions, my time is limited."

"As you wish. We are working on gathering information to honor the crew members of the USS South Carolina that was lost at sea seven years ago. I first want to share my condolences for your son."

He nodded.

"I would like to know more about your son, Babur. His service records were exemplary."

"He was everything a man would want in a son. His loyalty was matched by his love of family."

"What made him want to serve in the United States military?"

"He was ready to see more of the world. He wanted an education in that country."

The '*that country*' remark seemed to hit something as he said it. Bisma sensed this father felt no love for '*that country.*'

"Why did he pick Nuclear Engineering for his course of work?"

"It may have picked him. He went to the Academy with an open mind. His love of mathematics and physics seemed to take him that direction."

"He was top of his class," Bisma said.

"Yes, we were very proud."

"Tell me about the rest of your family?"

"I have a son who is now studying at the University of Michigan and I'm married."

"How does he like Michigan?"

"He is doing well."

Every answer was short and to the point, much as Bisma anticipated. She'd been advised not to stray too far from the line of questioning for each family, that might cause more harm than good.

One last question, Mr. el-Tariq, "Did your son ever give you any reason to believe he might be worried about a traitor among his crewmates?"

His eyes told her she'd hit a nerve. "No, never. What are you saying, this was no accident?"

"I'm not saying that, but we've felt the need to explore all options. We look at these men and women as heroes."

That didn't seem to make him happy and he was using this as a good time to end the interview as he gathered up his coffee cup and plate. He slid out of the booth and stood to face her.

"Thanks for your time Mr. el-Tariq."

With a small bow, he turned and headed for the door. Bisma watched him go. She wondered what it would be like if she could ask Mrs. el-Tariq to share a few words about her lost son. Maybe she wouldn't be so stoic. Bisma made some notes, finished her coffee and paid her check. She watched Mr. el-Tariq leave the store and head to the right. She plugged his home address into her phone, walked out and turned left. After a fifteen-minute walk, she was standing two houses down from his Edwardian style two-story home. It was on a pretty tree lined street with plenty of foot traffic and a short walk to several mom and pop type stores including a local market and butcher shop. She found an unoccupied bench and decided to just sit and watch for a while.

It was ten minutes to twelve when the front door opened and a woman left the house. She turned to walk right past Bisma. She decided to not confront her like this, instead she pulled her magazine a little closer. Bisma hoped this was Mrs. el-Tariq and not a housekeeper or someone else. She gave her plenty of lead and then got up to follow.

Five minutes later she walked into a small bistro. Bisma found another bench and sat down to wait. Thirty-five minutes later she came out and made her way farther up the street. It wasn't long before she turned into a market. This was exactly what Bisma had hoped. Bisma entered the market and quickly found the woman in the produce section with a basket hanging from her left arm. She walked up to her and said, "Mrs. el-Tariq?"

She looked up, "Yes."

"Mrs. el-Tariq I met with your husband this morning."

She looked confused, "What about, I didn't realize he was meeting with anyone this morning."

"You were invited, I just assumed you couldn't make it."

"No, I'm sorry I didn't know anything about it, but that's not surprising, that's how things work for me."

"I'm sorry to hear that, Mrs. el-Tariq, but I understand."

As Mrs. el-Tariq looked at Bisma's face she somehow knew that Bisma did understand.

Bisma said, "I met with your husband to discuss your son Babur and his service in the U.S. Navy."

The look of confusion was still there but she gave a half nod.

"We discussed his excellent academic record and service record. We also discussed your other son studying at the University of Michigan. He is also doing well."

Mrs. el-Tariq smiled.

"I am wondering if you ever heard Babur speak of having any crewmates he thought could be a problem?"

"No, I do not understand what do you mean."

"We are still investigating the loss of the submarine. I know it has been extremely painful for you to lose a son Mrs. el-Tariq. Please take my card and give me a call if anything comes to mind you'd like to discuss."

Bisma handed her the card and she accepted it and put it into her purse.

"I'm sorry to have bothered you but thank you for talking with me." Bisma reached out and lightly touched her arm before turning to leave.

Bisma's mind was racing as she left the market and began walking. She knew she was probably reading more into it than she should. She sat down for a quick lunch and to make notes at the same Bistro where Mrs. El-Tariq had stopped. Turned out there was little to write, she'd done most of the talking.

Nafeesa el-Tariq returned home with her dinner ingredients. Her mind was on her son, Farid. Babur was gone, he was sent to his death by her brother-in-law, and her husband had done nothing to stop it. Babur had all the potential in the world and he was gone forever. Farid was still with them but might well be going down the wrong path as well. Her husband never stood up to his older brother, Asis.

Greenville

After less than one month in the Hampton County jail, things were progressing quickly. One arraignment hearing and one hearing to discuss negotiations in a plea bargain. After repeated requests by his court-appointed attorney to ask for a trial to fight this, Tyler Harper was ready to talk plea bargain. It turned out he was especially afraid of needles and that was enough to have him thinking. He maintained he was not guilty but believed he was in big trouble and had too much going against him. The prosecutor was contemplating the death penalty and made sure this information was in the papers. It had also become well known the cost to try a death penalty case was over a million dollars and would take months, probably well over a year to complete the trial. For this reason, the prosecutor was willing to take the death penalty off the table and keep Tyler off the table as well.

There was talk around the county this was a "railroad job" but there was not much love loss for Tyler and even less for Roger Knight. FBI agents, Nat Jackson, and Tim Dailey had testified at the Probable cause hearing and were happy to move on to other work. Tyler's attorney was on record saying he did not agree with this course of action and wanted Tyler to stand trial, but it was Tyler's decision and he was ready to stipulate to the murder for life in prison with a possibility of parole in twenty-eight years. The hearing was set for three weeks from now in early March.

Rockton

Kurtz had been monitoring the proceedings and was amazed at the swift justice happening in Hampton County. This was better than he could've ever imagined. His biggest worry was that a judge might say no to the deal. He didn't think that would happen unless someone brought in a high-power attorney who would argue otherwise to the judge and want a change of venue. He'd keep a close watch and do what it took to keep the path clear from anyone wanting to change its course.

This payday would have him at a point where he might not need to work anymore, but he was thinking a larger nest egg would be a good thing and he enjoyed what he did.

London

Steve's mood was going downhill. He and Bisma would be leaving in two days and he was already missing Fiona. He was thinking of ways he could get himself back here as soon as possible, realizing this was not going to be easy. Tonight, at dinner he would bring up things of a personal nature.

They'd made little progress on the money trail but felt there were possibilities here. It seemed they would need to catch the wave of the transfers actually happening versus trying to track transfers that had already occurred. If they could catch one in progress, see the funds flowing, they might locate some of the stops or gates where the money flowed through.

Bisma was ready to get back to school in Bethesda. She felt they had done good work in London but was ready to return to her studies. She'd found a couple of potential leads but also knew whoever they were looking for was well insulated. His security was tight and had been in place for a long time. She had googled detective work before coming over here and discovered there was a lot written on technique and theory, but not a lot written on how old-fashioned luck was often times the best factor. She felt that good luck could be increased by hard work. Things like this can go hand in hand. It was difficult to put into words, but you could feel it, plant enough seeds and some will grow.

Greenville

Mike was driving one day and found himself on the road where his Baker grandparents had their small farm. The times there usually involved cousins and playing baseball in the yard north of the house. There was a hand pump that brought up the best cold water he could remember. Someone used to say, "if you want a cool drink of water, you've got to dig a little deeper in the well," who said that? He used to remember how many pumps it took to get the first water and it only got colder from there. An old metal enamelware cup hung on a nail. He couldn't imagine how many times he drank from that cup.

In the mid to late fall, they'd all go to the farm for a big wiener roast back in the woods. Grandpa would set a big brush pile ablaze sometime in the afternoon and by the time everyone got there and carried everything back to the woods, it was perfect for roasting hot dogs and marshmallows and keeping warm. All the cousins would play and laugh and run into the woods to pee, there had been times poison ivy happened in the aftermath. Poison ivy in places you especially didn't want poison ivy. Mike believed there were two places a hot dog tasted the best, at a wiener roast in the woods and a baseball game. He slowed as he passed the farm and then the house and barn. What memories. That house would be so full of aunts, uncles, and cousins at Christmas they could hardly get around each other; but they did and it was great. They were all farm families, and everyone lived fairly close. Grandma made homemade candy at Christmas. Mike's favorites were the fudge and divinity, more than one kind of each. The younger crowd liked the candy without nuts in it, the older crowd professed to like the nuts. He still would prefer treats without nuts. If he wanted to eat nuts, he'd go get a handful of nuts.

He remembered other farm families as he drove these roads. He could still name many of the locals, most of them were now gone but a few remained, and some were being farmed by a fourth or fifth generation family member. If a farm stayed in a family for 100 years, the state of Indiana would call it a Heritage Farm and put a special plaque out for all to see. These were few and far between and made them special. There were two within five miles.

Mike saw a flash off to his left and realized an early spring storm was making its way into the western side of Hampton County. Technically it was still winter for a few more weeks but they were having a warm snap which could always boil up some precipitation.

Chapter 27

Over the Atlantic Ocean

They were three hours into the eight-hour-ten-minute flight home. Steve had his eyes closed but sleep would not come. His mind was on Fiona. Nat and now Fiona. He must have a need for this type of woman. At least he lived in the same country with Nat, but she was not interested in him as far as he could tell. He would be happy to have a relationship with her but just didn't see that happening. Fiona, on the other hand, was showing some interest in knowing him better. They'd had some frank discussions over the last couple of dinners. Neither one had an answer for the 3,600 miles that separated them. They agreed to keep in touch personally as well as professionally. A nice breakthrough on a terrorism ring might get them some extra perks like more time together. Fiona had never been to the States, so they decided she was due for a visit later this year.

Steve was impressed with Bisma. She'd made the most of her three-week mission as evidenced in her report to Moe Keane. They each shared their accounts of preliminary goals versus progress made. Bisma had been methodical in her steps. They both reported they'd ruled out more than they'd learned but this was expected, ruling things out decreases the list of probabilities usually.

Steve anticipated there would be a day or two spent with Keane before getting back to his office at Fort Meade. He'd stayed current on his emails which made him feel much better about the first morning back. He'd still have a full inbox, but two-thirds of it would get pitched. Keane would be interested in what they'd learned about money flowing around the world.

He looked over at Bisma sleeping like a baby. Three weeks had either exhausted her or relaxed her. She was going to be an exceptional agent for DHS. She'd lived in a terrorist cell and wanted nothing more than to put them all out of business. He could barely see the scar on her neck where the jihadists had slit her throat and left her for dead. She was a survivor.

They were met at the airport and driven directly to their hotel. The driver handed each an envelope with a message from Moe instructing them to get some rest, get some food and they'd be taken to his office tomorrow morning at 8:00 AM. Bisma was ready to start her debriefing immediately but she listened to reason. She took a warm bath, drank some hot tea and went to bed. She was awake at 5:15 AM having more sleep than she could ever remember. She was refreshed and ready to go.

Washington

Chris had been back in Washington for nearly two weeks. He hadn't received any messages on his new phone. Keane had involved him on the initial stages of a new plan to move forward with the war on terror here in the States. No one wanted to believe there was a war happening on our own soil, but Moe Keane knew it was happening. He knew we had to beat terrorists at their own game starting with recruitment. Keane had recruited him right out of college. Terrorist cells were recruiting anywhere the internet reached, which of course was everywhere.

The secure phone on his temporary desk came to life.

"Powell."

"Chris, this is Nat Jackson."

"How you doin', Special Agent?"

"I'm good. I'd be better if you told me you had any leads on your favorite terrorist."

"My favorite terrorist will only be my favorite when he's in custody or the morgue."

"Strong words," she said.

"I meant every one of them."

"I'm sure you did and I agree."

"You got something for me?" he asked.

"No, I need some advice."

"Go ahead."

"You talk in about the same length of sentences as your boss," she said.

"I didn't use to. Too long living with my favorite terrorist, less said the better for all that time."

"I can't imagine."

"Ask your question," he said.

"I've had more than one discussion with Mr. Keane about my coming to work for DHS."

"You leave the bureau? How long you been with them?"

"Twenty-three years. Our negotiation is that I would not be based in Washington, I'd stay in the Midwest."

"Is that what you'd want?"

"Yes, it is."

"What do you want my advice about?"

"Anything you'd advise me about DHS and working with Keane?"

"Funny thing about that is, you've spent more time with him than I have. I spent a short time with him after being recruited and was fast-tracked for my mission. I had virtually no contact with him for over four years until a few weeks ago. You know he is a no bull shit warrior on terror. This is a big agency, but we operate with autonomy. I like the idea of you staying in Indianapolis or wherever and not locating in the Washington machine."

"That's a huge part of this, Chris. A one-week meeting in D.C. coming up and I'm ready to move along."

"I understand, I was raised in rural Iowa."

"I also like the idea of being focused on the fight against domestic terror. I've sure been exposed to it in my current position but there are a lot of other things here I'm tired of."

"It sounds to me like you've made a decision," Chris said.

"I guess I have, my biggest worry may be if Mr. Keane would leave the agency."

"That could sure change things for all of us I agree. That could always happen," Chris said.

"That's true."

Chris was leaning back in his chair reaching for his coffee when he heard the tone. He grabbed for the phone and said, "Nat, I'll get back to you."

He quickly made note of the number on his phone and hit answer, "This is Chris."

After several seconds of silence, "You okay?"

"For now, who is this?"

"That doesn't matter, now listen to me. You've proven yourself over time, you need to get out of Chicago and reestablish."

"Reestablish what?" Chris said.

"Just yourself for now."

"Can I come to see him? Where is he?"

"It's not going to work like that Chris. If he wants to see you, he'll come to you. You relocate and let me know where you are."

"Give me an idea of…"

"Enough for now. Do not call this number, it won't work. I will call you."

Before Chris could get out "when?" he clicked off.

He immediately began making notes even though there was not a lot to write down. He was called from a phone that would immediately be destroyed. A cell tower expert would be able to get a general location, but Chris was sure whoever called would not be anywhere near Hazaq. At least he'd gotten a response, now he'd have to figure a way to get Hazaq's attention.

Keane would appreciate any news like this and maybe this could get him out of Washington and on the road. Two flights of stairs and he was standing in front of Moe's receptionist.

"Hi Jenna, is he in?"

"Yes but he's with someone."

"I just need two minutes."

"Let me buzz him, Chris."

"Mr. Keane?"

Moe picked up his phone, "Go ahead, Jenna."

He hesitated after hearing her message.

"Mr. Keane?"

"Send him in Jenna."

He looked across his desk, "I've got a little surprise for you and a bigger one for him."

The door opened, and Chris walked in. Bisma turned to see him and Moe watched each of their faces.

"This is not how I planned to do this but here we are. Chris have a seat."

"I thought you were dead," Chris said.

"I thought you were, I don't know what," Bisma said.

They both turned to Moe Keane.

"You both deserve an explanation and you'll get it."

The next hour was spent with Moe doing most of the talking. They both asked a few questions along the way. Moe made certain to explain how Bisma had wanted him to recruit Chris because he was different.

"Bisma didn't think you were cut from the same cloth as the other cell members. Honestly, Chris, this worried me. I thought if Bisma was seeing it or feeling it, how could Hazaq not see it or feel it? You've told me he wouldn't think twice about killing one of his own."

"That is true," Chris said.

"On the other hand, Bisma your observations always impressed me about you. I frankly had to get over the possibility that you were so good that you were playing me with your sincerity or empathy or whatever you call it."

"I'm thinking there is a compliment in there somewhere," she said.

Moe smiled, "It's a compliment, but you were coming to me for asylum not for me to recruit you. This vetting process is more complicated."

"I understand," she said.

She noticed that Chris was staring at her and she turned to him with a smile, "I knew he was a good guy."

This made them all laugh. Chris shook his head, "I was sure they killed you."

Bisma held her head back and brought her hands to her neck. "The surgeons did some good work, yes?"

It was hard for Chris to see. She'd done everything Hazaq had asked of her and he repaid her with a knife and left her to die.

"I just got a call from Hazaq's fixer."

"Anything worthwhile?" Moe asked.

"Not really. They want me to reestablish myself somewhere besides Chicago and they'll contact me when the time is right."

"Okay, you do some thinking on how we should play this info. Be here tomorrow morning at 8:00 with your thoughts. Change course for a minute. A lot changed for you both in the last year. It was a year ago you two were meeting at Starbucks to talk about the cell. Chris as you know, we let the world know that Bisma died in her Indianapolis apartment. This was to keep her safe as well as let her begin to help us. Bisma you know that we didn't make any splash about Chris when the Chicago cell broke up. We don't intend for him to go back into that life, but we want him to be able to track down Hazaq."

They were both looking at him taking it all in.

"Chris let Bisma and I continue to debrief. I know you two have a lot to talk about so dinner's on me tonight."

"Sounds good where are we all going?" Bisma said.

"We're not all going anywhere, but you two are, unless you had different plans?"

"Not me," said Chris.

"Dinner works for me," said Bisma.

"Now give Bisma and me another hour to talk."

Chris got up and shook Moe's hand, "Thank you sir."

He looked at Bisma and smiled, "See you later."

As the door closed she smiled at Moe, "So my instincts were correct?"

"I knew you'd say that. He's a good man and he's been through a lot to say the least. He's been to see his family, they were relieved to know he's alive and well. The cell targeted his hometown and college so he wants to find Hazaq in the worst way."

"I understand."

"Let's finish up our discussion and you can get out of here for today."

Fifty minutes later Bisma was gathering her things. "Thanks again for dinner, Mr. Keane."

"Have a good time and don't keep each other out too late," he smiled. "You'll find him two floors down."

Bisma walked into Chris's office. He looked up and smiled. "Where you staying?" he asked.

"The Kirkpatrick Hotel."

"Me too."

"I'll text my driver," she said.

"I've got a DHS issued SUV, I'll drive."

"Let's go."

Twenty-five minutes later they pulled into the parking garage. "Meet in the lobby in half an hour?"

"Sounds good. Where did he want us to go?" Chris asked.

"Our choice."

"Okay, be thinking, I'm not from here."

"Me neither. They have a nice restaurant here on the eighth floor."

"I haven't tried it, but I've heard it's good. Let's do that."

"See you in thirty minutes," as she got off on the third floor.

Shit lightning and crap thunder he thought to himself. What a day!

Thirty minutes later she walked up to the restaurant in the best outfit she had with her from traveling.

"I apologize I'm not dressed up more. I've been living out of a suitcase for three weeks."

"You look great."

They followed the hostess to their table and Chris held her chair. She couldn't think of a time when a man had done that for her. That was the beginning of a wonderful evening. Neither one remembered what they ate, the conversation went late. They already knew quite a bit about each other, but there was a lot they didn't know. They both felt a real connection, it just seemed inevitable. They laughed about their Starbuck's meetings and how they both enjoyed that time together after spending all their other time with jihadists.

"I knew from the first time we met you were a kind man, you didn't fit their mold," she said.

"I can be a cold-hearted jerk when I need to. I honestly shouldn't have let my guard down around you. You could've burned me with Hazaq. Truth is you were the only bright spot I'd had in many months."

"Same here, Chris. Spending time with the college crowd in the city kept me sane. I spent my time coming up with a plan to get away from the cell."

"Making contact with Mike Baker?"

"Exactly, and that didn't go as I expected at all. He's a force. I guess I shouldn't be surprised, we killed his wife and dozens of others in cold blood."

"He's a man who wants to help us and knows that many times our hands are tied. I respect that, but he'd be dead now if I hadn't been in the right place."

"When he and his son confronted me, I was amazed at his honesty. I could tell he hated what we represented, but when I told him I wanted out and needed his help he was willing to listen and see what he might do."

"Did you know he came to the farm by himself to talk to us?"

"I learned that later."

"I recognized him the day he was captured in Chicago, the others didn't, thank God."

Bisma shook her head, "So here we are, in no small part due to Mike Baker."

Chris lifted his glass, "To Mike Baker."

Bisma clinked her glass to his.

"I guess we should invite him to the wedding," Chris smiled.

This got him a look he'd never forget. Surprise, smile, nervous laugh.

"Did we just get engaged?" Bisma asked.

"Not yet. Keane hasn't given me time to go ring shopping, but more importantly, until about nine hours ago, I thought you were dead. A lot has changed for me in those nine hours."

"Meet me for breakfast?" she asked.

"Sure thing. Six-thirty...ish?"

She nodded her head and they asked for the check.

"It's taken care of," the waiter said.

"Really? How's that?" Chris asked him.

"A Mr. Keane said he'll see you in the morning."

They both smiled at each other.

"He's everywhere," Chris said.

Chapter 28

Lexington

Hazaq was not pleased to be contacted by Chris. He was content to cut any tie with Chicago. So far he'd only come up with problems as he thought about reconnecting with Chris. He decided to have him killed if he could get him into an isolated situation. He'd gone to extra measures to make sure he was protected in these communications. The recruit he was using to take a call like this was trustworthy as well as knowledgeable with the cell phone network. He'd made a contact back to Chris to keep him engaged. This bought him time for now.

He was still blending in with the local crowd. This was a much different town than Chicago. Things were slower here and people noticed each other. He was still unsure of this choice. He'd changed his appearance again with a clean-shaven face and he'd let his hair get longer but it was usually still covered under a stocking cap as he was out and about. His flow of money had resumed when he was able to reconnect with Asis as well as the other brothers he'd found in Syria. The job he'd found at a warehouse was only to look good for his apartment rental contract and possible recruiting.

Bethesda

After three days at the DHS Bisma asked Chris if they could drive to her apartment in Bethesda, she was ready for a wardrobe change. They made the forty-minute drive and stopped for dinner along the way.

"You said you enjoyed your first semester here."

"Very much, just being able to be a college student is more than I could've wished for. I dreamt about it, but never let myself get carried away."

After dinner, they got to her place and went in to look around. He was impressed at how clean she left it, not a dirty dish or glass in the sink. It was sparse but functional. Chris sat down as Bisma went back to her bedroom. He noticed she had no pictures in her apartment, she wouldn't have any from her family. She came out a few minutes later with a short stack of clothes and put them in a small bag. It was easy to see she did not have a lot but she wasn't complaining. Compared to her life up until now, he assumed she felt like the luckiest person around. He knew Moe had her on a monthly stipend so that she could be relatively comfortable. Her education was being paid by the government and she'd be indebted for a certain amount of service afterward.

"Can we sit a few minutes before heading back?" she asked.

"Sure," he said. "I like your place."

"It's small but I like it."

"I can see why you deserve a place of your own after what you've endured, Bisma."

"Can I get you anything?"

"No, I'm good, thank you."

They sat for a while in silence. Chris was starting to doze off.
"Think we should head back to D.C.?" Bisma asked.

"Yep, I'm going to be asleep."

He helped her carry things to the car and they were off. They were getting very comfortable with each other.

A small town in Italy

This area was gorgeous, heaven on earth. She'd been decorating for three months with local shop owners. The food was amazing and she'd noticed several of her favorite items of clothing were getting snug all of the sudden. She'd have to watch that and do some more walking. She was also enjoying her new bicycle, everyone had a bicycle with a front basket to bring things home from the market. Janet felt she'd chosen well. Her olive complexion fit in nicely with the locals. Her Italian was approaching fluent, but you could always hear English spoken by the vendors. There were many student groups who passed through the area doing social work, playing soccer with the kids and enjoying the area.

"Good morning, Bufasta."

"Good morning, Miss Claire, beautiful day."

"Yes, it is, coffee please."

"Just like you like it."

Janet Knight was now Claire Davidson, owner of the villa at the end of Heartbreak Street. It was actually Rosemary Street but a few of the locals thought there was heartbreak in her past. She sipped her cup of strong coffee and flipped through a magazine detailing an upcoming garden tour.

"Bufasta, make one to go please."

He smiled, she was a wonderful new customer. He handed her the coffee and an iced lemon cookie he knew she favored.

"Bufasta, you spoil me," as she laid her money on the counter.

He gave a slight bow, "See you tomorrow."

She made her way down the street enjoying the stroll. This place was heaven.

Washington

Friday morning came with news for Chris Powell. Moe was sending him to Kansas City to follow a lead on the phone call he'd received.

"You'll fly out Monday morning," was the final instruction he received after the thirty-minute briefing with Moe Keane. "You'll find all intel we have along with your itinerary in an email."

Chris rose and turned to leave. Moe thought of asking him about Bisma but chose not to. Chris walked directly to Bisma's office to tell her about this mission. They agreed they'd have a nice weekend together and they'd talk later. Bisma watched him go and wondered if a relationship could ever work. Things seemed to be moving fast between them. She couldn't help but wonder if that was because of the life both of them had led up until now. Neither one of them had been in a situation where they could have a boyfriend or girlfriend, have dates, go to movies, chat on the phone or send funny texts. They'd skipped that part of their late teenage years and the early part of their twenties. For herself, she wanted to make the good choices going forward, television was filled with people who hadn't made good decisions which was why she rarely watched.

They spent the weekend seeing sights in Washington D.C. and the surrounding area. Moe made sure they had nothing scheduled to do. He'd told Bisma she'd be heading back to Bethesda early next week to resume her studies. She'd missed a large chunk of the spring semester already but there was plenty of online classes and ways for her to get back up to speed quickly. Chris was glad she could get back into her studies.

"You did a nice job organizing our sightseeing," Chris said.

"I googled things to see in D.C. and found several top ten lists that were mostly the same."

"I like seeing it for the sake of history, it means more to me as I get a little older."

"I appreciate learning about the history of this country because I come from places where everyone wants to hate this country."

"That would be hard," Chris said.

"It was before, but not now for me."

"I guess I've always thought the United States tries to help others, but sometimes that ruffles feathers in other countries."

She chuckled at his words.

"What?"

"I love the way you all talk."

This made Chris chuckle.

"I have to tell you this is not a place I want to live. It's not my style and neither was Chicago for that matter."

"You want to be on a farm?" Bisma asked.

"That sounds good, but it doesn't have to be a farm, just not in a big city. I'd be good close to a city though. I would enjoy going to the city for a concert or to listen to an author speak or for a baseball game, stuff like that."

She just nodded.

"Do you want to live in a city?" he asked.

"No, not really."

"Where would you like to live?"

"I liked Indiana. When I was downtown Indianapolis, but I also liked what I saw outside of the city."

"That's cool. I grew up in rural Iowa, lots of similarities."

"I'd like to see where you grew up some time," she said.

Chris smiled and nodded, "I'd love to show you."

The weekend went fast and they had fun being together, they even did their laundry and had fun. As Chris was folding his stuff he was again realizing that for the time being he was homeless. His last place of residence had been the apartment house in Chicago. He had no desire to go back to that lifestyle. He decided this was a discussion to have with Mr. Keane when he returned from Kansas City.

Sunday night arrived and they chose pizza for dinner.

"This is just like a college student to want pizza on Sunday night," Chris laughed.

"I like pizza!"

"I like pizza too," he said.

After dinner they walked to his car, Chris opened her door and Bisma just stood there looking up at him. He reached for her and they stood there and held each other. They both knew the first kiss was coming, and it happened, and it was good. Real good.

"I'm going to miss you," she said.

"I'll miss you but I'll be back soon."

They kissed again and Bisma got in the car. Chris closed her door and had an extra bounce in his step as he made his way around the back of his car to the driver's side. They drove back to the hotel and he walked her to her room. This kiss lasted a little longer and may have drawn the attention of any security guard who was monitoring cameras on the fourth floor.

Chris awoke with 5:17 AM staring him in the face, his flight left at 9:05. The only good thing was he was not waking up in a house full of terrorists. He'd been dreaming about Bisma. He knew from the first time he saw her she was different. Dark eyes and dark hair with a tawny beige skin tone made her absolutely beautiful. She had always been held down by her society. Never been given a hope by anyone except her mother who'd been a strong woman and had saved her life fleeing Afghanistan after her father was killed by Russian troops. Bisma was now getting to realize her potential and her own self-worth. She was flourishing.

The trail to Hazaq had grown completely cold. Maybe not completely but Chris felt like it had, hopefully, this lead in Kansas City would get them back on his tail. He wanted to get his hands on him for so many reasons, his list had grown after the attacks on his home in Iowa, but it was long enough already. He would have value to them for intelligence gathering as well as a link to the London terrorist. Chris had lived with him for over four years and knew most of what they needed. He had to put his time with Bisma behind him for now and focus on finding Hazaq.

London

Asis had nothing to do except tie up a few loose ends. His small group of fanatical friends had grown much less fanatical after the extortion plan, he was now keeping them out of the loop with his future plans. The only person who knew what he was doing was his brother. Asis didn't care about his brother but he saw potential in his nephew, Farid. For this reason, he wanted to keep the relationship with his brother civil.

The home in Indonesia was purchased by Asis with cash, sight unseen. He had seen some pictures but hadn't flown there personally to see it. He was having updates made to the security system. His thoughts went to Alberto Mulina who he'd set up with a beautiful villa in Portugal. The assassin Asis first sent was killed by one of Mulina's bodyguards. Mulina's men were no match for the assault by the Navy Seals sent by the United States. He wanted no part of Navy Seals.

His home would have an escape tunnel inspired by the drug kingpin, El Chapo. The tunnel emerged three houses down the mountain. It was actually more of a slide. Once he dropped down through one of three trap doors he'd slide his way five hundred and fifty feet to a safe house. He had a camera system like no other. Redundancy built into more redundancy. If something failed there was a backup. He would have two dogs that had been trained as police dogs. They'd patrol his property and house day and night. There would be two employees for cooking and cleaning, both trained in all areas of self-defense and firearms. This move would happen soon.

Chapter 29

Rockton

He finished reading the third account of perhaps the swiftest justice in Indiana history. Tyler Harper was sentenced to life in prison with the possibility of parole in thirty years or so. He sent the carefully worded email to his contact. Payment had always happened within forty-eight hours of a completed job in the past. He'd already decided he would move this money as soon as possible. He'd picked his investments after considerable study and had decided to use a group of index funds to give himself both domestic and international exposure over a wide range of companies and sizes of companies. He was going to put very little to fixed income investments, bonds were boring to him and still carried their fair share of risk with the low-interest rate environment the country was now experiencing.

These funds put him over the top on financial independence. He had worked and saved in the same legitimate ways as all Americans with his 401k that was now going to the Roth choice. The earnings in his line of work as an assassin all came tax-free which was a real boost. There was no withholding on contract killings.

Indianapolis

Wes Maxwell forwarded the email to his assistant, Tess Acklin. Let Tess take care of it, Tess would take care of anything for
Mr. Maxwell, she adored Mr. Maxwell. This was the transaction
she'd been waiting for, she knew it was coming because she'd
been following central Indiana news. Tess had been planning this
transaction for months. She punched in the account and routing
numbers and hit send. She printed a hard copy of the transfer and
walked to his office. She could hear him finishing a phone call,
she gently knocked on the door.

"Come in."

Tess turned the knob and gave him the shy smile he loved.

"Is it done, Tess?"

"Yes, Mr. Maxwell."

"Good work."

She slid the paper across his desk giving him a nice view as
she leaned forward. He lingered as he reached for it and signed
his name barely seeing the paper.

"Anything else, Mr. Maxwell?" she asked.

"No, Tess, thank you."

She smiled as she turned to leave.

"Tess, I forgot to date it."

"I'll take care of that, Mr. Maxwell," as she closed the door
behind her. That piece of shit has it coming to him she thought to
herself. She had endured three years of sexual harassment from
this jerk and she was happy with her decision to take this risk. In
his two-thousand-dollar suits, he thought he was God's gift to
everyone, not just women. She remembered when Roger Knight

used to come to visit. What a pair they were. She was amazed there was a room in their suite of offices that could hold their egos. She knew her boss had been doing work for Roger Knight that was questionable at best. There was an Illinois Holding Company that had bought farmland at auctions for below market values, sometimes well below.

She kept copious notes over the last three years. Personal and business-related things she'd seen and been a part of as his personal assistant. She knew they'd hired an assassin to do what law enforcement had not been able to do, catch Knight's killer. She'd thought how creepy it was that Knight had put this plan into place. He must have had a premonition that he'd be hurt. He was right, he was executed in his own backyard. This assassin was handpicked by Knight. He was being paid but he also must have been indebted to Knight in some way. This was not in any records and for good reason she was sure. She figured her boss didn't want to know.

She had built more than one switch back into this transaction. All evidence would point directly to Wes Maxwell as the double-crossing attorney who kept the money for himself. She imagined this assassin would be very upset he didn't get his five million dollars.

Greenville

The trip was booked, and time was drawing near. The only thing he was not excited about was the twenty-hour flight to Sydney and the twenty-hour flight home. He had always wanted to see this part of the world, Australia and New Zealand had been on his bucket list before he knew what a bucket list was. He'd suggested it to Sarah and she was ready to go anytime. Mike suggested it to Brian and Pam and they too were onboard with the idea. The other person who would have made it perfect was David and that couldn't happen at this point. He'd have a furlough soon, but he wanted to just come home and rest. They'd come up with another adventure someday.

They'd all spent time online getting tips and tricks for this type of flight and cruise excursion. One of them would find something good and share it with the others. Mike had more websites marked than he would ever recall what was on them, but this was part of the fun of going. Sandy had always enjoyed the planning and anticipation of a trip, that was a big part of the fun. That was absolutely right, they used to have so much fun planning a vacation and being excited for it to start. In her honor, he'd do the exact same thing. He'd keep her in mind as he made decisions. At times he'd go about chores or cooking or anything else around the house and find himself talking to Sandy. If this wasn't mentally healthy, he didn't care one bit. She was a part of him and this conversation could center his thinking about a lot of things. He thought more than once about the 'What Would Jesus Do?' bracelets people used to wear. First, he thought people should still be wearing them and secondly, he liked to think about 'What Would Sandy Do?'

Ann Arbor

Asis had asked Farid to monitor the social media accounts of Mike and Sarah Baker as well as Brian and Pam Miller. He did it even though he felt it was below his pay grade. Someone else could be doing this mundane task as far as he was concerned, but he gave it all a quick look about every third day. Today something did catch his eye. A friend of Pam Miller was sending her information on cruises to the South Pacific and telling her to have a great time in New Zealand. There was also mention of the Bakers having fun. He flipped over to Sarah's page and found nothing there. Mike did nothing with his pages except wish friends, happy birthday. He made a note of this and decided to check again later to see if Pam responded or if anyone else said anything.

That evening he checked again, Pam had responded with a smiley face and thumbs up emojis. Another friend commented how nice it would be there and another said how nice it would be for the Bakers to get away for a couple weeks. He made notes of everything and put it into an email to Asis. He didn't have much to report lately on the extortion investigation, so at least he was sending something.

London

Asis opened the email from his nephew. As he read it his frustration grew, he needed information on the person or persons who cost him $100,000,000. He didn't give a damn about these Americans going on a cruise and living the good life. Maybe he should go on a cruise after he got away from London. He'd paid the money but would never feel safe again. He still needed to find the extortionist and have them killed. Maybe he'd just do it himself.

His flight was booked, and he was ready to be gone. He second-guessed himself on a daily basis but once the flight was booked it couldn't get here soon enough.

Lexington

Hazaq was now living in horse country. He always wondered what Asis would have said if he ever found out it was Hazaq who ordered the horse to be slaughtered for the attack on the Purdue Vet School. Asis thought they had found a random horse and set it all up. Asis didn't know they'd killed a perfectly good stud horse. Asis loved horses and racing. He regularly traveled to the Newmarket Racecourse as well as Ascot Racecourse. Both are easily accessible by rail. Horse racing is the second most attended sport in the United Kingdom after football. If he ever learned what Hazaq set up to happen he'd probably have him killed. For this reason, Hazaq was even prouder of his accomplishment.

He was finalizing his plan to get Chris Powell out in the open. He'd like to do it here in central Kentucky but knew he should not risk bringing the authorities to his new base of operations. His recruiting efforts were coming along slowly. He knew this area would be tougher than Chicago, it was not as diverse here, but he wasn't just focusing on this area. Hazaq knew better than to try and build a copycat version of what he had in Chicago. That would be what they were searching for, making him more vulnerable. He was now going to put himself into a situation like Asis where he didn't live with his own jihadist army. He'd have much less day to day worries like how to feed and house ten men.

He was going to build a network that would span the United States.

Hazaq was thankful he'd learned some old school techniques from Asis. All the current technology was great but left him susceptible to discovery. The government had people who were cell tower experts and spent all their time tracking people through cell phone calls. It was down to a science. Granted this all worked best when you were communicating with someone on your side, not an adversary like Powell. Two of his recruits were hackers. They probably had no real zest for the jihad but had a great desire to cause problems for the government.

Bethesda

Chris had been gone for a few days and she was missing him. Having missed most of the semester she'd immersed herself into three online courses to get some spring credits. She nearly missed the call but got it on the fourth ring.

"Hello."

After a pause, Bisma said a little louder, "Hello."

"Yes, is this Miss Bisma?"

"Yes, it is."

"Bisma this is Nafeesa el-Tariq."

"Hello Mrs. el-Tariq, how are you?"

"I don't have long to talk, can you meet me?"

"Mrs. el-Tariq I'm back in the States."

"I cannot do this by phone. I have important information you should know."

"Okay, I need a few hours to make arrangements. Can I call you when I know my arrangements?

"No, I'll call you when I can."

"Are you in danger?"

"Just hurry."

"Okay, take care."

"You too."

She immediately called Mr. Keane.

"Keane."

"Mr. Keane I just had a call from Mrs. Nafeesa el-Tariq. She asked to meet in person to give me important information. I told her I was in the States and asked to tell me by phone but she refused, she'll only talk in person.

"Then you have to go. You felt this was the most promising lead from your time in London. Get packed and I'll send a driver, I'll text your itinerary," he clicked off.

She was powering her laptop down and heading for the door. The text came before she'd made the eleven-minute walk to her apartment. She was packed and watching for the driver as he pulled up.

"Hello Bisma," he said.

"Hello, Clint. Do you need my information?"

"I already heard from Mr. Keane, I'm good."

"He's amazing."

Thirty-five minutes later they pulled up to a private hangar at a private airport.

"If this place could talk," she said.

Clint smiled, "If it could talk we'd have to kill it. Good luck and safe travels."

"Thanks, Clint."

She grabbed her bag and was up the steps with the door pulled shut behind her.

"Make yourself comfortable the co-pilot said, there's food and drink in that small fridge."

She noticed he did not wear a name badge, this was now 'need to know' time. She was clicking her seat belt when the engines were spooling up. They were wheels up in less than three minutes. She reclined and closed her eyes.

London

The next morning Nafeesa waited for an hour after her husband had left for the day. She dialed Bisma's number and let it ring.

"Bisma," she answered.

"This is Nafeesa."

This has moved to a first name relationship Bisma thought to herself. That has to be good.

"I'm in London."

"That's good, I need to see you right away."

"Where we met before?" Bisma asked.

"No, I'll be in the park two blocks from my house. I'll be watching for you."

"I'll be there in thirty minutes," Bisma said.

"Watching for who?" he asked.

Nafeesa nearly jumped out of her shoes as she quickly turned. "Uh, a friend," she stammered.

"Who?" her husband asked again as he grabbed her arm.

"I said a friend, you don't know her."

"A friend from the United States? What are you up to Nafeesa?"

She just stared at him.

"Nothing to say to me?" as he backhanded her across the face.

She raised her free arm to protect herself and tried to pull away. He pushed and she stumbled backward against their kitchen table. She looked up at him to see what was coming next, he just stood shaking his head.

"You're not going to see anyone."

"She's just a friend."

"If you want to live, you'll shut up and know your place."

"Are you going to kill me like you killed my oldest son?"

He just looked at her, "Get up. You are not leaving the house. If anyone comes to this house you will tell them you don't know what they're talking about. If you say anything Nafeesa I'll make sure you wish you hadn't."

Her eyes bored a hole in him as she got up and straightened herself up.

"Do you understand me?"

She gave a slight nod.

"Do you understand me?" he said louder as he moved toward her.

"Yes."

Bisma was in place ten minutes early. She sat to watch. Twenty minutes later there was no sign of Mrs. el-Tariq. Twenty minutes after that she was half an hour late and Bisma had a bad feeling. She'd been insistent on the phone they meet in person as soon as possible. Something was not right. Bisma knew Fiona was watching in a white van down the street. They had not wired Bisma for sound, so she sent Fiona a text to say she was worried. Fiona asked what she'd like to do. Bisma said she'd wait for fifteen more minutes and then walk towards the house.

‣Fifteen minutes later she stood and walked east. She passed the white van and strolled on, it was a quiet day in the neighborhood and except for one young man walking a dog she saw no one. She passed the house and stopped three houses down and crossed the street for a better sightline. She seemed to pay attention to a house for sale and took a few pictures of the street. There was a car parked in front of Nafeesa's house and she got a picture of the license tags on the front.

The car behind it was close enough that Fiona would not be able to see the tags on the back. Bisma stopped to send a text, '*I'm going to the coffee shop down the street. Here's the car in front.*' She included the picture. Fiona read the text, saved the photo and emailed it to her associate at the office. After a quick conversation with the two others in the van, she climbed out of the side door and headed for the coffee shop. Fiona saw Bisma sitting in a side booth and sat down. As the waiter brought Bisma coffee Fiona ordered a double espresso. Her phone buzzed and she read out loud. The car was registered to Mr. el-Tariq.

"Nothing illegal for a man to be in his own home," Fiona said.

"No, but I'll bet he wasn't home when she called this morning."

"How do you want to play it, she's your contact?"

"Let's watch the house today, you okay on resources?"

"Yes."

"I need to call my boss at Homeland Security."

"I've got two people in the van watching. Let's get back to my office."

Fiona called for a driver.

Chapter 30

London

Bisma got Moe Keane on the line and filled him in with every detail.

"I agree with you not to go to the door, she didn't make your meeting for a reason and that reason most likely has her in danger. I say we give her a couple days to make another contact and set another meeting."

"I've looked into her neighborhood to find there have been problems with gas lines they use for heating. I'm thinking we might approach the house in the uniform of the local gas company," Bisma said.

"It can't be you, you've met both of them."

"If we make sure her husband is gone, we can give her a phone to use. He may have her phone now."

"Okay, have one ready, but we have to assume he has her under every type of surveillance. It needs to be concealed."

"Understood. So, you're okay with me moving forward like this?"

"Yes, keep me posted. Is Fiona on board with this?" He was assuming they'd already discussed it since she'd been researching the local gas company.

"Yes, we've done this before."

"Good luck and keep me posted." He clicked off.

"He's okay with it, can we contact the utility company?"

"There's no need, we already have uniforms and one of their vans in the garage. It comes in handy," she said.

Bisma smiled and shook her head, "Impressive."

"Nothing you guys don't do in the States," Fiona said.

"I'm not sure."

Nafeesa was on lockdown in her own home. She'd figured out her husband had been monitoring her phone calls through their own account. She was upset she'd not considered as much but she hadn't. She didn't realize until now she was not trusted. She always knew she was a second-class citizen to her husband and Farid for that matter, but she never realized they didn't trust her. She had to assume her email account was possibly even less secure than the phone, so she was not sure how to proceed.

She'd overheard enough of a conversation one evening between her husband and his brother to know this was all worth the risk. If she did nothing to stop whatever plan was in the works, her other son would also be lost forever. Farid was all she had and she'd fight to save his life. She did her best to cower under her husband's harsh threats to make him think she was harmless. This had bought her some freedom in their home and she was keeping to herself with a multitude of thoughts swirling in her head. She slid her hand under the middle drawer of her dressing table to find the card from Miss Bisma. She studied the card deep in thought and then a smile came across her face.

The utility truck was parked down the street, its driver began knocking on doors. The agent came to the door, knocked and waited. He casually looked around for cameras and saw none. He knew full well they could easily still be there or listening devices. He recognized Nafeesa from her picture when she answered the door. He introduced himself and asked if she had noticed any power issues in the house, she said no.

"We've had some minor power issues in your neighborhood."

Nafeesa watched as he opened his work pad giving her a clear view of a picture of Bisma. He made a note and looked up to catch her eye. She gave a slight nod.

"Is there any information you can give me, or have you heard from any of your neighbors?" he asked.

"Please wait a minute." She turned and went into the house.

She made her way back to the bedroom, found her carefully hidden small journal and put it into her front pocket. She was also wondering if there were cameras or listening devices in the house? She knew she had to be monitored in different ways for her husband to know things he seemed to know. She walked back to the front door and gave the man her journal realizing she may be having to answer questions about this.

"These are some notes I've made over time about problems we've experienced, nothing major mind you."

"Thank you for your time."

"Thank you for checking on us."

He turned to leave as she closed the door, he made his way to a few more houses down the street before crossing and working his way back to make things look legitimate. He got back to the truck, got in and took off hoping this little book in his pocket would be a help.

Back at the office, he turned the book over to Fiona and they gave a quick watch of his bodycam video. It was easily apparent that she was nervous but still willing to help. They started reading the journal and realized how valuable this was going to be.

After twenty minutes of reading, Bisma excused herself to call Mr. Keane.

"Keane."

"Mr. Keane we've obtained a journal from Nafeesa that looks to be valuable intelligence. I'd like to come back for your help."

"I'll arrange travel as soon as possible. I'll text you details."

She went back to Fiona and told her what was said.

"I'd like copies of this," Fiona said.

"Of course. Thank you for making this possible."

"Let's hope it does both of us some good."

Copies were made and Bisma was getting her text from Mr. Keane. A driver was due in fifteen minutes and she'd be off to the airport.

"Tell Steve I say hello," Fiona said.

"Will do."

Bisma made her way to the front sitting area to watch for her ride. She'd have a few hours to read and think.

Washington

Chris was back in Washington after chasing leads in Kansas City that yielded nothing. He knew Keane had sent Bisma back to London. He didn't yet know she was coming back with a potential powder keg of intelligence. He was no closer to finding Hazaq than before he left.

It had gotten the better of Moe Keane. He called Fiona and had her send the journal contents by secure email. He was reading it and highlighting passages in yellow. This troubled mother had lost one son and was determined not to lose the other. There were a lot of holes in the information, she had evidently overheard pieces of conversations but had done a remarkable job of documenting what she'd heard. It was easy to see that if her husband had discovered this journal she would've been dealt with in the most extreme measures. It was easy to see how much it meant to her to hand it over to the man who came to her door after he let her see Bisma's picture.

The journal verified Nafeesa's son, Farid, was attending school in Ann Arbor, Michigan. Moe immediately began to assemble a team to begin surveillance on him.

Cirebon, West Java, Indonesia

The home was just as beautiful as he'd hoped and imagined. The security system was state of the art in every way along with some old-school tricks. Asis loved it. It took only a few days before he was thinking operationally again. Despite the huge loss from the extortion plot, Asis still had friends in the Middle East. There were two distinct groups involved, the money people and the operatives. The money people were still mad, the operatives appreciated what he'd accomplished and would still accomplish.

Word would get back to both groups quickly that he was not in the United Kingdom, this would upset the money group even more. The true jihadists would understand why he left. He made contact and within twelve hours he had everything he needed. They were intrigued by his request including the logistics and geography involved. They asked no questions, if this was good enough for Asis it was good enough for them. He would let them take credit for his plan as he always did.

He contacted his nephew to verify the details and by the end of the day, Farid had given him exactly what he needed to finalize the plan. He was now ready to rest up a couple days as he put the finishing touches on the attack. He needed to rest from his travel from London to Cirebon. What would have normally been a tiring 16-hour flight turned into a four-day excursion involving planes, trains, automobiles and one rusty old container ship carrying things no one could probably fathom. He had concocted the most convoluted travel plan to avoid surveillance.

Asis had felt the need to fly under the radar for a while and had done just that, but he was also enough of a narcissist to want another big attack to his credit. He'd been thinking about this plan for a long time and now he knew how to do it. This would bring terror to the entire world, not just in the United States.

Rockton

He was now well past annoyed, anger was building, and internal alarms were going off. He'd checked his foreign account more times than he should have, someone could be paying too close attention to his inquiries. A small amount of what was due him had come through as planned, but not nearly enough. If there were some kind of problem or hold up they should've told him. Being left in the dark was getting to him. He'd love to make a visit to this paymaster but had no idea who it or they were. Communication was sparse and included a sophisticated email server.

He had access to some amazing search engines in his line of work, he'd figure this out in a way that at least appeared legitimate.

Tess Acklin was at the time in the process that made her the most nervous. She knew the assassin would be coming for his money soon. She had thought for months on how she wanted to lead this person to her boss. It had to be subtle, the assassin would be painstakingly thorough in his search. She shuddered to think what he would do to Wes Maxwell, but whatever it was he deserved it for many other things in his life. The shudder also included what he might do to her.

The news she'd learned about Janet Knight vanishing from the area was just a plus as far as she was concerned. The timing was perfect to add another layer of suspicion to the assassin. It was not that much of a stretch to think Janet Knight might also have his money. The last thing Tess considered was hiring someone to kill the assassin. She'd found a former client of Wes Maxwell who was a real low life. Maxwell had gotten him acquitted on a murder for hire charge, she was sure he'd return the favor. She knew if she sent this man to kill the assassin, the assassin would stop him, question and torture him and learn quickly he'd been sent by Wes Maxwell. This would further ensure Mr. Maxwell would not fare well in the coming days. After a lot of thought, she decided against this plan for now but kept it on the back burner.

Chapter 31

Washington

Bisma and Chris were as excited as two young kids. Moe Keane had basically been a surrogate father to both of them, especially Bisma since her rescue in Indianapolis. Her path to him was one she could have never imagined but his mentoring and care, while she pulled through her near-death injuries, turned him into a father figure. Chris and Moe had more of a mutual respect kind of relationship. Moe had recruited him and had great respect for what Chris had been willing to do for his country. They'd spent little time together up until the last few months. Chris knew this man had given his life to protect this country. He was a tough old bastard and the kind of man you want protecting your family.

They saw him come through the door, tie pulled loose and sleeves rolled up two turns showing forearms that looked like how dairy farmers used to look. He was in his late sixties and Chris would not challenge him to arm wrestle or any other type of wrestling for that matter and Chris was an accomplished college wrestler himself. He crossed the restaurant and settled into the other side of the booth with a smile, "Good evening you two."

"Hello Mr. Keane," Bisma said.

"I'm Moe tonight or you're buying."

"Sounds good, but this is our treat," Chris said.

"It's a treat to just get away from the office for a while but especially with my two favorite agents."

"So shall we discuss our next operation to save mankind?" Bisma asked.

"No way!" Moe said.

"Thank goodness," she said.

"Let's all get a cold beer and order dinner," Chris said.

Two other heads were shaking yes and they waved the waitress over. They made quick work of ordering a beer and studied the menus as she brought three frosty mugs. They each ordered and Moe proposed a toast.

"Here's to people who've seen bad things and can truly appreciate the good times."

Glasses clinked and they each enjoyed a long drink.

"We're really looking forward to enjoying this meal together. We're also wanting to share something with you."

Moe smiled and Chris thought he actually saw a twinkle in his eye.

Chris looked at Bisma, she said, "Go ahead."

"We're going to get married. We've not set a date but want you and Mrs. Keane to be a part."

"And I want you to walk me down the aisle!" Bisma said.

Moe sat for a few seconds smiling. He held his hands in front of him with palms facing inward, "First of all, Congratulations and second, I'd be honored to walk you down the aisle, honored."

"Thank you so much, Moe," Chris said.

Talk then revolved around future plans until the food came to the table. They all ate and just enjoyed the fellowship of the evening. Moe ordered ice cream sundaes for everyone, turns out he was a big ice cream sundae man. Chris ate his entire meal like he'd never had food before, including the ice cream with hot fudge.

"Can I get you another one?" Moe asked as he watched in amusement.

"No sir, I'm stuffed!"

They all sat and talked a little longer with Moe calling for the check. The waitress came over and said it has all been taken care of. Chris smiled as Moe looked over.

"I knew there was no way to do this except do it ahead of time. You always seem to have things taken care of ahead of time, looks like I learned from the best."

Moe gave him a faux tip of the hat and he stood to leave. Bisma and Chris followed as they headed for the door. There was little traffic on this side street at this time of night. No one had noticed the backpack that had been left at the front door minutes before. Moe held the door and Bisma and Chris stepped out on the street. Before he let go of the door the deafening explosion happened. Chris was knocked forward into Bisma and both hit the street with Chris on top of her.

Two men in the car a half block away pulled out onto the street and slowly headed west, the driver was watching from his side mirror as his passenger watched over his left shoulder.

"Allah Akbar," was repeated by both men as they gained speed to leave the area.

Chris did not lose consciousness, but it might have been better if he had. He was regaining his senses as he realized he was pinning Bisma to the sidewalk. He raised himself up and tried to speak. His ears were ringing so much he could hardly hear himself.

Bisma turned her head to look up at him mouthing the words, "I'm okay, are you okay?"

He blinked his eyes a few times to clear the dust and was nodding at her. She saw blood coming down the right side of his face. Chris rolled to her right and reached for her shoulder. She winced as he touched her and he moved his hand to her back. He was getting himself up and knew he had to be looking for other threats. He quickly scanned the street in both directions and saw no one. He helped Bisma to her feet and saw an odd shape close to her shoulder, she possibly had a broken clavicle from him falling on her. Again, she winced as he helped her get her arm into a sling-like position so she could hold it against herself.

"Where's Moe?" she asked.

Chris turned back to the restaurant to see a hole where the front door had been. The air was still filled with dust and they could not see into the restaurant. They knew immediately Moe had to have taken the brunt of the blast and Chris began pushing back debris. There was a small fire burning on what was left of the door frame. He saw what was left of a body and knew there was no way he could have survived the blast.

Chris reached into his coat pocket to find his cell phone still working and showed a signal. He dialed 911 and told them there had been an explosion and gave the restaurant address. He asked them to send an ambulance and please hurry. Bisma was fighting back tears as this was all sinking in. Chris reached down and realized he was touching Moe's right arm because he was seeing his watch. He gave a tug to confirm his arm was not attached to his body. He removed his watch and slipped it into his pocket which seemed odd and the right thing to do for some reason.

Emergency personnel and D.C. police were on the scene within five minutes. Chris made sure they were checking on Bisma first, he knew they could not help his boss. He began telling the story to two detectives as well as telling them Mr. Keane's position with the Department of Homeland Security. An attack of this type had to be considered terrorism but was never labeled as such without special investigation. The local FBI office was immediately notified to send a team to begin processing the scene for bomb residue and anything else they could find to determine the signature of the device. They needed to know if it just detonated at that exact moment on its own or was detonated by someone watching for the right moment.

EMTs quickly determined Bisma had a fractured clavicle, a tender wrist that did not appear broken but had been instinctively reaching out to lessen the impact of her fall and a lacerated knee that would need to be stitched up. She likely had cracked or bruised ribs as well. They could see she was holding her other arm tight against that side. They'd x-ray that area in the hospital. Chris seemed to survive the ordeal pretty well except for a few small wounds in his back and backside. This would more than likely be shrapnel from the bomb and would be dug out and used as evidence.

Local police now had the area cordoned off and secure from sidewalk traffic as locals were now gathering to see what happened. Two local news stations were pulling up and set up to broadcast. Chris did not feel like talking to them at this point. He especially didn't want Bisma's or his face on any local or national news feeds, he asked to climb on board the ambulance with Bisma. He stepped up into the back and the doors shut behind him. It was hard to leave Moe Keane behind like that, but it's exactly what Moe would have told him to do.

FBI agents carefully made their way into the rear of the restaurant to find employees in the kitchen uninjured but dazed. They moved into the main part of the restaurant which was mostly intact. They found a waitress laying in between a table and booth who had sustained a head injury from the impact after being blown towards the booth. She was conscious and had no idea what had happened.

Agents got contact information for the owner and had him on the phone. He was shaken to hear the news and would be at the scene as soon as he could get there. He confirmed there were no security cameras in the restaurant.

After a seven-minute ride to the hospital, Chris was by Bisma's side as she was brought into the emergency room. She knew Moe Keane was gone and could not imagine how she was going to deal with that, she was also extremely thankful Chris had not been killed as well. She held his hand tight and just closed her eyes.

The two cell members had made the drive back to their Baltimore house in an hour and a half. They'd taken extra time to drive the speed limit and made a stop at a fast food restaurant on the way back. It was good to be involved in something again. Their major coup had been the destruction of a government safe house last year using two drones with explosives. They had no idea this attack killed a man that had also been present at that house. Moe Keane had narrowly escaped that day by being in the basement doing an interrogation. They did know the communication and plans for this attack had come from another source, someone likely based in the States. All previous orders came from out of the country. It was good to know that jihad leadership had finally moved into this country.

Lexington

Hazaq was hoping to get confirmation of Chris's death. The email he received included three pictures that were poor at best. He could definitely make out Chris in one of the three. There were two other people with him, another man and a woman. The detail was not good as he studied the pictures and made them as large as possible to view on his laptop. He had no idea about the man, but the female looked vaguely familiar. There just wasn't enough detail but it was nagging at him enough to get an internal radar buzzing in his head.

He'd wondered before if the plans he'd been given while in Chicago for an attack had also been to target a specific individual. The attack at the Indiana State Fairgrounds had likely been to specifically kill Mike Baker and his Boiler Club friends. This attack was to kill Chris Powell and Hazaq was glad to be done with him. He was the biggest threat and should now be gone. He could move on to bigger plans. He also was wondering what he should do about taking credit for this attack. His London source had always let a group from Saudi Arabia take credit in their usual "put on masks and put it on the internet" fashion for the world to see.

He did not have these connections and was not that willing to give up the credit for this latest attack. This happened at the capital of the infidels and he'd made it happen.

Hazaq was up early and finished his morning prayers. After brewing his favorite coffee, his only western vice, he logged on and began his search. News out of Washington D.C. was giving details of an explosion at an area restaurant with one known casualty. This casualty was a top-level official at the Department of Homeland Security. He pushed back and stood to get his cup of coffee. Different scenarios were running in his head. Was his former cell member with the DHS? Did they kill the wrong person? He had to get confirmation of Chris's death, but as he searched he learned the name of the victim was not being released pending notification of the family.

Indianapolis

Nat Jackson was still getting used to seeing the name Chris Powell. Moe had spoken of him with great admiration while he was embedded with the Chicago cell. This had all come to light after the State Fair attack last year and Bisma was being brought in as a new agent after she was nearly killed by the same cell members. It was late but she clicked answer.

"Special Agent Jackson?"

"Hi Chris. What can I do for you?"

"I'm very sorry to tell you this, Moe Keane was killed this evening."

She was stunned and sat looking at her phone.

"Natalie?"

"Yes. What happened?"

Bisma and I were having dinner with him. As we were leaving there was an explosion at the front of the restaurant and he was killed instantly. Bisma was injured but will be fine."

"Someone wanted him dead. Or wanted all of you dead. There is no way it happened randomly."

"I've honestly not had time to think much of this through, but you are probably correct. It was a hit instead of a terrorist attack. A local FBI squad is on the scene."

Even though she was thinking it, she didn't want to say out loud this hit could have been meant for Chris from his former cell leader Hazaq. She knew Moe had Chris working on leads for Hazaq and he would have known they were looking for him. Moe had shared this with her and it was a worry for him. He'd been working his intelligence assets hard looking for Hazaq. She then settled on the idea it was undoubtedly meant for everyone there tonight even though no one from the former cell should know that Bisma was alive.

"Okay, Chris you take care of Bisma. I'll do anything to help from this end."

"Thank you, Nat."

She sat back in her chair and felt the emotions inside. Mostly she just wanted to feel rage for the animals that do things like this with no regard for human life. She thought that wasn't fair to animals, they wouldn't do something like this. People who do this are evil, nothing but evil. They didn't deserve to have their rights when they were caught. She wasn't supposed to think things like this, but she was. They deserved to be dealt with in the harshest way possible. They deserve to feel some terror like they are so good at making others feel. There would be little sleep coming her way tonight. She decided to call Mike Baker in the morning to let him know. Colleagues would be amazed if they knew how she kept Baker in the loop when appropriate, she felt he'd earned it. She also didn't want him to hear about the death of Moe Keane on the news or internet. Mike knew and had worked closely with Keane in Indianapolis, there was mutual respect between the two of them.

Mike was of course extremely sad to hear the news.

"They never stop, do they?" he asked Nat.

"No, they don't Mike."

"I guess I knew little about him personally, but I sure respected him professionally."

Nat agreed, "Me too."

"Thank you for letting me know. Would it be okay if I let my friends know?"

"Sure, she respected the Boiler Club. Let them know."

"Thank you again, you take care, Nat."

"You too, Mike."

She had not told Mike anything about Chris and Bisma being with him at the attack.

Washington

The next week was one of the toughest Chris had ever experienced. He was not prepared for the mental toll the loss of Moe Keane was having on him. It seemed to bring everything to a heightened sense of urgency, he wanted to bring the responsible person or persons to justice. He was also worried for Bisma, she was doing okay but very sore and dealing with the pain of her injuries. She too was taking the loss hard. He had somewhat stepped into a paternal role for both of them. Bisma asking him to walk her down the aisle made that clear. Chris was also dealing with a crushing sense of "how can we beat them?" He wouldn't stop trying but wondered if it were possible.

DHS leadership agreed to let Chris and Bisma take the lead in setting the course of action to pursue the London terrorist until Keane's successor was in place. Fiona's people were already watching the business and apartment and had not seen him once. They were also keeping tabs on his brother's house and business along with watching Nafeesa. It seemed she was hardly leaving the house. They were also interested in seeing what Nafeesa's son, Farid, was doing in Ann Arbor, Michigan.

They put together a three-person team out of Indianapolis to befriend, surveil and bug Farid's apartment in Ann Arbor. The nephew of a London terrorist who was at the top of the most wanted list gave them enough probable cause to get the necessary Federal warrants. Local FBI agents started the surveillance before the DHS team arrived. Living arrangements were booked and the team was operational the next morning.

Chapter 32

Italy

The fee that came with the report made her blink her eyes a couple times. It was three times what she imagined, but she would have paid even more to get this information. This was impressive, to say the least. Asis had gone to great lengths to cover his travel tracks. Her people had gotten lucky on finding him after a four-day journey including 16 hours aboard an old container shipping vessel in the Indian Ocean. She even had pictures of his new home which was a fortress in disguise. Her people had contacts who had worked on hardening the property. His assumption that people didn't talk in this part of the world was wrong, just like in every other part of the world when money was involved. Janet's people were now down the road as neighbors of Asis and keeping close tabs.

Indianapolis

The call came from a man Natalie had only heard about from Moe Keane. This man was second in command at DHS and someone Moe respected. This was the highest-ranking person in the agency who was not political. This man had his roots deep in the military along with national intelligence.

"Special-Agent Jackson, this is Jake McBee."

"Hello, Under Secretary McBee, my condolences for the loss of Moe Keane."

"Thank you, I guess you know who I am."

"Moe Keane spoke very highly of you."

"And he spoke very highly of you."

"Thank you sir. How may I help you?"

"I want to sit down and talk in person, but I'm going to get right to it. Moe Keane and I talked several times about you. He told me he wanted you to come work for the DHS as his next in charge. We both agreed on this and were preparing to make you a formal offer. With the loss of Moe, I want you to take over as the Director of Counter-Terrorism. I know for a fact this is exactly what he would want as well. I know this is a lot to take in. I'm not asking for an answer, I'm asking you to come to Washington to talk further."

A few seconds passed, "You there Jackson?"

"Yes sir. How soon do you want me there?"

"I'll have a plane ready for you within two hours of you letting me know." He gave her a callback number. "Any questions for now?"

"No sir."

"I'll await your call." He was gone as quickly as Moe always ended a call.

Nat physically looked down and shook her head. She thought back to a quick conversation she and Moe had about a year ago. He'd mentioned her working in Washington someday. She'd not dismissed it but had not dwelled on it either. She owed it to Moe Keane to listen.

Greenville

With the exception of mosquitos and chiggers, Mike couldn't find anything wrong with fishing. He wasn't much of a fisherman, but he was good at feeding the fish. The fish needed to eat and when he did pull in the occasional bite, he'd then let it go. He went fishing with a childhood buddy when they were kids. Fishing was only part of the outings. This gave them a chance to sneak out and smoke a cigar. They'd talk about girls and things they knew nothing about at that age. They also had one evening they sat in the tall grass and by late that night they'd both learned what a chigger was and how this little bastard could cause so much agony. That was summertime and they were both wearing jeans that had been cut off a few weeks before when school let out. Sitting in shorts in tall grass on the bank while fishing was a huge mistake. Why chiggers like to bury themselves in your privates was a mystery, how to get relief from this occurrence seemed to be a bigger mystery.

Mike remembered that once was enough to learn the hard way on this one. After that, a camping stool or five-gallon bucket was in the back of the truck to sit on. It probably happened another time or two over the years, but the cigars and good fellowship made up for it. Years later he still went fishing with this buddy who had also gotten him into FarmHouse Fraternity at Purdue. They still laughed about the chiggers. Their conversation now focused on their kids, the economy and farming.

Today he was by himself enjoying a beautiful Indiana morning. He was a bobber fisherman. He'd put a worm on a hook and toss it out there to sit. After the initial splash, the water would settle down with the bobber sitting perfectly still. When a bite finally happened the bobber would go down and the ripples would start. This was the cat and mouse part. If you pulled too soon the fish was gone. If you waited too long he'd get your worm. Mike was fine with that for a time or two then he wanted to catch that little fish. He didn't mind just as long as there were at least some bites, that was fun. His thoughts drifted to his kids. He'd taken them fishing a few times when they were little. He now wondered why they hadn't gone more times.

His thoughts then went to Moe Keane. They could call it a terrorist attack, but it was cold-blooded murder. You could be sure he was targeted, had to be. This was a murder covered up by a terrorist attack.

Washington

Nat landed in Washington and was taken directly to her hotel. She welcomed the idea of having a restful evening to think about her meeting tomorrow morning with Under Secretary McBee.

She continued adding to notes she had started immediately after getting the initial call from McBee. She realized that even though she had gotten to know Moe Keane fairly well on an operational basis, she knew little of what his job entailed inside the DHS hierarchy. She knew the FBI channels and how things had to follow those channels almost perfectly. Anyone with her background had to bump against the sides of those channels from time to time. No policy could be written to perfection. People who wrote those policies would disagree. She looked at those policies as potential for painting yourself right into a corner many times.

She'd gotten herself into difficulty more than once trying to get out of that corner. She assumed the DHS also liked to paint you into corners. Her optimistic side made her hope this relatively new agency left their people with more freedom to fight their enemies. She planned to ask.

She awoke early with a better night's sleep than she imagined. After a nice hot shower, she had a good breakfast with two cups of coffee. She finished fifteen minutes before her ride was due and went to the front desk to check out.

"Good morning, Ms. Jackson. You are booked for one more night."

She smiled, "Well okay then, this trip happened in a hurry."

"I hope everything is okay," the woman behind the desk said with some concern.

"It's fine, thank you."

Nat grabbed her backpack and made her way to the door. It was no time at all before the standard government black SUV pulled up. The driver got out and came around the back. He caught her eye, "Special Agent Jackson?"

"Yes."

He opened the door and she got in. He was down to business as they made the twenty-minute trip to the DHS. She was familiar with the entrance at the rear. This was the entrance they'd used for Janet Knight when Nat had first come to Moe Keane's office. She thought back to those days and wondered how Steve was doing. She'd not had contact with him for a few months now. He'd shown interest in her almost to the point of making her uncomfortable. While being a little flattered, she had not reciprocated and hoped he had moved on. If they had spent time in London together as planned the situation might have turned out differently.

"This way, Special Agent Jackson," the driver said.

She'd been lost in her thoughts, now she needed to get focused. "Thank you," she looked at his badge. "Clint."

He smiled and pointed the way. She got on the elevator and noticed they were going up one floor higher than Moe's office which seemed appropriate. She stepped out and immediately saw the man she was there to see. He was coming her way and the first thing she noticed were highly polished cowboy boots. He extended his hand and she put her hand into a big paw that had more than enough grip. She was relieved she got her hand back thinking he could have yanked her arm off. His suit was cut to accommodate whatever sidearm was holstered underneath. His easy smile fit perfectly with a southern accent that could melt butter.

"Jake McBee, please call me Jake."

"Natalie Jackson and I'm fine with Nat."

"Nat, this way."

They made their way down the hall and turned into his office. He motioned her to a leather wingback chair and asked, "Anything to drink?"

"No sir."

"You mean, Jake?"

"Yes sir, Jake."

He stuck his head out the door and asked his assistant for two glasses of ice water. He came back in and took the chair across from her with a small coffee table between them.

"Were your travel and accommodations satisfactory?"

"Yes, sir."

His assistant brought in two glasses of ice water and set them down between them. "Thank you, Sylvia, would you please close the door?"

She smiled as Nat mouthed "thank you" to her and turned to leave.

"Sylvia's been with me for thirteen years. She's a wonderful mother and the wife of a Marine who's on his third deployment."

"So many people sacrifice for this country. Many times we forget the sacrifices of the spouses and families left behind."

"Very true," Jake nodded.

"And I want to offer my sincere condolences to everyone here on the loss of Moe Keane. In the short time we worked and spent time together he had my highest respect."

"He was killed by the very people he was protecting us from. He will be greatly missed. As I told you on the phone you are here because Moe had the highest respect for you. He wanted you to come work with him. He would be pleased you are here."

Nat nodded as she looked at Jake McBee, "I've made some notes, do you mind if I get my yellow pad?" she asked.

"Not at all, I'm doing the same. I use technology as everyone does but still need pen and paper close by at all times," he reached for his pad on the coffee table. "I invited you, so I'll start, and you're welcome to ask anything."

The next seventy-five minutes were filled with a lot of infor-mation. Nat appreciated his frank nature, he didn't mince words and was a man she could respect. He was not afraid to say the things that frustrated him about our government and about the world. He mixed the right amount of optimism and realism for her taste as well. She felt anyone who leaned excessively to either side did not fit with the way she saw our world. He was about having the DHS do their best to keep the American people safe but also taking a few punches during the fight if necessary. She liked his pace of speech as well as his southern accent. His thoughts were measured and grounded in what she saw as good common sense. Even though she'd planned to ask for a couple of days to think it all over, her mind was made up.

"Nat I'd like to show you around, even though I know you've spent time here in the past when we brought in Janet Knight from St. Louis."

"I'd like the tour."

They walked and talked as Jake introduced her to people he'd picked out. He was cognizant she might feel a little overwhelmed so he kept that in mind. He liked the way she met people easily but was guarded as well. That's not a bad thing he thought, he'd seen the type who wanted to be your best friend after a big hand-shake, he always wanted to rein in that type. Not a problem with Nat Jackson.

"Shall we stop by your office?"

She smiled up at him as he cocked his head to the side. "We've packed up Moe's personal items after having his family here for some private time with me and two close staff members they all knew. It was extremely emotional for Mrs. Keane, but she thanked us for getting to have that part of closure."

They made their way through the outer office and spoke to Jenna, Moe Keane's assistant. Nat felt a wave of emotion as they entered and walked around. The emotion was deep sorrow mixed with the raw anger you kept packed away to only show when you're alone. Jake could see there were things on her mind and chose to stay quiet as she looked around. They closed the door quietly behind them and walked down to the elevator. He rode to the lobby with her and extended his hand.

"You probably know I've got you booked for another night."

"I do. What's the plan for tomorrow?"

"I'd like you to come back with any questions you have for me. I'd also like you to look at the file we have on the attack that killed Moe. Lastly, I've got a couple more people who'd like to talk to you."

"Okay," she said.

"Your driver will take you back to the hotel or anywhere else you'd like to go. Have a good evening and I'll see you tomorrow. Dinner is on me at the hotel, if you'd prefer to go somewhere else just bring me your receipt tomorrow."

"Thank you, Jake. See you tomorrow."

He smiled and was on his way, cowboy boots shining.

It was a beautiful day and she asked to be dropped several blocks from the hotel. She wanted the time to walk and think.

The next morning was a carbon copy of the first. Jake led Nat to a sitting room where she could look at Moe Keane's file. "Buzz me on this when you're finished, as he pointed to line one on the desk phone. You remember where you can get coffee and snacks?"

"Down the hall and to the right."

"I'll leave you to it," as he closed the door.

She sat down and opened the file. She started with the autopsy, she shouldn't have. She'd seen a lot, but it was too much to see pictures of the scene and what they found. She pushed it aside and got up. She left the office and walked to the restroom. She stood and looked at herself in the mirror for several minutes when someone else came in. She looked at her in the mirror and smiled.

"You okay?" the other woman asked.

"Yes, thank you, I'm fine."

Nat washed her hands and dried them, willing herself the strength to push forward. She decided a cup of coffee sounded good and headed that way. She returned to the room and began reading the police and FBI reports from the scene. Ninety minutes later she was through the entire file. She'd made notes along the way as she recalled details from the safe house attack that nearly killed Moe months before. They'd never found whoever was behind that attack. She pushed the button to buzz Jake McBee, she was ready to talk.

She didn't even hear the door open, but Sylvia was saying, "Come with me."

Nat followed her to Jake's office. He rose to meet her and she handed him the file as she smiled at the two others in the room.

"Meet your team," Jake said.

Bisma gave her a hug as Chris was extending his hand which turned into a hug. Jake looked at his watch. "I've set up lunch for the three of you downstairs. You've got some talking to do."

They rode the elevator with nothing more than small talk. Nat was glad to see these two together. She was only imagining what their reunion must have been like. Bisma thought Chris was a homegrown terrorist and Chris thought she was dead at the hands of his Chicago cell members. They were served a salad followed by garlic bread and spaghetti served family style.

Nat knew from the report that Chris and Bisma were with Moe the night of the attack, she didn't know what they had discussed. She knew Bisma had been sent to Great Britain with Steve Bradshaw to search for any leads on the London connection. She had not talked to Moe since Bisma returned but was hoping they gained information.

"You've read the report, you know we were with Moe the night of the attack," Chris said.

"Yes, I don't have the words to express how sorry I am. I'm so glad that neither of you was severely injured. How are you feeling?"

Bisma said, "I'm fine, Chris saved me from worse."

"I'm fine too, few bruises and some burns but nothing more. They checked me for a concussion but my hard head saved me."

Nat smiled, "Hard heads are good for something." As she raised her glass of water in a toast.

"We want you to know we were meeting with Moe that night to talk about something besides business."

"Okay," Nat said.

"We were there to tell him we are getting married," Bisma smiled as she said it.

Nat's eyebrows raised, and she broke into a big smile, "That's wonderful."

"He, of course, was happy for us," Chris said. "We're not convinced he didn't know before we did. You know, he was Moe."

Nat shook her head.

"We want you to come here and take his job. We want to work as a team to fight for our country and we have a few scores to settle, each one of us," Chris said.

Again, Nat shook her head and then reached for her fork. The rest of the meal was small talk and wedding discussion. Bisma did tell Nat she had asked Moe to walk her down the aisle and this put a knot in her stomach as she reached out to give her hand a squeeze. Bisma had tears in her eyes. Nat knew she was deeply affected by this senseless act of violence. After lunch, they made their way to the seventh floor and they all shook hands. Chris and Bisma said goodbye and were on their way. Sylvia escorted Nat into Jake's office.

"How was your lunch?" he asked.

"Very good and enlightening."

"Do you have any questions for me?" Jake asked.

"When can I start?"

He smiled and started looking at his phone, "Let's make some calls."

Chapter 33

Indianapolis

Talk around the FBI office was running hot. After about ten days of 'water cooler' talk the word came down that Special Agent Nat Jackson was leaving the Bureau and going to Washington to work for the Department of Homeland Security. Tim Dailey was glad to see her go. He had always looked at her as a threat. It seemed every time he was about to get a career break she was there to scoop up the ball in front of him and make the highlight throw to first. She also had a knack of being able to read people like no one he'd ever known, he didn't want her looking at him too closely. Good riddance.

Nat was getting used to the idea of leaving Indiana along with her sister and two children who were her only family. Her sister was taking it harder than she was letting Nat see. She spent most of a day with her sister, her niece and her little nephew.

"I'll be back to visit soon," she told them.

She wished she believed what she was saying. There was a lot of work to do. In an interesting twist of fate, she learned from Jake McBee that Chris and Bisma had asked to make their home in central Indiana. This is where they had met and this is where they wanted to make their home. With a little reservation, Jake had gone along with their request to be based out of Indianapolis.

The city had a nice airport and they'd be out of the scrutiny of Washington. This might come in handy down the line. Nat decided she could combine trips occasionally to see her agents as well as her family.

There was not a lot of packing to do in her office, and she had a good last day talking to fellow agents she'd known for years. The Indianapolis office had always seemed like family to her and for the most part ego got checked at the door. They had their riffs as all offices do and she'd dealt with plenty of testosterone along the way.

Her thoughts also went to the Boiler Club. She had a special bond with Mike Baker and his daughter, Sarah. She'd not gotten to know Mike's son David very well, he was now deployed overseas with the Marines. She'd miss seeing Mike but promised herself to stay in touch. She had called to tell him about her career change. He was excited for her and wanted her to do Moe Keane proud. She'd promised to do that.

As she was buttoning up her email she saw an interesting one from the St. Louis office. They sent it as a courtesy to the Indianapolis office. It seemed that Janet Knight had retired from her investment firm and had left the area. No law had been broken, she was never under arrest or indictment, but it was strange indeed. One of those things she'd file away for another day.

Two doors down, Tim Dailey was reading the same email with great interest.

Ann Arbor

Surveillance on Farid had not yielded much at this time, just bits and pieces of seemingly unrelated things. He'd made inquiries about South Pacific cruises and inquiries about shipping methods from sea to land to air choices. Apparently, he was also a big fan of computer dating, he spent a lot of time looking at girls. He was going to his classes and from what they could tell was an excellent student.

Two of the surveillance team members had met him more than once at the student union. They were dressed as students and were young enough to pull it off, backpacks hanging from one shoulder. They found him to speak excellent English with a British accent they expected from his upbringing. He was well versed in the English Premier Soccer League which seemed to be a passion.

The team was now reporting directly to Chris and Bisma. One of the team members was wanting to open the door to discussing Farid's recruitment into a cell. Chris quickly said no to this one. They'd spook him for sure. This would take gaining an inroad into an activity where he was showing some kind of extremism. At this time he'd shown none of that on campus or online.

Greenville

Chris was always trying to connect the dots in any way possible. He was feeding everything he got to Nat and Steve Bradshaw. Chris was using a laptop and lots of intuition, Bradshaw was using the computer power of the National Security

Agency. Chris thought he and Bisma made such a good team it was a little scary. It seemed daytime business migrated into evening dinner table conversation.

One evening he said to Bisma, "We're going to have to learn how to turn it off."

She looked at him with the look that always melted him, heck any look she gave him melted him.

"I mean geez, we hardly talk about anything but terrorists."

"It's what we do," she said.

"Yeah, but we deserve a personal life."

"You're right, it seems I'm still learning how."

He nodded, she was right. Her life had been one crisis after another. She'd spent most of her time in survival mode, not chatting with friends about dating or who had the best pizza in town. She deserved to know what it felt like to relax once in a while. He hoped this home in Indiana would start that process for her.

The next day they received an email from Steve Bradshaw, he'd found a link from a few months earlier showing Farid had been watching the Facebook page of Pam Miller. She'd made a comment about a cruise. The only thing that piqued Steve's interest was the fact Farid had taken an interest in it.

Chris had talked to Mike Baker since they'd moved to Hampton County but had not met Brian and Pam Miller. He knew their names from info Nat had given him on the Boiler Club and from his days with the Chicago cell. He made a note to see if any of them might be planning a cruise.

Rockton

Kurtz's day job had taken most of his time and energy the last couple weeks. He came home this evening and grabbed his mail as he turned onto the long lane. He loved living here and enjoyed the peaceful setting. He flipped through mostly junk mail and then saw the picture on the front page of the Indianapolis paper. Special Agent Natalie Jackson of the Indianapolis FBI office was going to Washington as a big whig with Homeland Security. He looked closely at the picture to see Tim Dailey in the background. He tossed the paper aside and logged on to his home laptop. He saw an email and hoped it was the one he'd been watching for. He opened it to see a statement showing a series of transactions, the name was Wes Maxwell. He then opened another attachment showing a newsletter with a picture showing Maxwell standing with another man he knew. The caption identified the other man as Roger Knight. It seemed they'd both participated in a seminar for ag lenders several years ago. It looked like he was getting some help, and he wondered who it was coming from.

He did extensive searching the next few days at work. Wes Maxwell was no stranger to controversy with his law practice. In his personal life, he was as much a narcissist as Roger Knight had been. Nothing was too good for him and it seemed nothing was out of his financial reach. He was sure Maxwell would have moved the money meant for him out of the country, he'd have deniability, no proof to show what he'd done. He didn't plan to just walk up and ask him even though that might work. He had a place in mind where they could talk until he had all the information he needed to get his money back.

Greenville

Chris was focused on the task at hand. This was hunting down the London terrorist and bringing him to justice. He was not sure what bringing him to justice meant. He hoped to himself justice ended with violence. This London man they called Asis deserved to die, no question. He was now gone, and they had no idea where he went. He fully understood that Nat Jackson had to be focused on the big picture of Asis, but she also knew about Chris and Bisma's past with Hazaq and how important it was for Chris to get him out of the picture. It was not only the right thing to do, but Chris needed to do it to protect Bisma and himself. Chris knew this was a worry for Bisma, even though they hardly ever talked about it. They all knew that someone had planned the attack that killed Moe. Was the London person behind this or was it Hazaq? It could be neither but more than likely it was one of them and Chris felt in his gut it was Hazaq. His gut also told him that attack was meant for him. He hoped that Hazaq still thought Bisma was dead and would do his best to keep that information safe.

Nat had introduced Chris to Steve Bradshaw at the NSA. Bradshaw had developed a questionnaire he'd sent Chris concerning the Chicago cell and specifically Hazaq. Chris was amazed at what Bradshaw had put together. It asked questions as specific as what Hazaq watched on television, liked to eat, what he looked at online and importantly what he ordered online. Bradshaw used these nuances in his search engines to dial in on specific targets. Patterns were what he was searching for. Chris knew this was both an art and a science and it would take time.

The science part involved algorithms, Chris didn't have to understand it, but he wanted it to work as soon as possible.

Washington

Nat quickly settled into her new surroundings. She didn't skip a beat on getting to work. Jake had found her a more than suitable townhouse minutes away that would work until she found something permanent. The furnishings were nicer than she'd ever had before in her sparse Indianapolis home. She'd just never taken the time to decorate and truthfully had no idea where to start.

She kept in close contact with Chris and Bisma as well as Steve Bradshaw. As far as she was concerned this core team along with the supporting cast at DHS was going to be amazing to work with. Forensics teams from the FBI and DHS were coordinating efforts on the restaurant explosion that killed Moe Keane. Nat had asked them to compare any bomb residue evidence with everything they'd obtained from the explosion at the safe house in Virginia two years earlier. Moe had almost died in that explosion, he had been heading up the interrogation of a known terrorist, Alberto Mulina, at the time. That house had been attacked by two drones that had been retrofitted to look like large birds. They hadn't yet found what cell carried out that attack.

Lexington

Hazaq was continuing to check the internet daily for more details on the attack in Washington. At this point, he was convinced his team hadn't killed Chris Powell. It did appear they'd gotten a high-level DHS individual which made it all worthwhile, but if Powell were still alive, he couldn't rest.

He'd decided not to contact the Baltimore cell for a while. He couldn't risk being tied to this attack. His biggest problem now was quickly becoming finances. He had ample funding when he left Chicago, Asis had sent funds that he was able to protect in several different accounts. Money flow and transfers were always a weak spot in security, they could be tracked, eventually.

He knew little about Asis' source of funding but had learned it was from the Middle East which was no surprise to him. He had no idea if he could tap into this source himself, they might like someone living among the infidels in the United States. He was also wary about even trying to make an inroad, this could get back to Asis and give him a trail to find him. He was at a point he didn't want any further dealings with Asis. He was ready to lead, not take orders.

Hazaq gave Powell credit for keeping his name off the grid. He'd searched for him all kinds of different ways with no success. The night in Washington was pure luck. The team in Baltimore had gotten a tip when Chris Powell had made a reservation in his own name. He still didn't understand but it was a friend of a friend kind of thing that was once in a million. He'd get him, it was a matter of time, but he'd get him.

Cirebon

Asis had the final piece in place. The cargo plane would be made ready out of Noumea, New Caledonia. Could it be flown as a drone? The only crewmembers were a pilot and co-pilot.

They could be rendered unconscious and someone then flies it the rest of the way. No chance for a change of heart.

It was obvious Asis felt he was completely secure. He was taking no measures not to be followed. Shahed and his son had been following him for fifteen minutes before he arrived at the airfield. They watched as Asis entered the office they'd bugged two days earlier in the old hangar. Voices were muffled and then became clear. Greetings were brief, this was a business meeting.

"Are you clear on what I expect?" Asis asked.

"Yes I am, it will be as you say."

"Is all of the technology satisfactory?"

"The plane has been retrofitted as you instructed. All modifications worked as planned except for two braces in the cargo compartment that had to be cut to size. No stability was compromised, it's as strong as you wished. Nothing will move about in that compartment."

"Excellent."

"The cargo arrived and was off-loaded onto the two trucks. They are secure and far from any customs officers or bomb-sniffing dogs. They will not be moved until they pull up to the plane."

"We will be operating in a 48-hour window. I will get your final time and logistic info a few hours before mission launch," Asis said.

The older man nodded, "You've picked well. New Caledonia is a very keep-to-yourself type of place, and this airstrip is important to the island. All supplies come here with shipments arriving daily."

"Flight time should be nearly thirteen hours, do you agree?" Asis asked.

"I agree. I've calculated by hand and with my software to only be minutes different. As we've discussed weather could be an issue."

"That is part of the 48-hour window."

The old man shook his head.

"The first half is in the account you chose," Asis said.

Again, a shake of the head.

"You know how to reach me." Asis stood and extended his hand.

The old man shook his hand and gave a slight bow. Asis walked out the door, everything was in place. The old guard in Saudi Arabia would be sorry they ever doubted him. Asis didn't even turn his head to see the parked Toyota Highlander as he passed it, he was in his own world.

Shahed smiled at his son. "Looks like the old man will stay alive after all."

"He gave us all we need," the boy said.

Italy

Janet read Shahed's report and was more than pleased, her people had done well. This was more than she could've hoped to learn. She had Asis by the balls in every way possible. She'd set up her communications in a similar fashion as she'd used in the extortion plan including using the most current security available. She decided to work as long as it took to get this ready. She had no idea when the attack would happen, so time was critical to keep this information as fresh and valuable as she needed it to be. She was still weighing the option of whether to tell Natalie Jackson she didn't know the date of the attack or letting her think it was being withheld for additional leverage.

She'd already decided on most of the wording for her proposal. She, of course, had no idea how good the intelligence was going to be, she would parlay this into as much as possible. She'd decided not to give Jackson Asis's new location. She was keeping that to herself for now.

Chapter 34

Western Hampton County

Wes Maxwell thought it was a strange request but he agreed to meet a realtor friend who dealt in farm real estate. Something about a 1031 exchange that might benefit Wes. It would have him sell one of his farms at a high price and then buy many more acres of lower-priced land to rent out. Why not hear him out?

He arrived on time and headed down the long lane after seeing his friend's real estate sign in the side ditch. He was surprised there wasn't a vehicle by the tool shed but the door was pulled open a few feet. Wes got out of his Escalade and headed toward the door.

"Hey, Ross? You need a new sign..."

He never saw what hit him, the headache he'd wake up with would be the least of his worries tonight.

Kurtz loaded him into a body bag and put him into the back of his crew cab. He made the forty-minute drive and pulled up to the barn. He opened the doors and pulled his truck inside to find his friend, Steve, waiting to take over. Maxwell started to stir as Steve drug him out of the back, he pulled him out feet first and he let out a grunt as he hit the ground. He was never in danger of suffocation, but he didn't know that, as he came to his senses looking up at Steve through the clear plastic over his face. His face showed panic as he began to struggle. Steve let him struggle a bit before unzipping the bag.

"Water," Maxwell said as he sat up.

Steve knew the injection Kurtz had given him to stay sedated would make him thirsty. He threw him a bottle of water and Maxwell couldn't open it fast enough to down it. As soon as he was nearly done, he turned and wretched half of it back up. That ramped up his headache. He wiped his mouth with his sleeve and lowered his head. Kurtz had searched him for any type of weapon in the first barn and Steve didn't see him as a physical threat.

Maxwell was trying to process what was happening without much luck, he knew this was bad. Didn't take much to figure that out. He had no idea where he was or how he had gotten there in a body bag. His nature was to speak his mind and put anyone else in their place, but this time he decided to stay quiet.

"Get up and sit here," Steve pointed to a chair.

With a lot of effort, he did as he was told, as he rubbed his temples to the back of his head while he sat down.

"More water?" Steve asked.

He shook his head yes and took a small drink to wash out his mouth, spitting it on the dirt floor.

"Okay, Wes, let's get to it. If you're alive by morning is your choice and yours alone."

"I don't understand."

"You're startin' off on the wrong foot," Steve reached down and picked up a nail gun he'd left laying on the barn floor and pounded it down on top of Wes's right foot. He jumped and let out a scream at the same time. He immediately realized he was not hurt as he looked up to see this man slide a sheath of nails into the gun, now it was loaded. Steve reached down and shot one through the end of his expensive Italian loafers. Wes could feel it just barely between his first two toes.

"I got your attention?"

He got a spirited shake of the head.

"I know you have my money, Wes. I'm not sure if I should be impressed that you had the balls to do this or amazed at how stupid a smart attorney can be."

Wes was shaking his head from side to side.

"You think I'm going…"

"My assistant sent the money to your account."

"Bullshit, don't blame your assistant. I've seen where it went and it's in your account and by now it's out of the country I'm sure."

"I swear, I."

"Here's what's going to happen. You will have the entire $5,000,000 in my account within 48 hours plus an extra $250,000 for my trouble. Failure to do so will result in things worse than a nail gun."

"What if…"

"Shut the hell up! This isn't a negotiation. Find whatever way you need to get this done and get it done. Failure to do so will involve not just you Wes, but those close to you. Do you fully understand me?"

"Yes, but I don't see how I can do it."

"You'd better figure it out, I'll be watching my accounts. Do I even need to tell you not to go to the authorities?"

"No."

With that, he jammed a needle into the side of his neck. Five seconds later his head drooped. Kurtz walked into the barn to join his friend.

"Good job, buddy."

"Convincing?"

"Yep, he knows what he has to do. I'll get my money whether he's dead or alive. It'll be easier if he does it for me though."

"You want me to stay around a couple more days?"

"Yes, we'll see how he does. Might need more of your help."

They loaded him back into the body bag and into the truck. Kurtz would drive him back to his car. He left him on the floor of the first barn and unzipped the bag part way. Letting him wake up again in a body bag would surely soak in pretty deep. He checked two pulse points and watched his breathing for a minute. He'd feel like crap but he'd be fine.

Washington

Natalie got to her desk early, opened her email and began to scroll. Nothing out of the ordinary until she checked emails that had been quarantined in her spam file. At 11:30 PM last night she received an email she wanted to see. She opened it to find information concerning a probable terrorist attack. While having precious few particulars it gave her enough information to have serious credence with her.

Without a lot of thought, she forwarded the first part of the email to Steve as well as Chris and Bisma. She wanted all of them to see it and begin their thought process. Within fifteen minutes she heard back from all three. She asked if they would basically drop what they were doing and focus on this information and be prepared to talk at noon today.

She had removed the second half of the email before forwarding, it was extremely interesting. The second half was a proposal by the author, Janet Knight, to provide more information if Natalie would provide her with written guarantees she would be held harmless for everything in her past. This was problematic for Nat. First of all, she didn't see how she'd have that authority and secondly, she didn't want to make a deal with her.

At noon they all dialed into a secure line for a video call. Brainstorming had already started, and each person put similar ideas on the table. Early on Chris asked, "How reliable is your source?"

"I believe it to be very reliable. For reasons not pertinent to this discussion I'm not going to reveal the source. I feel we are on the correct path."

The discussion continued for another hour. At that point, it seemed they'd gotten as far as they could go. Natalie said, "Everyone keep going on your own, let's reconvene at 5:00 PM."

She clicked off and began thinking about Janet Knight. They were off to a good start connecting the dots. Janet had given them what seemed to be valuable intelligence. What Janet didn't know was that they'd also received good intelligence from Asis's nephew Farid. This new information from Janet was fitting nicely with info from Farid. She would not respond in any way to Janet until her team had assembled everything they'd now acquired. Steve Bradshaw was developing his algorithms and would turn his computer loose to follow these leads. Chris and Bisma were looking into angles they understood from their first-hand experience with terrorists and attack planning. Yes, she'd let the team work.

Five o'clock arrived and everyone was back on board. Updates were given, and the progress was impressive. They were basically down to two main thoughts and those were not too far apart, thus making everyone feel they were on the right track. They had narrowed their geographic search down to a particular area and assignments were given. All agreed to keep each other apprised with any news until they reconvened again as need be. Natalie thanked them and they all logged off.

Indianapolis

Wes Maxwell awoke to the worst headache of his life. He'd had some rough nights before, but nothing like this. He lay there a couple of minutes without moving and started to go through the night's events in his head. He was wishing this was all a bad dream, but he knew it was real. He needed to find out what happened to the $5 million dollars sent to Kurtz. As he tried to sit up he realized he was back in the body bag which immediately gave him the creeps. He unzipped it and rolled out. He worked to get himself standing and made his way out of the barn and over to his car. His keys and phone were right where he left them, he closed the door and started the engine.

As he drove south to Indianapolis he called his office's answering service and left a message saying he'd be in sometime mid-morning. His first thought was that Tess would have some explaining to do.

He knew how dangerous this person was and for that reason, he had no choice but to get the money. As bad as he'd like to go to the FBI, how could he? Even if he wanted to do it, he'd be implicating himself in a murder conspiracy. He had considerable assets in offshore accounts he'd accumulated in various ways over the years. This would put a pretty good dent in it, but what choice did he have? None.

When he knew Tess would be in the office he called her direct line.

"Good morning Mr. Maxwell."

"Be in my office at 10:00 AM with all paperwork from the transfer that happened recently. "

"I'm not sure which..."

"You know the one, the big one."

"Is there a problem?"

"Just be in my office at 10:00 AM," and he was gone.

This was the day she'd been expecting. She was ready to get on with it. She was sitting in his office when he walked in at 10:07 AM. He looked like hell, she inwardly smiled to herself. Whatever he'd been through had set him back on his heels and no one deserved it more. She knew it would be best if she just kept quiet and answered what he asked, so that was her plan.

"Show me the documentation on the transfer."

She opened the file on her lap and laid out three pieces of paper in front of him, remaining quiet. He took nearly five minutes studying each page line by line. Without looking up he said, "I see nothing wrong here."

She still remained quiet which began to annoy him. He looked up at her and stared for several long seconds looking into her eyes and watching her face. He saw nothing to make him think there was anything wrong. She knew this was the real test happening right now.

"Okay, I'm getting worried, is there a problem?"

"Yes there is, the funds did not get into his account."

"I did everything as I've always done it."

"It does look that way. I'm not sure what's wrong, but we've got a big problem."

Tess certainly picked up on the word we and just nodded her head slightly giving him the most concerned look she could muster.

"I want you to retrace every step along the way to see what happened. Don't plan to leave here today until we get to the bottom of this."

Just as she rose to leave she turned back to him saying, "Mr. Maxwell I'm sorry I have always been meticulous in handling your affairs."

"I know you have Tess, just see if you can help me out."

When he was alone he decided it was time to make a call to the person he never truly wanted to call. Roger Knight had given him the name of the man who could be extremely helpful in situations like this. He'd told Wes he could be trusted, but he was not someone to upset. Wes was having a hard time with it because this man was an FBI agent.

In the next hour, he carefully scripted what he wanted to say to Tim Dailey. He kept contacts like this on the most secure and encrypted flash drive technology available. The password was committed to memory. He unboxed a burner phone he kept for times like this and made the call.

Tim answered his personal cell phone even though he didn't know the number, "Dailey."

"Mr. Dailey, my name is Wes Maxwell. I was told you are a man who I should call if I needed help."

"Do I know you?"

"No, you don't know me, but we have a mutual friend, Roger Knight."

Tim paused, "Is your line secure?"

"Yes, this phone will only be used with you."

Tim knew no phone was fully secure. He didn't want to meet this man in person and didn't want a lot of phone conversation either. "Give me a quick idea of your problem."

He gave him a rundown that he'd lost a lot of money by problems with a wire transfer. "Do you want the particulars?"

"Give me the amount, phone and account numbers only."

Wes gave him what he asked and waited.

"I will give this a look and call you back. My number will be different when I call. Don't call me again before I call you."

Before Wes could reply the line went dead. People like this don't make small talk.

Greenville

Pam sent Mike a text asking how packing was going.

'I'm pretty much done I think. I'd made a list over the past few weeks and have fine-tuned the list. I did realize I had to buy more underwear. I know, TMI, but you asked', he wrote back.

'No problem, I bought Brian more too!'

That made Mike chuckle. *'Your kids still taking us to the air-port?'*

'Yep, we're all set. We'll be at your house at 6:30 AM.'

'Thank you, see you then.'

Mike couldn't wait, this was going to be an adventure.

Washington

Twelve hours had passed and still nothing. Wes was running out of time. He'd made inquiries to check balances in different overseas accounts and would be able to do this on his own if need be. He'd wait until the 36-hour mark before initiating with his own money. He was mostly sure Tess was innocent of any wrongdoing, but he hadn't asked her to help on any of his personal accounts. She knew enough already. At 10:45 PM his phone buzzed.

"Maxwell," he answered.

"Are you safe to talk?"

"Yes."

"I've spent more time on this than I should've. Everything I ran was a dead end. I cannot help you."

"Nothing?"

"You heard me, all dead ends. You need to destroy the phone you're using, get rid of this phone number and never call me again. Do you understand?"

"Yes, but Roger Knight said you would be a help."

"Knight, as you know, was murdered. Executed. People like the man you're dealing with won't give you a second chance. I'd suggest you pay him and close that chapter of your life." Without one more word, he was gone.

Well thanks, old buddy, Maxwell thought to himself. Seems his friend Roger hadn't given him any help at all. He had no other choice but to pay the assassin from his own funds. Transfers were all waiting on him to hit send. He finished a glass of bourbon and sat a couple more minutes, he pushed the enter key and it was done. There was no way he'd close this chapter, he'd keep digging to find who'd taken his money.

Washington

It had been forty-two hours since the last video conference and they couldn't wait any longer. She sent them all a group text to be ready to talk in six hours.

Chris and Bisma had been going non-stop. They would brainstorm and then work separately; bounce ideas off each other. They were making some big assumptions with the biggest being the target of the attack. This assumption led them to search a geographical area where the cargo plane could launch. If they were correct they'd be quickly running out of time to prevent the attack.

They all linked on at the set time and started giving reports. Nat was relieved to learn they were basically all on the same path, albeit from different angles but leading to mostly the same place. Already knowing the part of the world they were all focused on, Nat had made solid contacts with law enforcement and a military liaison in the area. Steve was working on satellite imagery and planning to vector the maximum coverage in the suspected area.

Chris and Bisma had been narrowing down shipping businesses using flight times to the area to create a circle of the highest probability of launch sites.

Twenty minutes into this meeting and they'd all given their thoughts. No fluff, no bullshit, just we need to act immediately.

"It's clear we all think our intelligence connects to the same point. If we're correct, time is critical to get assets in place to stop that plane. Steve, keep on the satellites and radar, I'll call you as soon as I've made my contacts. Everybody pray I can convince them to help."

Rockton

Kurtz waited until hour 46 to check his accounts. He smiled to himself seeing a total of $5,250,000 tax-free dollars. He immediately initiated the transaction to send $250,000 to his old Marine buddy who'd done a good night's work convincing Wes Maxwell this was life or death in the barn two nights ago. His buddy was now back home in Oregon and probably strolling into a craft brewery for his favorite IPA.

He assumed Maxwell would not give up on looking for the missing five million dollars. He couldn't blame him and didn't care as long as it didn't bring him anywhere near him. The bank teller in St. Louis was a loose-end over $5,000. Maxwell was for sure a much bigger loose end. Maybe Maxwell should go out like his old buddy Knight? A crossbow bolt would shake things up with Tyler Harper having a perfect alibi this time. He didn't care at this point, he had his money. Let Harper out, he didn't do it anyway.

Chapter 36

Tasman Sea, South Pacific

Mike couldn't get enough New Zealand. They had sailed through the Cook Strait and were going to dock at Aotea Quay. This put them between the Inter-Island Ferry Terminal and the train station serving Wellington. This gave them access to basically anywhere they wanted to go on the North Island. They'd be at Auckland day after tomorrow so there was no need to try and get that far north. This cruise was everything he'd hoped. Everyone was having a good time, the food was great, and he was sleeping better than he had in months.

They were standing at the rail on the port side this morning. Another beautiful day was on the way. Mike was looking to try and find a cloud in the sky. There was a layer on the horizon which had given some extra color this morning. He looked left to see Sarah standing with Pam. They were watching for dolphins or great white sharks or any type of marine life. To his right was a woman with a bikini top and stretch pants with heels. He figured she'd not been to bed last night, at least not to sleep.

"You guys see anything?"

"We might have just seen a great white."

"Wow, I'm going to stay on the boat."

"Good idea, Dad. Why don't you lean over the rail just a little more?"

"I would but I'm late for Goat Yoga."

Sarah chuckled at this since it came along with a mental picture. Mike turned to get one more cup of coffee. They were coming into port and getting ready to dock. He had offered to parallel park the ship with no acceptance. Those side thrusters would have made it a breeze. He got another cup and headed back down to his room. He pulled on socks and tennis shoes. He wanted to walk all around Wellington today. Everyone agreed to go their own direction today. He didn't plan to come back to the ship until late afternoon and then he'd go back into the city for dinner this evening.

Mike spent several hours at Te Papa, the National Museum. It was fascinating. He felt like he knew so much more about their culture. He had a great lunch and then took a twenty-minute ride to the Tussock Ridge Farm Tours. He got to see three working farms, and the countryside was amazing. Central Indiana farms couldn't be more different from this rolling pastureland that dropped off to the sea. A constant breeze was a cooling relief on this warm day. He imagined how it might feel during the cold winter months soon to come. He was not surprised to see all the sheep grazing in the countryside. The sheep must have outnumbered the beef herds ten to one. He saw no hog farms but several dairy herds along the way. There were no row crops in this area and he learned hardly any grain was fed to livestock, they were all grass fed.

They took the same road back to the port and he showed his ID to get back on the ship. He had time for a short nap before changing for dinner. Everyone arrived on time and they were all seated. Brian raised his glass, "A toast."

They all raised their glasses.

"Here's to a wonderful adventure with wonderful friends. Here's to New Zealand, a beautiful country with friendly people."

Glasses clinked all around their table and a New Zealand couple seated next to them joined in. Stories were shared about everyone's excursions for the day as dinner was served. It seemed everyone had a great day wandering around the city of Wellington and the surrounding countryside.

Tomorrow they would be at sea. They'd be cruising away from the two big islands out in the Tasman Sea. The New Zealand archipelago consisted of over six hundred small islands surrounding the two main islands. Mike had read stories of the backpacking possibilities on many of these smaller islands. They are practically all uninhabited and many are just a few square miles, less than a township back in his home county of Hampton. It's good to know there are still places on the planet where no one lives. They are unspoiled.

Brian, Pam, Sarah, and Mike all walked back to the ship. They convened on deck five for a nightcap. Brian ordered Scotch neat, Pam and Sarah got a Wellington brewed Yeastie Boys Porter and Mike ordered a Woodford Reserve neat with ice water. They sat mostly in silence as they watched the lights of Wellington.

"Dad, why do you put about half of straw full of water in your bourbon?" She'd seen him do this a few times on the trip.

332 · TERRY BARNETT

"A good buddy back in Greenville taught me it opens up the drink. Brings out the flavor."

"Does it work?" she asked.

"I don't know, I guess. It looks cool, right? Makes people ask me about it."

The waitress came by to learn no one wanted another.

"Lightweight," Brian said.

Mike scratched his nose with his middle finger.

"Dad!" Sarah said.

Brian and Mike both smiled. The girls got up to head down to their rooms.

"Rest well, Sweetie."

"See you in the morning, Dad, love you."

"Love you, too."

"I'll be there soon," Brian said.

"Don't stay out too late."

Brian raised his glass. The girls turned the corner and Brian waved to the waitress. She smiled and two minutes later delivered two more drinks.

"This bourbon and scotch traveled a long way and sure tastes good."

"Damn good," Brian said as he raised his glass. Mike clinked his glass against Brian's. They were good at just sitting together without filling every minute with conversation. They could just sit. Mike knew full well Brian liked to hear a story almost as much as he liked to tell one, but this time was just quiet.

After twenty minutes Brian reached over and hit Mike on the leg, "See you in the morning buddy."

"Night Bro."

Mike watched him round the corner. The waitress caught his eye, Mike shook his head no. He sat a few more minutes and then made his way upstairs for some fresh night air. He stood at the railing and listened to the gentle noise of waves brushing the side of the ship. He looked back at the deck chairs lined up and then saw blankets stacked back by the pool towels. He considered laying back in one of those chairs for the night. What the heck, maybe one of the crew would run him off in a few minutes. He moved a chair a little closer to the rail and sat down with a blanket over his legs and closed his eyes. He immediately thought of the woman this morning with the bikini top, stretch pants and heels.

He woke a half hour later and satisfied that he'd given it a try got up to head to his room. After about twenty steps he was working the stiffness out of his lower back and thinking how he would have felt if he'd spent the night here. As he passed the bar area he was pretty sure he saw Miss Stretch Pants chatting it up with anyone who'd listen or pretend to listen.

As it often happened, his thoughts turned to Sandy. He missed her so much. He could be surrounded by wonderful family and friends as he was and still feel lonely. She would have loved every second of this trip especially being with Sarah and Pam. She would have immersed herself in these experiences and surroundings. She would have bought several magnets from places like the Te Papa museum as souvenirs and would have accumulated a short stack of local newspapers by now. He fell asleep on his right side with his back against a pillow in the middle of the bed.

Sunrise came at 7:12 this time of year and Mike had been on deck since 6:20 drinking coffee. That coffee had washed down some scrambled eggs and bacon he'd brought out on deck with him. It was as peaceful as it could be with a light breeze out of the north. A few clouds on the horizon were making minute by minute color changes since the first light of dawn. This could either delight or thoroughly frustrate the avid photographer if they weren't ready to capture the perfect light they'd miss it in a heartbeat. That made it even more special. Mike always felt morning was the best time of the day, a time not to be missed. An entire day in front of you. Dusk was a close second, the day behind you and memories made. Boy, he was feeling philosophical this morning, a few decades of living and experiences made you that way sometimes.

"Want some company?"

He was smiling before he even turned to see Sarah walking up with coffee in one hand and a plate of scrambled eggs and bacon in the other. She did have a banana on her plate, just like her mother.

"Sure do. Have a seat," as he pulled out her chair.

"Pondering life on the high seas?"

"Yes I am. This is very spiritual to me out here on the South Pacific."

"I can see why. It's a good place to reflect. There's not much to divert your eyes, water and sky and clouds."

"I also get lost in the wonder of what's below the surface. A whole world."

"I know you're thinking of the positives Dad, but I also know you think of Uncle Scott. I want you to know I think of him."

He nodded, "Thank you, yes, I think of Scott. I miss him. When he left for the service he was basically gone. We didn't get much time after that and then when he became a submariner even less time."

"I'm sorry, Dad."

"Yeah, me too. Terrorism has devastated our family."

They sat in silence as Sarah picked at her plate. She cut the end and peeled back the banana and broke it in half handing over one half to her dad. Mike smiled at her as he took it. He saw Sandy in her as she did this.

"Another cup, Dad?"

"I'll go get more for us both. Finish your eggs."

She slid her cup to him.

"Doctor mine just like yours."

He knew that already. As he made his way to the coffee station it was busy as usual, Mike saw Brian and Pam in line for breakfast. He caught Pam's eye and she smiled. Mike pointed towards the aft deck and she nodded. Five minutes later they were sitting under an umbrella enjoying a little conversation and everyone having their chance to soak in the surroundings.

"A day at sea 'mateys," Brian said.

"We're going to have to go into port for more oranges as much juice as you've had," Mike said.

"It just tastes good out here," Brian said.

"It does, doesn't it," Sarah agreed.

"What's everyone's plan for this day at sea?" Mike asked.

"I'm spending as much time out on deck as I can stand," Sarah said.

"I'm going to stay out until it begins to get hotter," Brian said.

"I'm going to stay out somewhere in-between these two," as Pam pointed to Sarah and Mike.

"Guess I'm with you all, but I'll set back in the shade more. I plan to read and drink tea and beer. There's probably a nap in my near future."

With that, they began to stir and head back for magazines, sunscreen, and more cold drinks.

Forty minutes later Mike found himself back on deck and standing at the rail. He planned to just sit and read but he just loved to stand at the rail and look out. It was amazing to watch the wake that was generated from the massive engines and how long it trailed behind. It made him think of the contrails in the sky he'd see with his dad while doing evening chores especially in the fall of the year. He decided to walk for a while. Families were gathering around the pools and children were laughing and playing. A big waterslide was a major attraction on the stern of this ship. It was actually its own waterpark with three different tubes of twists and turns.

He stopped again to look into the eastern sky and the sun felt good on his face. He closed his eyes and let the sea breeze blow through his hair. He startled himself back to consciousness realizing he'd momentarily dozed. Nap time was going to come sooner than later he chuckled to himself. He looked out to see a plane in the distance and decided to see how long he could watch it before it disappeared on the horizon. He watched for a couple of minutes to see it getting closer and then banking to its left putting it on a course towards them. He wondered if planes out here liked to fly over a ship and wondered what the maritime rules would be for something like that. He thought of Top Gun when Tom Cruise would request a fly-by with his fighter jet, have his request denied and then do it anyway scaring the officer on the bridge as he spilled coffee on himself. Funny every time.

He continued to watch and started wondering about this plane. It was a large prop plane and he was now hearing its engines in the distance as it drew closer. He was wondering how fast it was traveling since he'd been watching now for several minutes. It was now growing in size and still getting closer. Mike cocked his head and began to look around to see if anyone else was watching this happen. Thirty seconds later it was still coming their way and he had some alarm bells going off in his head. He about jumped out of his skin when the ships horn began blaring two decks above him but sounded like it was right behind him. He turned to look up but could not see that deck.

At this time the plane had descended low over the water and appeared to be heading right into the ship. Mike was turning to get off the deck when he saw a bright flash come from his left. It seemed the explosion was so close he could touch it and was sure he did feel a blast of heat. It was happening so fast he was having trouble processing it all, but he was sure he saw one of the wings blown off the aircraft. The plane immediately turned, and its other wing lifted up veering it to the right. At this point, it was on them and that wing hit the ship's waterpark tearing it off the back of the ship. Mike saw the waterpark debris falling into the ocean and could hear screams. The aircraft hit less than a hundred yards behind the ship and immediately exploded into a giant fireball.

Mike ran towards the stern to see if he could help. He knew this section was full of families. Fire alarms were blaring, and it was mass chaos. Ship crew members were already launching lifeboats off the lower deck where they were housed. As he reached the back of the ship crew members were already tending to wounded passengers and it appeared many were children as he feared. His thoughts were also on Sarah, Pam, and Brian and he began looking. Two minutes later he found Sarah, she was helping crew members with a little girl who appeared to have a broken leg after falling from the water slide.

"Sarah," Mike hollered.

She turned to see her father and gave a weak smile. Her right arm was bloody and Mike reached for her. She'd gotten cut and needed attention herself. Mike helped her up and put his arm around her as they moved from the immediate area. As they moved toward the nearest door to go inside they saw Brian.

"Where's Pam?" Mike asked.

"I don't know. She was sitting out here. Let's go."

They all turned to begin searching. Brian was doing a good job keeping positive, he was down to business intent on finding Pam. Mike watched Brian take the lead and then motioned to Sarah to head to Brian's left, Mike went right. Six minutes later they had not located Pam. This was not a large area to search but there was a lot of confusion. Brian looked at Mike and raised his hands.

"Let's go down one deck," Mike said.

Brian agreed, "Let's go."

"I'm going to see if they've set up some type of triage area," Sarah said.

The Captain of the cruise ship was on a secure line with an officer of the Royal New Zealand Navy. He was being assured the threat was over but still being closely monitored. The missile that downed the cargo plane had been fired from a Kaman SH-2G Super Seasprite helicopter with the Royal New Zealand Navy. Though they sustained damage and unknown casualties the aversion of a direct hit by the plane had likely saved the ship. Royal New Zealand Naval ships were steaming their way at top speed to offer medical assistance to the wounded passengers as well as help with damage to the superstructure. The captain had made more than one announcement assuring passengers the wounded were being treated and the ship was stable and seaworthy. Further information would be released as more information was available.

Mike and Sarah were trying to keep Brian from going into panic mode even though each of them was silently also going into panic mode. The next deck down had several wounded passengers who had been swept off the above deck as the water slide structure was torn from its mounts and swept into the sea. It was going to take time for the crew to determine the whereabouts of all passengers. Families were being interviewed for missing persons and the list was growing at an alarming rate.

"I need to let them know," Brian said.

Mike shook his head and got in line with Brian.

Twenty-five minutes later they were nearing the table to give their information. Brian was lost in his thoughts and not saying much. Mike and Sarah respected that and just waited with him.

Sarah was the first to hear his phone buzz. After three times she reached out and tugged on his shirt sleeve. Brian looked at Sarah and she pointed to his front pocket, "Your phone."

Brian realized what she was saying and reached in his pocket to see UNKNOWN on the screen. He was about to just put it back in his pocket when Sarah shook her head to get it. He pushed receive and lifted it to his ear to hear a faint voice.

"Brian, it's me."

He couldn't believe it, "Pam?"

"I'm okay, I'm in a lifeboat."

"Lifeboat? Thank God."

"They said they're taking us to deck two on the starboard side to bring us aboard to be checked by medical staff."

"Okay, we'll be there."

"I love you."

"I love you too," he said.

He clicked off and relayed the info to Mike and Sarah. They had already decided she was okay by the look of relief they saw on his face while talking. Without another word, they were heading down to deck two. They took the stairs instead of the elevator and were in the deck two hallway in four minutes. They asked a steward to learn where passengers would be brought onboard and made their way to that point where they immediately found themselves roped off from going any further. Crew members were keeping an area clear to get people to the room where the medical staff had gathered. Mike saw several people he recognized as fellow passengers who must be doctors and nurses.

They strained to see as the first three people were brought in on stretchers. The next person was walking and the next person was Pam.

"Pam!" Brian hollered.

She turned her head and managed a weak smile and wave. She mouthed the words, "I'm okay," and nearly collapsed as a female crew member steadied her. Brian raised his eyebrows as he looked at Sarah and Mike.

"She's tough, Brian," Mike said.

"Tougher than I am," Brian said. "You may have to hold me up."

"You've done that for me plenty of times," Mike said as he put his hand on his shoulder.

Fifteen minutes later a crew member was calling for the family of Pam Miller.

"Here," Brian raised his voice.

They were ushered into the room and taken to her. She was laying on a cot with her eyes closed. Brian reached for her hand and she smiled before opening her eyes.

"Hey guys, I took an unplanned swim. Boy have I got a story for you."

"I'll bet you do. Are you okay?" Brian asked.

"They say I'll be fine. I feel like I was run over by a truck. Pretty bruised up on my back and left side. Not sure if that was from the impact of being swept over or hitting the water."

"Shit, I didn't think of that," Brian said.

"A crew member said that would have been a sixty-foot fall into the water."

"Wow," Sarah said.

"I was able to get somewhat oriented as I fell and pretty much went in feet first but I still hit my left side. Not a belly flopper though. Then whatever breath the fall didn't knock out of me the concussion from the blast did. It took all the strength I had to get reoriented and back to the surface."

Just hearing that made all three of them wince. At that point, they were told she'd be kept there for a while longer for observation and asked that only one of them stay. Mike and Sarah hugged Brian and squeezed Pam's hand, "See you both later."

They walked out of the room and decided to go get a bite to eat. Neither of them were hungry but they decided they needed something to settle their stomachs. They made it to the Lido deck where they were serving food and it looked like they were business as usual when it was actually anything but. They both got iced tea and Mike picked up a small basket of rolls with butter and jelly. They were pretty quiet while they ate. This kind of life-threatening emergency sends your body into an adrenaline dump that leaves you spent. It meant the tea and rolls tasted like the best thing they'd ever eaten. They sat back in their chairs content to just rest.

"You saw that plane coming right at us, didn't you?" Mike asked.

"You saw it first, but yes."

"They were going to crash right into the broadside of this ship causing a huge explosion."

"We'd have gone down," Sarah said.

"But something shot it and threw it off course enough to save us."

She shook her head.

"Think about it, someone knew what was happening and took it out in the nick of time to save us!"

"When you've just been attacked it hard to think you're lucky, but I guess we are lucky," Sarah said.

"Well, there's quite a story behind all of this for sure."

Chapter 37

Cirebon

Asis was looking for any information on the cruise ship attack. This ship should be on the bottom of the Pacific Ocean by now or at worst sinking quickly. Timing had been planned to ensure they were far enough off the coast to not get help quickly. The cargo plane was filled with enough explosives to sink two ships. He was careful with his search wording, no need to send out any red flags for analysts who'd be watching for anything, however small. It will show up, he thought, it takes time to get information on an event in a remote location.

His thoughts turned to Chimera. He'd contacted her after his arrival in Cirebon. She invited him to come for a visit in Jakarta and he was ready to firm up the date. He was still getting used to the idea that he had no calendar to check, no business to run or deadlines to meet. He could go whenever he pleased. Is this what every retiree felt and then decided it scared them? You could only play so much golf and he was not much of a golfer. Yes, spending time with someone like Chimera sounded like a nice diversion.

He made contact by email and suggested an arrival date. She responded asking to make it one day later due to a business commitment and he let her know he'd be there that day. He'd let her know his arrival time after making travel arrangements. After checking Google Maps, he learned it was only a three-and-a-half-hour drive, 219 km. This would be a nice drive and he could see the countryside of the island of Java. There would be no need for a bodyguard on this trip, he was ready for some alone time as he drove.

That evening he was seeing reports of an incident with a cruise ship off the coast of New Zealand. News sources were saying the ship had been attacked and was now making its way back to Auckland for repairs. This was not good. It should have been three miles down on the bottom of the Tasman Sea by now. There were no reports of casualties being given yet. One feed had a video showing the damaged ship still under its own power steaming along. It showed damage at the back where the water park slides had been ripped from the ship. The plane that caused the damage had been hit by a missile a few hundred yards out and veered off at the last second.

"Hit by a missile, from where and by whom?" he thought to himself. He'd give this serious thought, but it could not be a co-incidence. He logged off and shut down his desktop computer, opened the bottom drawer of his desk and pulled out a laptop. He powered it up and waited for the login screen. Safely on, he clicked on the map. Three glowing dots appeared. He pulled up the cruise line itinerary and the projected track of the ship. He entered the current time and guessed they'd follow the same course back to New Zealand. The only thing he was missing was real-time satellite imagery for the Tasman Sea.

He double-checked everything he'd entered and was ready to arm the mines. Two weeks ago, a mid-size cargo ship had deposited three mines into the shipping lanes of this area. These weapons were a hybrid design having features of the old mines used during World War II and had a state-of-the-art guidance system using GPS coordinates. They each had their own propulsion system giving them features of a torpedo, only much slower. They had been hovering at one hundred feet below the surface for the last two weeks. This kept them below keel depth for any ship that may have passed their way. He clicked on each glowing dot to now have a slowly blinking dot telling him they were armed and in search mode.

Tasman Sea, South Pacific

The New Zealand Royal Navy sent the HMZNS Wellington out of the Devonport Naval Base at Auckland to offer offshore support to the damaged cruise ship. She was running at 20 knots to get on scene as soon as possible, her maximum speed was 22 knots. Her crew of 46 was near capacity. She would not be able to carry many passengers but did have three 50-person life rafts if needed. The cruise ship was traveling at 18 knots and they were within 40 nautical miles of each other leaving them about an hour apart.

"Still on course, Captain, maintaining."

"Thank you, Quartermaster."

Everyone was deep in thought knowing the cruise ship had been attacked. All eyes were in the sky. The cruise ship attack had the characteristics of the kamikaze pilots in World War II, flying their planes full of explosives directly into a ship. They were armed with two .50 caliber machine guns and a complement of surface to air missiles. The Super SeaSprite Helicopter they had onboard could be launched carrying four torpedoes and anti-ship guided missiles.

Forty minutes passed, and they had good visual contact with their charge. They'd been in radio contact and knew the cruise ship bridge was pleased with their progress. The sun would soon be dropping away into the distant ocean. The Captain stood with one hand on the rail and the other holding a fresh cup of coffee. He felt it before he heard it. His ship seemed to abruptly move sideways a few feet. The sound immediately following, it was muted but still audible. The Quartermaster did a half turn to meet the Captain's eye.

"Sound the alarm." The Captain said in a calm voice.

"Aye, aye."

The horns began to blare, and the Captain was asking all departments for a sitrep. Situation report. The first three reports came in with no damage, the fourth was a different story.

"We're taking on water. Damage to at least two compartments. We've started search and rescue for crewmembers before sealing compartments."

"Keep me posted and let us know what help you need," the Captain said.

"Aye, aye sir."

The final three reports came in with nothing more than minimal damage, so it was concentrated in the one area. That was somewhat of a relief, but still bad enough.

"Shut off that horn."

Thank God thought the Jr. Officer on deck. The call came back letting the Captain know all crewmembers were out of the damaged areas and accounted for and those two compartments were sealed. Conversation ensued on the bridge of how taking on water in these two compartments would affect their seaworthiness. All agreed they'd lose at least 30 percent of top cruising speed.

"I don't have to say we don't want another incident with a mine. This will be a long night. Everyone able needs to be standing watch on deck with every light we have available."

"Aye, aye, Captain."

Within five minutes the Captain could see most of his crew stationed around the deck. He'd make sure they had food and plenty of coffee as needed all night long. The Captain had briefed the cruise ship Captain on the most secured line they could muster. He offered his support and then offered the advice to keep watch for mines in any way possible without creating panic aboard his ship. He also told the captain he was launching the helicopter to search ahead of one vessel and then the other. He could explain that to his cruise ship passengers any way he wished.

Australia was sending a minesweeper at full speed to the area, this was a nice gesture but most likely redundant due to the time it would take to get there, but still a nice gesture. It was quiet on the bridge, everyone was on alert with eyes peeled.

At about twenty-one hundred hours they received a call from the helicopter. He assumed they'd be requesting a landing to re-fuel. Instead, they'd spotted something.

"Captain we have a partial visual on something unusual. It is mostly submerged and is not marine life. We have a heat signature that is suspicious. Request permission to engage with the machine gun?"

After a few seconds to think, "Either ship on a collision course?"

"Aye, aye. Cruise ship."

"Permission granted."

Everyone on the bridge focused out to the helicopter. It was about one nautical mile to their starboard. Machine gun tracer fire could be seen and seconds later they saw a flash of light. Six seconds later they heard the concussion of the blast. It reminded the Captain of the sound produced when a glacier is calving. An impressive rumble that makes you glad you're back a safe distance. It made him shudder to think of the cruise ship possibly hitting the mine with his ship having already hit one.

"Good job, Airman Simons."

"Thank you, sir. Request permission to refuel."

"Granted, get back here, son."

After a quick refueling, they launched to keep eyes open for the night. The cruise ship Captain had inquired and was told he'd know more later. He thanked them and signed off.

Mike and Sarah were sticking close together. They were keeping tabs on Pam by checking in with Brian and trying not to wear him out with their concern. It was a nerve-wracking night for sure. The explosion off in the distance had everyone on edge. The Captain had made an announcement that was just the right amount of vagueness, with some nothing of importance thrown in. No one believed it, but they knew that was all they were getting for the time being. It was comforting to know the New Zealand Navy was close by providing escort. None of them knew their ship was in better shape right now than the HMNZ Wellington. A partial moon-lit night on the ocean was dark and scary even when things were fine as far as Mike was concerned. Morning couldn't come soon enough.

They spent the night on deck and welcomed the cool ocean breeze. Both took turns cat-napping as the other kept watch. Mike kept thinking to himself they have another story to tell. He knew they'd been attacked but had no idea of the details or who was behind it. Craziness had come to all corners of the world, land and sea. The first morning light was just starting, it would have been a lot more beautiful if they all weren't scared they'd be attacked again. He was happy to have better vision for their crew as well as the New Zealand naval ship. The helicopter had taken the lead all night with two more refueling stops.

Looking off to his left he spotted Brian leaning against the rail.

"Are you ever going to shave on this trip?" Brian asked.

"Not sure now, might as well let it go. Still surprised to see how gray it is."

Brian smiled and stroked his chin, "Very distinguished."

"In my estimation, that's what people say when they mean damn, you look old."

That got raised eyebrows and a tip of the head from Brian, "Did you and Sarah stay out here all night?"

"Yeah, we didn't feel like being apart or locked in a stateroom. You stay with Pam all night?"

"Yes, but I came up here several times. I lost count. Couldn't rest or relax."

Mike rubbed both hands over his face and yawned for all he was worth.

"I'm getting you and myself some coffee, you stay here with Sarah," as Brian pointed her way. It appeared she was sleeping soundly.

"Me too," she said with eyes still closed.

"Three coffees," Brian said as he turned for the Lido deck.

Auckland, New Zealand

They arrived safely into port and were given priority docking by a harbor master who was former New Zealand Navy. Thirty-nine of the wounded were taken by waiting ambulances to every nearby hospital. Pam was one of the last to go meaning her injuries were non-threatening. She had already self-diagnosed as being okay except for feeling and looking like she'd been run over by a big cargo plane. The contusions had had time to show extreme bruising on her left side. She was able to walk with a noticeable limp and was in a lot of pain.

The flight home was going to be a double-edged sword. She was ready to be home, but the flight would be brutal. They would be on a different flight than originally planned due to having their trip cut short and leaving with a direct flight from Wellington as opposed to leaving from Sydney.

She was thoroughly checked and released to travel with some good painkillers that would hopefully provide lots of sleep time. Brian was thinking he might try a couple of those pills himself. All four were taken to the Wellington International airport for the fourteen-hour flight. After a 90-minute wait, they boarded to find

Mike and Sarah had been separated in their seating assignments. Mike looked to see Sarah would be sitting by a nice-looking women close to his age.

"Ma'am, may I ask a question?"

She gave him a smile, "Yes."

"Would you mind trading seats with me, so I might sit with my daughter for this long flight?"

"Of course," she said.

She unbuckled and came forward as Mike thanked her and offered his hand. "Rachel," she said.

"Mike Baker, this is my daughter Sarah." They shook hands.

Mike thought he might have lingered just a bit too long with the handshake, but Rachel didn't seem to mind. Everyone got buckled in and began pulling out reading material for the long flight. A smooth takeoff that was on time led him to push deeper into his seat, he'd get as comfortable as he could get. He looked over at Sarah to see she was already asleep. How'd she do that, he wondered? At least he was on the aisle, he'd be needing to get rid of some coffee before long. When he got up to find the restroom nearly an hour later, he saw Rachel was pecking away on her laptop. There was a novel laying on her tray table. He could see the cover and the author's first name was Rachel. He stepped up beside her and pointed to the cover. She looked up and smiled, "That's me."

"Very cool," he said.

"Thank you," she said. "I may put you in my next novel, I'm needing another victim."

He raised both eyebrows and held out his hands in submission.

"Just kidding. Well, maybe," she said smiling.

He smiled and turned for the restroom. When he got back to his seat he began to think about the time he and Brian had gone for their "man" weekend in Asheville, North Carolina. They'd met a young lady in the bar and later the hot tub who said she was a mystery writer. After a quick awkward moment, they'd all had a good laugh and shared a bottle of wine after she'd pulled the cork out with her teeth. Mike was just glad she had teeth, and it all ended well. He always wondered if he ended up as a victim in her book. Maybe I need to write a book and put these ladies in my book. He liked authors, they were an interesting bunch.

His mind was on daydream mode which seemed appropriate gliding through the wispy clouds over the Pacific for hours on end.

Mike would have instances that made him think of something that happened in college or with one of his FarmHouse brothers. The older he got the more he treasured the time he'd spent with that group of guys. It also amazed him when he thought of how brief this time actually was in his life. He'd spent four years with this group of guys. About fifteen graduated each year and fifteen new freshmen came in each fall, thus you could count about one hundred friends you'd spent time with. He also got to know several alumni who came back from time to time so that number grew to over a hundred. Four years seemed like the blink of an eye at this point in his life, but what a time it was. He kept in touch with several of them over the years, this had become easier with social media. There were many he'd not seen since he graduated. It was funny to him that even though they were his age they were all 21 years old in his mind. That should come as no surprise, everyone who had ever gone back to a class reunion had those moments before they saw an old friend who was twenty years older.

Sandy had been an Alpha Xi Delta at Purdue and shared the same sentiments. She kept in contact with a few sisters. He'd heard from many of them after her death. The sisterhood lived on, they cared deeply and grieved. Her pledge class had already set up a scholarship in her name and he planned to add to it each year. It still hurt so damn bad, but he just kept reflecting on all the good times. He celebrated their life together. He continued to add good memory notes to the cigar box of memories. Someday he'd write the full stories.

Nearly fourteen hours after taking off they were preparing to land in Los Angeles. They'd have a ninety-minute layover. There were several of their cruise ship companions on board that had received injuries in varying degrees. The DHS had scheduled three doctors to give everyone a quick look before their next flight. If there were any problems, they'd get them to a local hospital.

Brian was almost as stiff as Pam when they landed, even though there had been more than one hike up and down the aisle. Even though she hurt, it felt great to get up and walk. She again was not looking forward to buckling back in for the last leg to Indianapolis International. She checked out with her doctor and they headed for their next gate. Everyone got a quick bite, it's amazing how good McDonald's fries can taste as a snack.

They took off on time and four hours later they'd flown over Bloomington on the way to IND. Brian and Pam's daughter and son-in-law were there in a big Suburban to pick everyone up. All luggage arrived with them and they loaded up and headed for Greenville.

Chapter 38

Cirebon

He still couldn't believe it. That cruise ship should be the biggest news story since the World Trade Towers. The cargo plane was hit and directed off course at the last possible second. It had been close enough to do damage, but nothing like he'd planned. He knew the routes all along the mines were not foolproof, but still had a high probability of doing serious damage. The news was sketchy about what damage had been sustained by the New Zealand naval vessel, they had kept this quiet. That ship had still helped the cruise liner navigate back to the New Zealand mainland. Cruise passengers had posted videos of a Royal Navy helicopter evidently destroying at least one of the mines during the night hours.

His thoughts went to the different players in his plan. Farid knew nothing of how he'd planned the attack. His Middle Eastern financiers had not asked questions. That left the cargo plane owner and people he'd used to assemble the explosives. This did unsettle him a little, these people were in this area. It just didn't make sense, he was a master at keeping plans compartmentalized. The man who provided the cargo plane had purchased this plane in another part of the world. He, of course, didn't want to be one plane shy on his inventory when the authorities eventually came to visit.

Greenville

No town does the Fourth of July holiday like Greenville. This year the Bakers and the Millers were Grand Marshalls of the annual parade starting in the local high school parking lot. Mike had not let his hopes get too high but he was absolutely thrilled when he learned David would be home on furlough. The Marines strive to keep combat zone duty to a seven-month furlough schedule. It had been a little longer, but David was home for a couple weeks.

Pam had recovered from her injuries and was back to her old self. Brian told Mike he actually needed her to slow down a bit, she was wearing him out. She had that 'get things done' attitude happening after the scare she'd endured. "I guess getting swept into the ocean off the deck of a cruise ship does that to ya," Brian told Mike.

The week leading up to the Fourth had dinners in the park and some good entertainment. The Fourth was about as hot as normal and they finished the evening watching fireworks from the hill of friends in Greenville.

They still had six days before David had to head back. Mike, Sarah, and David had a nice restful week together. They grilled out nearly every evening and told stories that had been told before. David had a good time meeting Chris and Bisma who joined them one evening for a cookout. Chris was a few years older than

David, but it seemed they'd started a friendship that evening. David congratulated them on their upcoming wedding as they left that night, Mike and Sarah said, "We'll see you in Iowa."

David left two days later as they dropped him off at Indianapolis International. Mike knew it wouldn't be easy and it wasn't. He made his way into security at Gate B and turned to wave and he was off. Mike gave Sarah a hug and they headed for the car.

Iowa

The entire Boiler Club decided to make the trip to Iowa. Mike, Sarah, Pam, and Brian decided to drive together. It would be a nine-hour drive with stops. Tom and Charley and their wives decided to fly into Ames and rented a car. Natalie Jackson was as excited as she'd been about anything in a long time. She was just old enough to be a mother of the bride or groom and felt like it. They all carried the sadness of losing Moe Keane, he would have been walking Bisma down the aisle. She'd since asked Mike Baker if he would do the honor which he agreed to with tears in his eyes. The path that had brought them to this point was an amazing story. Starting with he and David kidnapping her at gunpoint on 86th Street in Indianapolis to walking her down the aisle. Amazing, Mike thought.

They all gathered in Chris's hometown of Mays, Iowa on Friday evening and had the wedding rehearsal. It was a small wedding, but Chris wanted Bisma to have a wedding. The dinner after the rehearsal was a wonderful celebration all by itself. Everyone was relaxed and glad to see each other and talk about anything except terrorist attacks. Nat did tell Chris and Bisma that Steve Bradshaw sent his best regards. He'd asked for some time off to visit Fiona in London and this made Bisma smile.

The next day was a special time, especially for Bisma. She'd never allowed herself to dream that her life might ever get to this point. Maybe a little. The wedding turned into the reception which was small but the most fun Bisma had ever had. They danced and enjoyed BBQ and danced some more. Dr. Sutherlin and his wife showed off some moves they'd perfected from a different time, they still had it. Pam Miller was nearly healed from the cruise ship attack and convinced Brian to bust a move or two.

Natalie and Mike offered toasts to the newlyweds that included both laughs and tears. No one here had known each other for a long time with the exception of the Millers and Bakers as well as Chris' small family, but it didn't show; it looked like they were one big family. A weekend Bisma would never forget.

Chris had asked Natalie two weeks prior if she would consider sending some help to make sure they were secure.

"I cannot trust Hazaq until I have him behind bars."

She already had it set up but didn't tell him. She told him this was a good idea and had a team of three watching different points in town all weekend. Most everyone gathered again Sunday morning for brunch before going their separate ways. Bisma had received more hugs in one weekend than she'd received her entire life. They had initially decided to take a cruise for their honeymoon but decided against it after New Zealand. Too soon. They'd fly out on Tuesday for a week in St. Lucia.

Washington

Nat was nearly finished writing her final draft of the cruise ship attack. She'd sent early notes to Chris, Bisma, and Steve for their input and to fill in holes. She still found it hard to believe the cruise line would not consider changing their itinerary. They felt like there wasn't enough evidence to change course for that many paying passengers. They were already dealing with some fallout as more questions were asked. It was not a stretch for reporters to wonder how the Navy was in the right place at the right time to shoot down a plane full of explosives without the cruise line knowing what might be coming.

Steve provided the documentation and processes he followed in being able to divert other air traffic in the last possible minutes using the satellite and radar feeds and the flight approach to the cruise ship. This was the perfect blend of new technology along with old school radar. One key was diverting other air traffic while not spooking the pilots of the cargo plane. The low volume of air traffic in that area between Australia and New Zealand was a help.

Bisma had already called Nat asking to discuss her plans for Farid. Nat had been thinking about their options knowing he was working with a foreign terrorist while residing here in the states. Bisma convinced Nat to let him stay in Ann Arbor for now in deference to his mother, Nafeesa. They'd continue to monitor what he was doing and make sure he didn't leave the states.

Nat shared her contacts in the report. She had a contact in the Ministry of Foreign Affairs and Trade in Wellington. This gentleman was aggressive in his help and immediately involved the

Royal New Zealand Navy. Nat was especially impressed with their cooperation and swift action. They worked well with Steve Bradshaw and implemented his intelligence.

Everything the Navy accomplished in avoiding the mines was through their own defensive measures. The helicopter had been a huge help, it may well have saved the cruise ship from a direct hit.

She finished writing, did some minor editing and hit send. Chris and Bisma were still working and read it quickly without many surprises. It was good to see the cooperation between Nat at DHS with the New Zealand Counterterrorism people and their military. This would not have worked without them, absolutely no hesitation on their part. Steve read and was amazed at how they'd pulled it off. He liked this team.

Everyone responded this all looked good and they had nothing else to add. Nat thanked them and told them she'd be forwarding it to Jake McBee first thing in the morning. She knew she'd be copied in on any questions he might have for any of them.

Indianapolis

She was on him when he came through the door. He deserved it, he was expecting it.

"Tim, where the hell have you been this time? You know you missed soccer last night, Kyle was devastated."

"I'll make it up to him."

362 · TERRY BARNETT

"I've heard that before. If you start in with how I knew what I signed up for, I may be out the door for three days without you knowing where I've been or when I'll be back if ever."

"I understand Mag."

"That's it? You understand?"

He headed up the stairs with his bag over his shoulder. It was exactly what he expected. He'd scripted his lines, but knew they were all wrong. The only answer was to make a change and show them all. She watched him walk away and then heard the shower come on.

Twenty minutes later he walked into the kitchen. Mag didn't turn around, she kept stirring whatever was in the pan.

"That smells wonderful."

"Don't even start, Tim."

He opened the cabinet and began getting plates down. He walked them over to the table.

"Where are the kids?

"Playing at the Walkers, they're due home in fifteen minutes."

"Maggie, let's talk."

She turned her head. She looked defeated, he wished she looked mad.

"I've been working extra as you know. I can't talk about it as you know."

She turned back to the stove.

"Everything you said is true and I've made a change in responsibilities at work to take effect immediately, it will change things."

"What?"

"I cannot tell you, but I promise you things will be better. I cannot say that I'll never have to be gone on short notice again, but things will be different now."

"I heard immediately," she said.

"Yes, you did. Summer is ending, and I've asked for the next two weeks off. What shall we do?"

Maggie shut off the burner.

"The kids have been talking about Disney World all summer."

"Then let's do it Mag, let's book flights and head out this Saturday."

"I need to cancel a couple play dates and one dentist appointment. Tim, can we afford it?"

"Let's not worry about the cost, let's do it."

"Can we tell them at dinner?" she asked.

"Absolutely, you tell them. I have one more night to button things up from this current assignment and then we'll be off as a family."

Dinner was as happy as it had been in many months. Tim gave them hugs and was out the door. He made the seventy-minute drive to the farm and pulled into the long driveway. He was going to miss this place a lot. He got everything buttoned up knowing it would be a while. He opened the fridge to see three beers and a small brick of cheese. He'd leave the beer and pitch the cheese. He packed up his laptop and set it by the front door. He opened the big safe in the back bedroom to look at his arsenal. Three sniper rifles, four handguns and a Remington 870 shotgun that his dad left him. It would all stay here for now. He pushed the safe closed with a thud. His days as Kurtz were over for a while.

Lexington

Hazaq was getting restless. He knew he always had to have his guard up. He knew they'd always be looking for him. He was spending way too much time on the internet. He was getting good at optimizing search engines, being creative with keywords and phrasing. He kept a list of sites he'd look at on a periodic basis including two towns in Iowa. This day he got a picture, it wasn't clear, but he was able to copy it and move it to his laptop to optimize it. Sure enough, he could make out a picture of Chris Powell. The local golden boy had gotten married in his hometown. It almost seemed they'd purposefully tried to hide his new bride. Hazaq studied her profile and jawline, he moved his attention to her neck to see what appeared to be a shadow or a scar.

He sat and just stared and begin to shake his head. He couldn't be sure but felt like he was seeing Bisma. He knew for a fact that Bisma had been dead for well over a year. Or did he? Had she and Chris been working together all this time? Conspiring against the cell and his leadership? They'd suffered more failures than successes during that period of time. He'd never trusted Chris fully but had trusted Bisma. He never liked her indignant behavior, she didn't know her place. His anger burned as he thought of them together.

Jakarta

Chimera ran her fingers through her long dark hair as she sat straddling Asis. Their love-making was now more intense. She threw her head back and let out a scream. Her hands reached for her chest. Asis initially didn't see the arrow that had penetrated her back, went through her heart and came six inches out the front. He just stared up at her in shock, he instinctively put up his hands as she began to fall toward him, but he couldn't catch her. She drove the arrow into his chest. The pain took his breath away as he fought to lift her off but could not do so.

She could not believe her good fortune as she slipped in through the lanai doors leading out to the pool. She moved closer to see him struggling. The entry wound in Chimera's back had produced very little blood. The sheet under Asis showed an enlarging area of dark red. The only light came from candles around the room that flickered from the light sea breeze. As she got closer his head turned enough to see her. His eyes narrowed as to ask why?

"For all the lives you've ruined Asis. For using my brother and then having him killed. Thought I'd return the favor. I do appreciate the one hundred million dollars you sent me with the help of your girlfriend here."

He could not speak; the life was quickly draining from his body. Janet turned to leave and let him die. It took every ounce of strength he had left to bend his arm down. Janet never saw it coming as the bullet tore through her lower back on the left side. She spun to her right as she fell, hitting the floor facing back in his direction. The last thing she saw was Asis smile.

Please consider leaving a review on Amazon.

Made in the USA
Lexington, KY
30 January 2019